The Christmas Quandary

Hardman Holidays, Book 5
A Sweet Historical Holiday Romance

by
USA TODAY Bestselling Author

SHANNA HATFIELD

The Christmas Quandary

Copyright © 2016 by Shanna Hatfield

Shanna Hatfield
shanna@shannahatfield.com
shannahatfield.com

*To the brave who follow
where their hearts lead...*

Books by Shanna Hatfield

FICTION

CONTEMPORARY

Love at the 20-Yard Line
The Coffee Girl
The Christmas Crusade
Learnin' the Ropes
QR Code Killer

Grass Valley Cowboys
The Cowboy's Christmas Plan
The Cowboy's Spring Romance
The Cowboy's Summer Love
The Cowboy's Autumn Fall
The Cowboy's New Heart
The Cowboy's Last Goodbye

Holiday Brides
Valentine Bride

Rodeo Romance
The Christmas Cowboy
Wrestlin' Christmas
Capturing Christmas
Barreling Through Christmas

Women of Tenacity
A Prelude
Heart of Clay
Country Boy vs. City Girl
Not His Type

HISTORICAL

Baker City Brides
Crumpets and Cowpies
Thimbles and Thistles
Corsets and Cuffs

Pendleton Petticoats
Dacey
Aundy
Caterina
Ilsa
Marnie
Lacy
Bertie
Millie

Hardman Holidays
The Christmas Bargain
The Christmas Token
The Christmas Calamity
The Christmas Vow
The Christmas Quandary

Hearts of the War
Garden of Her Heart

NON-FICTION

Fifty Dates with Captain Cavedweller
Farm Girl
Recipes of Love
Savvy Entertaining Series

Chapter One

Eastern Oregon, 1900

"Welcome to Hardman, folks," the driver bellowed as the stage rocked to a stop near the mercantile.

Tom Grove grimaced as one final jolt caused the man sitting next to him to bump into his broken arm.

"Sorry," the man said, scrambling to his feet and out the door.

Weary and in pain, Tom waited until the rest of the occupants exited the stage before stepping down and reaching for the bag the driver handed to him.

"Take care of that arm, Tom," the driver cautioned as he regained his seat and picked up the reins to take the horses to the livery for the night.

"I will, Mr. Alder. Have a nice evening." Tom nodded to the driver then stepped onto the boardwalk. A deep breath filled his nose with the scents of pine, wood smoke, and roasting meat.

Gas street lamps illuminated the thoroughfare, reflecting off the windows of businesses lining both sides of Main Street and shining on glistening piles of snow.

Beyond the sounds of a few dogs barking and the stamping of hooves from the horses tied outside the Red Lantern saloon, the town remained quiet. At that time of day, most residents gathered around supper tables, glad to be home for the night.

Home.

Tom hadn't been back to Hardman in more than a year. Until that moment, he hadn't realized how much he missed it. Missed the quiet simplicity of the small town where he'd grown up. Missed the people who'd helped shape his future.

With a firm grip on the heavy bag in his hand, he started down the boardwalk, planning to walk out to the farm where he'd lived the first eighteen years of his life. Although he didn't relish trekking four miles out of town in the dark and cold, he looked forward to seeing his parents and surprising them with his unplanned visit.

"Tom? Tom Grove? Is that you?" a feminine voice called through the winter darkness.

Slowly turning around, Tom smiled as Ginny and Blake Stratton crossed the street and hurried toward him.

"It's me." Tom set down his bag and shook hands with Blake as best he could with his right hand held captive in a sling.

"What on earth are you doing here? If you were coming for Thanksgiving, it was last Thursday." Ginny offered him a teasing smile.

"I hadn't planned to come until spring, but this…" Tom glanced down at the sling supporting his casted arm, "left me unable to work for a while. My editor told me to take December off and come back to work when the cast is removed."

"How's life in the big city of Portland as a newspaper reporter?" Blake asked, lifting Tom's bag and holding an arm out to his wife.

Ginny wrapped one hand around Blake's arm and the other around Tom's uninjured arm. "Come join us for dinner, Tom. We're on our way to the restaurant. After we eat, we'd be happy to give you a ride home."

"I don't want to impose," Tom said, hesitant to continue to the restaurant with the couple.

Ginny tugged on his arm. "It's not an imposition, not in the least. We'd love to hear all about your work at the newspaper and how you broke that arm."

Blake gave him a knowing look. "You might as well come along. My lovely wife rarely takes no for an answer."

"In that case, I won't object to eating dinner with you both." Tom grinned and walked with the couple to the town's only restaurant. It was busy, but it didn't take long for a waitress to show them to a table. Blake set Tom's bag down and reached to help Ginny remove her coat.

When he did, Tom couldn't help but gape at her rounded shape. He wracked his mind to recall if his mother had written him about Blake and Ginny expecting a baby. If she did, it had slipped his mind.

He grinned again. "I see congratulations are in order."

Blake held out Ginny's chair as the woman beamed with pleasure. "Thank you, Tom. This little one gives me the strangest cravings. All day, I couldn't stop thinking about the roasted chicken they serve here at the restaurant. Fortunately, Blake agreed to drive me into town for dinner."

"Let's hope they haven't sold out of the chicken, though," Blake said, draping an arm along the back of his wife's chair.

"When will the addition to your family arrive?" Tom asked, removing his sling so he could take off his coat. He sat down and rested his broken arm on the table.

"February," Ginny said, placing a hand on the curve of her belly.

Tom hid his surprise, expecting Ginny's response to be more along the lines of next week from her protruding shape. The woman was short and slight of frame, so he imagined it made her pregnancy seem far more advanced than it was.

The waitress appeared to take their orders, keeping him from offering an inappropriate comment.

As they ate, many people Tom knew stopped by the table to welcome him back to town, making it impossible to carry on a conversation with Blake and Ginny. By the time they finished eating, Tom was convinced he'd said hello to half the population of Hardman.

"You look like you're about done in," Blake said, helping Ginny to her feet. "My wagon's parked over by the bank. I'll run get it if you don't mind accompanying Ginny."

"Not at all, Blake," Tom said, struggling to put on his coat and slip the sling back into place while Blake helped Ginny on with her coat. "I'd be happy to pay for the meal."

Blake shook his head, then left money on the table to cover their bill. "Absolutely not. It's our treat to welcome you home."

"Thanks." Tom lifted his bag and followed the couple outside into the frigid evening air.

"I'll be right back," Blake said and jogged off in the direction of the bank owned by his brother-in-law and one of their friends.

Tom gazed around the town as he ambled with Ginny back to Main Street. "Nothing around here really changes, does it?"

A cryptic look crossed her face. "Oh, I think a lot of things have changed since you were last here. When was that? A year ago in October?"

"Yes. I was here for my father's fortieth birthday." Tom recalled the party his mother had thrown, inviting friends and neighbors. His father seemed rather embarrassed by all the attention, but enjoyed it all the same.

"Since you were home, the bakery has new owners. A brother and sister bought it and moved here right before

Easter. The siblings rent Adam and Tia Guthry's house, since they decided to stay in Portland." Ginny looked to Tom. "Do you ever see Adam and Tia?"

Tom nodded. "I do. We attend the same church. Often, they take pity on me and invite me to join them for a meal. Toby talks about Hardman and little Erin Dodd all the time. And they all dote on baby Hope."

"She's such a precious little thing," Ginny said, absently rubbing a hand along her stomach as they walked down the street. "I'm sure Toby takes his role of big brother seriously."

"He does. The last time I had dinner with them, Toby was helping Hope learn to walk."

Ginny stopped as Blake approached with the wagon. "It's hard to believe she's nearly a year old."

Tom admired the horses hitched to the wagon. The team's midnight coats gleamed in the amber lights of the street. "It looks like Blake is still raising the best horses in the area."

"He is, when he isn't busy making furniture." Ginny accepted Blake's help in climbing into the wagon while Tom set his bag in the back.

"You don't need to take me all the way home. A ride to your place will save me a few miles of walking." Tom swung up to the seat and sat beside Ginny.

Blake slid onto the seat on her other side and flicked the reins. "It's no bother at all to take you home, Tom. With that arm of yours, I'd feel better leaving you at your door instead of traipsing down a dark road in the cold and snow."

"I'd protest, but I'm too tired," Tom admitted and settled back against the seat.

Ginny rambled on about people they all knew and activities taking place in town. When she stopped to catch her breath, Tom hurried to ask a question.

"Is the school planning another Christmas carnival this year?"

"Yes." Ginny clapped her gloved hands together in excitement. "Mother and Dad have agreed to host it at their house once again. I think most of the activities will take place in the ballroom, though. Remember the first year we had it, before they'd moved into the new house?"

"I do," Tom said, recalling the fun he had serving as the magician's assistant during the event. He'd also written a poem to contribute to the auction. Ginny painted a winter scene around his words and the piece sold for an amount of money that made Tom's eyes widen in shock. It was then he decided he wanted to write for a living instead of follow in his father's footsteps as a farmer.

Gratefully, his parents both agreed he should pursue his dreams and supported his decision to move to Portland, even though he didn't see them often. They'd come to Portland in the spring to visit him, but that seemed like ages ago.

"Is Miss Alex going to offer another magic show?" Tom asked. Five years ago, a mystifying woman arrived in town with a unique prestidigitation wagon and ended up becoming his favorite schoolteacher. She and her husband, Adam Guthry's brother, helped Tom prepare for his move to Portland. He received letters from Alex and Arlan almost as frequently as he did from his parents.

Ginny cast a quick glance at Blake before looking to Tom. "That has not yet been decided, Tom. Alex hasn't been well. In fact, she's missed several days of teaching the last few weeks."

Blake, who served on the school board, leaned around his wife. "We've been hard-pressed to find anyone willing to help out in her absence. Luke even had to fill in one day."

Tom laughed, picturing the good-natured banker leading the lessons at the one-room school. "Desperate times have surely arrived."

Ginny giggled. "It does my big brother good to wrangle the students all day instead of balancing accounts at the bank, or chasing cows, or tormenting me."

"But he does it so well," Tom said, thinking of all the times he'd watched Luke Granger tease his sister.

"That he does," Blake agreed, guiding his team past his place and continuing down the road toward the Grove farm.

Tom was eager to see his folks. He imagined the look of surprise on his mother's face when he walked inside the house and announced his plans to stay until the arrival of the new year. The letters she wrote often hinted at how much she and his father missed having him around, but he knew they were proud of him and his accomplishments.

The previous month, he'd won an award for an article he'd written exposing a shipping company that kidnapped foreigners and sold them into slavery once they arrived in Portland. Adam was the one who mentioned he thought something odd took place at the warehouse he passed every day on his way to work.

Thanks to Adam's tip, Tom pursued the story until he'd unraveled the mystery and earned accolades from his editor and others in the business.

For the next six weeks, though, Tom's career at the newspaper was effectively on hold until his arm healed.

Forcibly setting aside his dark thoughts about work, Tom glanced over at Blake as they neared the lane that would lead to his parents' place. "If you don't mind, I'd like to surprise Mama and Dad. If you let me out here, I can walk the rest of the way."

"Sure, Tom," Blake stopped the wagon.

Tom swung off the seat and lifted his bag from the back. "Thank you both, so much, for dinner and the ride."

"It's our pleasure. Stop by our place one day while you're home and I'll show you my new colt." Blake snapped the reins and the team leaned into the collars, easily pulling the wagon in a circle and heading home.

Tom looked ahead, glad the sliver of moonlight made it possible to see his parents' two-story farmhouse and the looming outline of the big barn in the background.

He stopped outside the gate set in the picket fence that surrounded his mother's carefully tended yard. In the summer, it was an oasis of flowers and lush grass, dutifully watered to keep everything fresh and growing. Since Tom was the one who used to haul the water, he wondered how they managed without his assistance. His father had mentioned hiring some help back in May. Tom realized he'd been so busy with work, he never even thought to ask if his father had hired someone.

Dismayed by how out of touch he'd become with his friends, and especially his family, he quietly opened the gate.

A furry blob raced around the corner of the house and Tom braced his legs for the impact as the dog jumped up, licking his face.

"Down, Jasper. Get down. That's a good boy." He dropped his bag and rubbed a hand over the dog's back. The canine plopped onto his hindquarters and wagged his tail, feathering the powdery snow. "You're a good boy, Jasper. Such a good boy."

The dog licked his hand and followed as Tom lifted his bag and hurried around to the kitchen door. He took the steps up the back porch in two long strides, gave the dog a final pat, and opened the door.

Warmth and a sense of homecoming enveloped him, along with the scent of cinnamon lingering in the air from something his mother had baked that day. The kitchen was dark as Tom set down his bag and removed his sling then shrugged out of his coat and hat. He left his outerwear on a hook by the door and stepped through the kitchen. Coals of a banked fire in the parlor cast a coppery glow around the room.

Fully expecting to find his folks sitting in front of a cozy fire reading or discussing the day's events, he didn't know what to make of the still house.

Muffled sounds from upstairs assured him his parents were home.

Perhaps they were ill. That would account for them being in bed so early in the evening.

Tom retraced his steps to the kitchen and lit a lantern with some difficulty. If he had to break an arm, he certainly wished it had been his left one, instead of the right. Unlike those talented few who were ambidextrous, he relied on his right hand for most everything. Now, simple tasks seemed nearly impossible as he tried to force his left hand to do the work.

With the lantern firmly in hand, he made his way to the staircase and started up the steps. He smiled as he avoided the fourth step up from the bottom, mindful of how it always creaked. The few times he'd been caught sneaking out of the house as a willful youth had been because of the telltale step.

At the top of the stairs, he turned to his left and noticed a circle of light spilling into the hallway from his parents' bedroom.

On silent feet, he moved down the hall then popped his head around the doorway. "Surprise!" he yelled, nearly dropping the lamp at the site of his parents engaged in an intimate moment.

His mother screamed and jerked blankets over her head while his father uttered words Tom had no idea the man even knew.

Heat rushed up his neck and seared his face as he abruptly turned around and clattered down the steps to the kitchen. Traumatized, he blinked his eyes several times to clear the vision of what he'd just witnessed from his mind.

"Tom?" his father yelled. The deep bass of his voice carried throughout the house.

Footsteps thumped across the floor above his head as Tom set the lantern on the table and reached for his coat. He pictured his father hopping around on one foot, trying to pull on his pants.

In his haste to leave, Tom jammed his injured arm in the sleeve of his coat. The cast caught on the lining, making him suck in a gasp of pain.

"Son? What are you doing here?" James Grove asked as he ran into the kitchen. Bare-chested with bare feet, he wore a pair of hastily donned trousers with his hair sticking out every direction.

"Nothing. I'll just... um... I'll head back to town. I can get a room at the boarding house."

"Nonsense. You're home and you'll stay right here, like you've always done." James lit the lamp in the center of the big kitchen table and stared at Tom. "Come on, son. Take off your coat and stay."

"I'm sorry, Dad. I didn't mean to... I didn't realize..." Tom wondered if he might die of mortification right there in the kitchen where he'd spent so many wonderful years as a boy. "Truly, I'm sorry. It might be best if I just leave."

His father thumped him on the shoulder then lit the wick in another lantern. "Don't be ridiculous, Tom. No apology is necessary. Your mother and I want you to stay. Please?"

Hesitant, Tom removed his coat and hung it by the door. By the time he gathered his composure and turned around, his mother appeared in the kitchen, fastening the last button on a wrapper that swathed her form from neck to toe. However, her hair still hung loose in long, golden waves that belied her age.

For the first time in his life, Tom looked at the two people across the room not as his parents, but as individuals. His father was a strong, strapping man and Junie Grove held onto her youthful beauty although she had entered her fortieth year of life.

"I... I just..."

Whatever Tom might have stammered was lost when his mother embraced him in a loving hug and kissed his cheek. "Welcome home."

She pulled back and glared at the cast on his arm. "What happened, sweetheart? Are you well? Have you eaten? How long can you stay? You didn't walk all the way from town, did you? You should have sent word you were coming. We'd have met you at the stage."

Tom relaxed as his mother pushed him toward a kitchen chair and quickly set about making hot chocolate. While the milk warmed, she lifted a towel covering a pan and slid a cinnamon roll onto a plate, setting it in front of him with a smile. "I woke up this morning and decided I needed to make cinnamon rolls. Since they are your favorite, I must have known you were coming."

"Thanks, Mama." Tom cut into the tender pastry and savored the sweet bite, laden with cinnamon. "That's so good."

James took a seat across the table from him with a cinnamon roll and cut off a bite. "What happened to your arm?"

Tom glanced down at the cast. "I was helping with the late edition on Tuesday. The press can be temperamental on a good day. Since I'm one of the few people there who knows which end of a wrench to hold, I sometimes work on it. I reached in to make an adjustment when it suddenly came to life and crushed my arm. It's broken in two places, but the breaks are clean and the doctor said it should heal quickly. Since I can't write or do anything with it for several weeks, my editor told me to take the month off and spend the holidays with my family. I wanted to surprise you both."

The humor of the situation caught up with Tom and he smirked at his father. "Guess I did a good job of that."

His father chuckled while his mother's face flushed pink.

James cleared his throat. "That you did, son. We'll um... make sure that doesn't happen again." The man waggled his fork at Tom. "You didn't walk out from town, did you?"

"No. Blake and Ginny coerced me into eating dinner with them at the restaurant and then they dropped me off." Tom looked to where his mother stirred the chocolate on the stove. "Did you mention the upcoming addition to their family in one of your letters?"

Junie shrugged. "Come to think of it, I'm not sure I did, honey. It may have slipped my mind to let you know. Lately, there's been news of so many babies."

Tom grinned. "That's for sure. Is there something in the water? At this rate, babies will start popping up everywhere."

James choked on the bite of cinnamon roll he'd just swallowed and pounded a fist against his chest to dislodge it. Junie whacked him on the back and handed him a glass of water, along with a pointed glower.

Unsettled by the looks passing between his parents, Tom studied them. His mother's face had gone from slightly pink to the bright raspberry shade of her favorite summer roses while his father shifted uncomfortably on his chair.

Stunned by the thoughts racing through his head, Tom knew they couldn't be true. "You two... you aren't... you didn't..." Tom stared at his parents. "Are you?"

Junie poured chocolate into three mugs and set one in front of Tom. "Would it bother you so terribly to finally get that brother or sister you always wanted?"

Unable to stop himself, Tom's mouth dropped open. Society frowned on the discussion of a woman's "delicate" condition, but Tom didn't care. "You're expecting?"

Junie squeezed James' hand and leaned her head against his shoulder as she sat beside him. "We are, honey. After all this time, we're finally going to have another baby."

"But, Mama, you two are..." Tom caught himself before he said his parents were too old to have a baby. They certainly weren't too old to engage in the activities required to create one, if what he'd unwittingly stumbled upon earlier was any indication.

"We're what, son?" James asked, with a narrowed gaze.

Tom sighed and forked a hand through his short brown hair. For years, his mother had ached to have a big family, but he had been the only child. By the time Tom was ten, they'd all given up hope of another baby coming along and learned to be happy with just the three of them.

No matter how much the announcement caught him off guard, he couldn't help but be joyful for his mother and father as they anticipated such a big, unexpected blessing. "You are going to be great parents, again. Congratulations. When will I officially become a big brother?"

Chapter Two

Tom sat at the table the next morning, eating cinnamon rolls and crispy bacon, mulling over the possibility of returning to Portland early rather than stay in the house where he currently felt like a stranger.

Somehow, in accepting his absence from their home, the people who had given him life changed from simply being his parents to a couple celebrating a second honeymoon. The loving glances and touches they shared unnerved him, although he knew it was ridiculous to feel that way.

Part of him admitted it was silly and childish to be annoyed by their regenerated infatuation with each other, but he couldn't help it. At their age, they should be past such things. Shouldn't they?

Then again, Tom was happy for them. He thought of all the people he'd met through his work with the newspaper — all the unhappy individuals, the men who'd cheated on their wives, the women who'd stepped out on their husbands and families. If only those people had even a fraction of the love and adoration visible in his parents, their lives might have been so much better.

No, he'd much rather have his parents act like giddy, lovestruck teens than grow apart from one another.

The notion of having a baby brother or sister no longer seemed shocking. In fact, Tom warmed to the idea.

He'd given up on ever having a younger sibling, but now that he was old enough to have his own children, he'd finally get one.

It was a good thing he remained single, or he might have produced a grandchild that would be older than the baby his parents eagerly anticipated arriving in early summer. That would really be something.

The same beautiful glow he'd noticed on Ginny Stratton last night at dinner softened his mother's face as she hummed and refilled his coffee cup.

As though she sensed the turmoil of his thoughts, she cupped his chin and planted a kiss on his forehead. She'd done the same thing ever since he could remember.

The corners of his mouth lifted in a grin when she winked at him and refilled his father's coffee cup before returning the pot to the stove.

"So, Tom, do you have any plans while you're here, other than letting that arm heal," his father asked as he leaned back in his chair.

"No, sir. Not really. I'm not sure what I can do to be useful, but I'm willing to try anything. If I sit around doing nothing for six weeks, I'll be bored to death and as flabby as..."

A loud rap at the front door interrupted him.

"I'll get it," Junie said, wiping her hands on her apron as she rushed from the room. She returned with Arlan Guthry and Luke Granger following her.

Tom and his father both rose to their feet. "What brings you two all the way out here so early in the day?" James asked, motioning for the two men to have a seat at the table.

Luke sat beside Tom while Arlan took a seat next to James. Junie poured them both cups of coffee and offered cinnamon rolls.

"Thank you, Mrs. Grove," Luke said, smiling at her as he took a bite of the cinnamon roll. "That's delicious," he said, forking another bite before turning to thump a hand on Tom's back. "Blake mentioned Tom was back in town and we have a proposition for him."

"A proposition?" Tom asked, glancing from Arlan to Luke.

Arlan nodded. "Yes. My wife has been unable to teach much the last few weeks. She's been quite ill, but the doctor assures us it should pass in another month or so. You see, she's… um… well, she and I are…"

Junie squealed excitedly. "Oh, Arlan! When is she due?"

Tom groaned and rolled his eyes. "There really is something in the water," he muttered.

Luke chuckled, but Arlan either chose to ignore his comment or didn't hear it. "We're going to have a summer baby."

Junie smiled. "Tell Alex I'm so happy for her… for you both. That's wonderful news."

"We think so." Arlan grinned then turned his attention back to Tom. "The doctor says Alex's illness should pass in a matter of weeks. In the meantime, she doesn't feel up to teaching. From what Blake shared, you're here through the holiday season. Would you be interested in taking over teaching duties through Christmas? The children will be on break for a few weeks and by the time school reconvenes, Alex should feel well enough to teach again."

Tom considered the possibilities. If he hadn't been so enthralled with the idea of writing for a newspaper, he would have gone into teaching. Thanks to Alex, he'd come to love learning and school, and thought it would be a wonderful thing to share that with others.

Now, it appeared he would have that opportunity. "I'd be honored to teach, if you think I can do a good job for the students." He held up his arm with the heavy cast. "And if you don't think this will get in the way."

"You'll be fine," Luke said, thumping his shoulder again. "If you need help writing anything on the blackboard, we can find someone willing to assist."

"And I'd be happy to help you grade papers, honey," Junie offered.

"Thanks, Mama." Tom nodded across the table to his mother.

"If you'd like, the teacher's house is empty. You could stay there so you don't have to make the trip to and from town every day," Luke offered. He recalled how hard it was to live under the same roof as his parents when he was Tom's age.

Although Junie and James frowned at that bit of news, Tom brightened. After three years of living on his own, it would require patience and a big adjustment to reside with his parents, especially in light of the current state of affairs. By moving to the teacher's house, he could spend weekends at the farm and maintain his sanity all at the same time.

Tom smiled. "I'd like that. With this arm, I'm not sure traipsing around in the dark every evening on a long walk home is a good idea. When would you like me to start?"

"Tomorrow?" Luke asked.

"I'll be there," Tom said, pleased at the prospect of having something to keep his mind and hands busy while he was in Hardman.

Luke and Arlan finished their coffee and cinnamon rolls then rose to their feet, offering to give Tom a ride into town if he wanted to check out the house next to the school.

"I need to run into town later, son," James said, walking with Luke and Arlan to the front door. "I could meet you there in a few hours."

"Thanks, Dad. That sounds great." Tom hurried to slip on his coat. His mother helped him situate the sling around his neck and held his gloves while he slid them on.

She grinned at him as he worked his fingers into the second glove. "Just like when you were a little boy."

He scowled. "Thanks, Mama. I needed the reminder I'm as helpless as an infant."

Junie laughed and patted his cheek. "Hardly, sweetheart. Go into town and have a good time. We'll catch up with you later."

Tom bent down and kissed her cheek then hurried out the door and across the front walk to the sleigh Luke had parked outside the gate.

James waved as Luke turned the sleigh and guided the horse back toward the road. On the ride into town, the two men inquired about life in the city. Arlan asked questions about his brother. Tom assured him Adam, Tia, and the children were well.

"I think Toby's cat has grown even more cantankerous," Tom said as they made their way to town.

"How could that be possible? I've never seen a cat that hated people as much as Crabby," Arlan mused, waving as they passed a slow-moving wagon.

"He doesn't hate all people. He likes Adam, loves those two kids, and tolerates Tia."

"Remember the time he attacked that thug who tried to kidnap Toby?" Luke asked as they neared town. "I still wish I'd seen him in action."

"Me, too," Tom said. He grinned as Luke guided the horse into the schoolyard. Smoke puffed from the school's chimney and footprints in the snow hinted that children had played in it before trooping inside for classes. "Is Alex teaching today?"

Arlan shook his head. "No. She's home in bed. Luke found a substitute for the day, although she is adamant in her refusal to provide a permanent solution to our problem."

"Is it one of the mothers?" Tom asked. Luke and Arlan led the way up the steps to the door of the schoolhouse he knew so well from the years he'd attended classes there.

"I coerced my cousin into teaching. She much prefers to play with the children than teach them, though." Luke opened the door and motioned Tom and Arlan to precede him.

As they stepped inside, Tom looked around the sea of young faces. His gaze rested on the beautiful dark-haired woman at the front of the room, gray eyes sparking with mischief and fun as she smiled at them.

Pain blazed across his chest with an unexpected force. He took a staggering step back, attempting to catch his breath.

Oblivious to his current inability to think straight, Arlan and Luke greeted the class.

"Good morning, students," Luke said, his voice carrying friendly authority. "We'd like you to meet your temporary teacher. Mr. Grove will take over classes starting tomorrow until Miss Alex is well enough to return." Luke waved his hand toward the front of the room.

Tom tried not to gape at the glorious creature standing near the blackboard smiling at them.

Luke grinned. "Tom Grove, this is my cousin, Miss Lila Granger. If you think my sister and wife can cause trouble, they don't hold a candle to the tomfoolery this one makes without even trying."

Tom watched as the young woman marched toward them, the train of an expensive gown the same color as her eyes swishing in the wake of her steps.

"Hello, Mr. Grove. It's a pleasure to meet you." She stuck her hand out to him.

Awed and thoroughly addled, Tom yanked the glove off his left hand with his teeth and let it fall to the floor as he took her hand in his. Although she meant it to be a handshake, the connection of their palms felt more like a caress as he held her delicate hand in his.

Fearful of what words might spill out of his mouth if he opened it, he was surprised when he spoke in a clear voice. "The pleasure is mine, Miss Granger."

Whoever named this womanly sprite had chosen her name well. Lila put him in mind of springtime and an array of brilliant flowers. The scent of lilacs wafted around him as she pulled back her hand and smiled at Luke. "How wonderful you've coerced someone else into teaching these little hooligans."

Luke laughed while Arlan chuckled. The students appeared to be as dumbstruck by the engaging Lila Granger as Tom. One curly-headed cherub rose from her seat and ran over to them, wrapping her arms around Luke's leg.

The banker picked up his daughter and kissed her cheek. "Do you want to go home with me, honey?"

The little one shook her head, sending her curls into disarray. "No, daddy. I's having fun with Lila."

"Then you keep right on having it, Maura." Luke set her down and gave her a nudge back toward her seat in the front row.

Lila leaned toward Tom and he inhaled a deep whiff of her fragrance, sending his temperature into a steady climb.

"Mr. Grove, are you sure you wouldn't like to take over classes right now? Why, these little rascals are likely to tar and feather me before the day is over." A sassy smile revealed white, even teeth in her brilliant smile.

Tom shook his head. "I doubt that, Miss Granger." He glanced around the room, seeing many familiar faces, including several he'd sat behind in classes when they were younger. "There hasn't been a tarring or feathering since I was in fourth grade."

Lila laughed, the sound shooting arrows of delight into Tom's heart. "And were you in charge of the tar or the feathers, Mr. Grove?"

"The tar, of course," he replied. Aware that everyone in the room intently listened to their conversation, he bowed to Lila. "We'll leave the students in your capable hands, but they better be prepared to have a hard taskmaster in charge tomorrow."

The students looked at him wide-eyed, but Lila winked at him. "I'll make sure they're ready for you." She turned to Luke. "And I'll see you at home this evening, cousin."

"Have a good day, Lila," Luke said, opening the door.

Cold swirled around them, blowing away the lingering scent of her soft fragrance. Tom snatched up his glove and shoved it into his pocket then followed Luke outside.

Arlan and Luke showed him the teacher's house. Although basic, it was furnished with everything he'd need. He knew he could get linens from his mother and a trip to the mercantile would stock the cupboards.

"Do you want a ride anywhere?" Luke asked as he climbed in the sleigh and lifted the reins.

"No, thank you, Luke." Tom remained standing in front of the little house. "I think I'll wander around town a bit, until it's time to meet my father."

"Thanks again for taking on the job, Tom. We greatly appreciate it," Luke said as Arlan slid onto the seat.

Arlan glanced over at Tom. "Be sure to stop by our house. Alex is most anxious to see you. She'll want to hear all about the newspaper and she'll probably have some ideas for lesson plans."

Tom nodded. "I promise to stop by later."

Luke snapped the reins and the sleigh swooshed across the snow back into town.

He watched it go. Slowly ambling out to the boardwalk, he wondered what sort of spell Miss Lila Granger had cast over him.

Never, not even once in his twenty-one years of living, had he experienced anything like the feelings coursing through him the moment he'd set on eyes on her.

Interest in a girl he'd only see for a few weeks, especially one related to the well-to-do Grangers, was pure folly. But she certainly was pretty and plenty feisty.

A self-depreciating smile touched his lips. "There really must be something in the water."

Chapter Three

Lila locked the door to the school with a click, dropped the key in her reticule, and rushed down the steps.

"Come on, girls. Let's go," she called to Erin Dodd and Maura Granger. Although unrelated by blood, the two were closer than most sisters could hope to be.

With dark curls and blue eyes, Erin was a little beauty full of sass and spunk. Maura's strawberry blond curls and pale green eyes gave her the appearance of a delicate doll.

At the ripe old age of nearly seven, Erin felt it her duty to instruct Maura in everything from the best way to swing to the tastiest bites of snow. Lila discovered a few of the busybodies in town frowned upon the pastor allowing his child to be so lively. Even if Chauncy and Abby wanted to subdue their spirited little girl, it would have been impossible to do so.

"Hurry, Maura," Erin encouraged, holding out a hand to the four-year-old. Although Maura was young to be in school, she begged to attend classes and her parents finally relented. Most days, the child was ready to go home at noon. On days when fun things transpired in the classroom, she lasted until school released for the day. At any rate, someone was there to check on her when the students rushed outside for their lunch recess.

Lila held out her hands to the children. Erin took her left while Maura latched onto her right. "Well, Miss Erin, what do you think of Mr. Grove teaching until Aunt Alex is feeling better?"

"I think it's splendid," Erin said, grinning up at Lila with a missing front tooth. "Tom, I mean Mr. Grove, used to play with us sometimes. And he helps Aunt Alex with her magics."

"Oh, he does?"

"Yep." Erin skipped along, curls bobbing with each bounce. Maura tried to mimic her actions, but had a hard time keeping up.

Lila slowed her steps for the youngster. "Does Mr. Grove live here?"

"No. He moved away to Portland, but he gets to see Uncle Adam and Aunt Tia and he visits my best friend, Toby." Erin turned her elfin face up to Lila's again. "I'm going to marry Toby when we grow up. He's going to be a doctor and we will live on a boat and eat Turkish delight every day!"

One shapely, dark eyebrow arched upward. "Is that so? Decisiveness is a grand trait, Erin. One that will serve you well."

"That's what my daddy says." Erin giggled and pointed across the street to where Percy Bruner held hands with Anna Jenkins. "Percy's been sweet on Anna forever."

"Forever," Maura echoed.

She looked at her cousin's daughter. "What about you, Maura? Who do you fancy?"

"Nobody!" the little girl said, jumping forward and landing on both feet with a solid thud. "I like Bart bestest."

Lila laughed. "I'm sure your father will be pleased to know that mangy dog is held highest in your affections."

"Bart's a good doggie," Maura said, giving her head one curt toss to accentuate her thoughts on the matter.

"Yes, he is." Lila agreed. She took a tighter grip on the girls' hands as they crossed the street and walked past the mercantile to Abby Dodd's dress shop.

Erin ran ahead and opened the door to her mother's store, racing inside.

"Hi, Mama!" Erin wrapped her arms around her mother's shoulders as she sat at a sewing machine, stitching a seam down the ruby silk skirt of a holiday dress.

Abby Dodd kissed her daughter's rosy cheek then heavily lumbered to her feet.

Lila grinned as Erin gently tapped her mother's tummy. "Hi, baby. Hurry and get here so I can play with you."

Abby looked down at Erin and cupped her chin. "Your brother, or sister, will arrive when he or she is good and ready and not a minute sooner." She glanced up at Lila and smiled. "Although, at this point later might be best. I still have four holiday gowns to finish."

"If you need help, Abby, let me know. I can't do the fancy stitching, but I can at least sew a straight seam." Lila backed toward the door before Maura decided she wanted to stay and play with the toys Abby kept in a corner of her shop.

"I might take you up on that, if Luke and Filly run out of things to keep you busy." Abby waddled over and gave Maura's little cheek a kiss. "Did you have a good day at school, sweetheart?"

"Oh, yes, Aunt Abby. Lila let us sing. I love to sing."

"Yes, you do." Abby smiled at the child. "Did I hear you'll have a different teacher tomorrow?"

"Yep! Mr. Grove is gonna teached us." Maura swung back and forth while holding onto Lila's hand.

"That will be fun, won't it?" Abby pressed both fists into her lower back.

"Are you well, Abby? Do you need anything?" Lila asked, concerned by the woman's continued rubbing of her back and the discomfort lingering around her eyes.

"I'm just a little stiff from sewing all day. Nothing to worry about." Abby turned to her daughter. "Erin, honey, will you grab Mama's coat? We need to head home. Your father will be there soon, ready for his supper."

"I best get this little one home, too," Lila said, tugging Maura toward the door. "She's had a long day."

"She has, but I bet it was entertaining with you in charge of the class."

"It was so fun, Mama. Miss Lila even played with us outside and helped us build a snowman!" Erin said, dragging Abby's coat across the floor.

Abby took it from her and slipped it on. "Tell Filly I'll stop by in the morning for a final fitting of her gown."

"I'll do that, Abby. Have a wonderful evening." Lila opened the door and stepped outside. Maura hopped on one foot then the other a few steps before she suddenly deflated like a flattened ball, dragging against Lila's arm.

She smiled and picked up the little girl, settling her on her hip. "Well, miss honey bunny, what happened?"

"I runned out of steam." Maura rested her head against Lila's shoulder.

"Yes, you did," Lila said, kissing the tiny dimple in Maura's chin.

Lila hurried through town, eager to return to Granger House. Since the day she set foot in Hardman three months ago, she'd enjoyed every minute of her time there.

When her parents died in a tragic boating accident the previous summer, she wasn't sure how she'd go on without them. Her father's favorite cousin, Greg Granger, and his wife, Dora, traveled from their home in Oregon to help her settle her parents' estate and invited her to visit them in Hardman.

Lila wasn't in a hurry to do anything rash or to leave behind the New York home where she'd been born and raised. A handsome young man who'd been courting her seriously for more than a year proposed not long after her parents passed away. Emerson Lylan confessed his timing was inappropriate, particularly for a girl who was grieving such a devastating loss, but he would soon leave to spend a year studying abroad. He wanted to ensure Lila's affections would still belong to him upon his return.

Once she agreed to marry him when he came back to America, he hugged her tenderly on New Year's Eve as the clock struck midnight. His kiss held warmth and promises for the future. The next day, he left with many vows to write often and miss her every moment while he was away.

The last letter Lila had from him, he elaborated on his plans to return to New York mid-January. He'd hinted at wanting to marry her in an April ceremony.

In truth, Lila wasn't sure a spring wedding was a good idea. She thought it wise if she and Emerson spent time becoming reacquainted before they made any further commitments to each other. While she'd been quite enamored of the dashing young man with vibrant blue eyes and thick golden hair, the many months apart gave her the time she needed to grow up and develop more certainty about herself.

As her self-confidence grew, so did her resolve that she would not jump headlong into marriage with anyone, even if she'd been engaged to Emerson for nearly a year.

She missed his wit and intellect, his courtly manner and attentive interest, but she wanted to be one hundred percent certain she was madly in love with him before they exchanged vows.

In an attempt to fill the emptiness left by the death of her parents and Emerson's departure, she'd joined committees, volunteered to help with any number of charities, and kept herself too busy to think.

One morning, as she rushed out the door, she'd realized she wasn't enjoying life. She wasn't living it. Rather, she was merely getting through one day then the next and the next.

That very afternoon, she'd sent a telegram to Greg letting him know to expect her arrival the following week. She packed her trunks, purchased a train ticket, set her business affairs in order, and made the trip to Oregon without a chaperone.

Scandalized by the fact she traveled alone, Dora Granger protested her travel arrangements, but her daughter, Ginny Stratton, encouraged Lila to be independent.

It took Lila all of a day to decide rather than stay at Dora and Greg's spacious house, she would live at Luke and Filly's home. Granger House was where everyone seemed to gather. Fun and excitement fairly filled the home to the rafters.

Lila stepped off the boardwalk and walked along the path Luke had shoveled to the back entry of his home. She rushed up the steps and smiled at the dog lounging by the kitchen door.

"Bart, my friend, are you keeping guard over Filly?"

The dog lifted his head and woofed, wagging his tail as he stared at her, waiting for the scratch behind the ears she usually delivered.

"My hands are full of our girl, Bart. You'll have to wait a minute," Lila said, opening the door and stepping inside the homey kitchen.

Filly glanced up from where she stood in front of the stove, stirring a pot of stew that filled the house with a mouth-watering beefy scent. Fresh bread cooling on the counter, redolent with a yeasty aroma, made Lila want to snatch a piece and dredge it in butter.

"That smells so good, Filly. I can hardly wait until dinner." Lila toed the door closed behind her and set Maura down on the end of the kitchen counter.

"Oh, baby, did you have a long day?" Filly asked, pulling off Maura's knit cap and unbuttoning her coat.

"I's tired, Mama," Maura whispered, eyes fluttering closed.

"I'm sure you are," Filly said, smiling over her daughter's head to Lila. "I knew she'd be exhausted when she refused to let her daddy bring her home earlier."

"She did have a busy day." Lila opened the back door and gave Bart several good scratches before stepping back inside and removing her coat and hat.

"I'm glad for that," Filly said, lifting her daughter and carrying her down the hall to the parlor where a merry fire blazed in the fireplace.

Lila washed her hands and peeked in the cradle near the kitchen table where little Cullen Granger slept.

The baby boy was only two months old and as sweet as he could be. Lila adjusted the blanket over the infant then hurried to set the table.

Filly breezed back into the room and smiled appreciatively at Lila. "Thank you so much for setting the table. As far as I know, there aren't any unexpected guests coming for dinner tonight."

Lila laughed. "When has that ever stopped Luke from inviting one or two or four extras along?"

Filly gave the stew a stir. "Never, but I truly don't mind. At least I don't now that I'm feeling back to normal."

Little Cullen's arrival had been a much more difficult birth than Maura's. Lila wondered how the lovely woman married to her cousin survived the ordeal. In truth, Lila had been as worried about Luke as she had Filly. He'd nearly gone mad with worry during the labor that stretched from one day into two as Filly battled to deliver the baby. Chauncy, Blake, and Arlan had all taken turns keeping him company while Abby, Ginny, and Alex alternated staying with Filly. Lila took charge of Maura and Erin with the help of Greg and Dora.

Much to Lila's surprise, once the healthy baby arrived, Luke rushed to Filly's side and refused to leave, promising he wouldn't put her through a similar ordeal.

Now, two months later, Luke nearly burst with pride any time someone asked about his son. Lila would have said he played favorites, except the man was equally as thrilled with his adorable little girl.

In spite of his obvious affection for both of his children, she couldn't help but notice his immeasurable love for his wife. Luke looked at Filly as if she floated on air.

The love the couple shared was the type Lila wanted. And before she agreed to set a wedding date with Emerson, she would make sure that's how he felt about her.

Emerson was wealthy in his own right, so she knew he wasn't after her money or social status. He'd been kindness itself after her parents' untimely passing.

Flattered Emerson had chosen her to wed, Lila wondered if part of her recent hesitation stemmed from the distance between the two of them.

In less than two months, she'd see him again. Most likely, love would surge through her the instant Emerson held her hand in his and gazed at her with his bright eyes. However, instead of picturing Emerson, her thoughts drifted to the pair of soulful eyes and a warm, callused hand that had captivated her earlier when she met Tom Grove.

Filly bumped into Lila, drawing her back to the present. "Were you wool gathering or daydreaming?"

Lila shrugged. "A little of both, I suppose."

"At least you're honest." Filly wiped off her hands and wrapped an arm around Lila's shoulders, giving her a hug. "If I haven't mentioned it lately, I'm so thankful to have you here. You've been such a blessing to us and I don't know what I would have done without you since Cullen arrived."

"My pleasure, Filly. I didn't realize how dull my life had become until I moved in with you and Luke. Thank you for giving me a place to stay." Lila gazed up at the woman who stood a good five inches taller than her height. "It seems life here in Hardman quite suits the Grangers."

Filly laughed. "That it does. Even Dora has stopped wistfully talking about returning to New York."

"That's because she's too busy doting over her grandbabies. She'll forget any other place exists by the time Ginny and Blake welcome their little one."

"You're probably right," Filly said, filling glasses with water and setting them on the table.

Lila cocked an ear and listened as Luke whistled his way around to the kitchen door. "It appears Luke is capable of coming home by himself," she said, tossing Filly a jaunty grin.

"Surely not," Filly teased. When Luke opened the door and stepped inside, Filly cast a coy glance at her husband. "Are you losing your touch, Luke? You haven't come home by yourself in weeks. Wasn't there some homeless degenerate or wayward stranger you failed to invite for supper?"

Luke smirked and stepped across the kitchen. He grabbed Filly around the waist and planted a kiss on her lips. Before she pulled away, he slid cold hands down the neck of her dress.

Filly squirmed away, shaking a spoon at him. "You best behave yourself, Mr. Granger, or you'll be sent to your room without any supper."

He waggled his eyebrows suggestively. "Only if you promise to come with me."

Lila laughed and filled a glass with milk for Maura while Filly flushed with embarrassment at his scandalous teasing.

Luke shed his outerwear, washed his hands, and then looked around the kitchen. "Where's my girl?"

"Asleep, in the parlor. She didn't quite make it home before she lost her pep," Filly said.

"I'll see if she's still sleeping." Luke hurried out of the kitchen.

While he looked in on his daughter, Filly checked on the baby then ladled the stew into a serving bowl and placed it on the table. Lila sliced bread and set it on the table, along with freshly churned butter and peach jelly.

Maura bounced on her father's back as he carried her into the kitchen, seemingly revived by her nap.

Halfway through dinner, she listed to one side and her head rocked back against the chair.

"Poor thing is just done in," Filly said, brushing her fingers across Maura's forehead, pushing back the child's mop of curls.

Luke started to scoot his chair back, but Filly motioned for him to remain seated. "Eat your stew, Luke. I'll take her upstairs." She rose and lifted Maura in her arms, cuddling her daughter close as she left the room.

After watching her go, Luke buttered another slice of bread and dipped a corner of it in his stew. "There's nothing quite like hearty beef stew on a cold winter day."

"I agree, cousin," Lila said, helping herself to a second slice of bread. It was a good thing she stayed very active or she'd gain ten pounds eating Filly's cooking. Lila had dined on some of the best food money could buy, but she preferred the delicious, simple meals Luke's wife prepared.

Despite Dora's continued insistence that Luke needed to hire a cook and full-time housekeeper, Filly enjoyed caring for her home and cooking meals. Mrs. Kellogg, a pleasant older woman, came three times a week to help with laundry, cleaning, and baking.

Lila liked to think her presence at the house helped alleviate some of Filly's work. She knew if the woman didn't enjoy it, Luke would have hired more help a long time ago.

He took pride in Filly's abilities and relished the meals she prepared, as did the endless string of guests who found their way to the Granger table.

Greg and Dora were frequent visitors, even though Dora had a full-time cook, a housekeeper, a butler, a gardener, and a lady's maid.

Lila was accustomed to having servants wait on her, but her mother also thought it important for her to learn all domestic skills. Grateful for her mother's wisdom, Lila could prepare a meal, wash a load of laundry, and remove crayon marks from wallpaper.

Thoughts of Maura coloring a picture on the wall in the dining room made her grin. The little girl had grown quiet one afternoon. After searching the house, Lila finally found her sitting on the floor behind the dining room table, contentedly drawing on the wall.

Lila watched with interest as Filly lectured the child on why that was not acceptable, took her crayons away for a week, and made Maura help clean up the mess.

"Well, what did you think?" Luke asked, covering another piece of bread with a liberal coating of jelly.

Lila pulled her attention back to the present. "My apologies, Luke. I missed the question."

He grinned. "Dreaming of Emerson again?"

She shook her head. "Not exactly."

The look he shot her held a bit of scrutiny. "I asked what you thought of Tom Grove."

"He seems like a nice man. Several of the students mentioned how much they like him." Lila swirled her spoon around in her bowl of rapidly cooling stew. "Do you think his arm being in a cast will hamper his ability to control the class?"

"No, not at all. Tom has a good head on his shoulders. I used to think he'd become a teacher, but then he ventured off to Portland to work as a reporter for the newspaper there. From the articles I've read, he's quite good."

"Did he give any thought to working at the local paper?" Lila asked. She knew Ginny sometimes wrote articles or created illustrations for Ed Daily, owner of the Hardman newspaper.

"He worked there off and on before he left for Portland. His father owns a farm and Tom's help was needed there most of the time." Luke took a bite of stew.

"How does his father manage now, with Mr. Grove in Portland?" Lila toyed with her bread.

"He hired two boys to help him this summer. There's not nearly as much work during the winter months." Luke glanced over at Lila. "I'm glad James and Junie encouraged Tom to leave. Not everyone is cut out to do what their father has done."

Lila tossed him a saucy grin. "And that's why you spend less and less time at the bank and more time chasing cows, playing with Blake's horses and begging your wife for cookies."

Luke snorted. "The third best decision I ever made was making Arlan a partner at the bank. He could manage it with his eyes closed and one hand tied behind his back."

"I'd like to see that. If he gives a demonstration, you must let me know." Lila grinned. "If that's your third best decision, what were the other two?"

"Accepting Filly as a bargain, and marrying her."

They remained silent a few moments, then Luke looked to Lila again. "I told Tom if he needed help writing lessons on the blackboard we'd have someone available. Would you mind? You generally walk Maura to school in the morning anyway. If you checked in with him then, it wouldn't take too much of your time. Tom is right handed, and that's the arm he busted. Until he gains more mobility with it, he can't do much writing."

"I'd be happy to help. In fact, I could check in with him at noon when I go to retrieve Maura. That way, if something occurred during the morning he wanted to add to the blackboard, I could do it then."

"That's a fine plan." Luke helped himself to another ladle of stew.

Curious, Lila wondered what made him appear so pleased. Eventually, she'd find out.

Chapter Four

After he stopped to say hello to several friends, Tom made his way over to see Alex Guthry. Although she looked pale and weary, she met him with a warm smile and questioned him all about his work. Arlan joined them at noon with sandwiches he'd purchased from Mrs. Ferguson at the boarding house.

As they ate lunch, Tom listened to the advice Alex shared about handling each of the students at the school, and how best to keep them interested and engaged in their lessons. Once they finished eating, he met his dad at the mercantile. Tom stocked up on supplies then James helped carry them back to the little house by the school.

He rode back to the farm with his father and spent the afternoon with his parents, talking about teaching, farming, and plans for the holidays. Junie made all his favorites for dinner. After she washed and dried the dishes, they all bundled up and gathered Tom's things to take into town.

His mom insisted on giving him plenty of warm blankets, two sets of sheets, fluffy pillows, and a stack of towels. She added butter, milk, eggs, and the last of the cinnamon rolls to a box of food. His dad tucked in half a smoked ham, a slab of bacon, and a beef roast.

The trip into Hardman passed quickly with the three of them recalling fun memories from past winter seasons. Before Tom would have thought it possible, they arrived at the house that would be his home for the next month. His parents helped carry in everything then his mother made the bed.

"If you want a ride out sooner than Friday evening, let us know," Junie said, giving him a tight hug.

"I will, Mama. I'll see you on Friday." Tom smiled at them both and waved his left hand as they climbed on the wagon and left.

Tom arose early, anticipating the day ahead. He built up the fire in the stove at his house, tugged on his coat, and stepped out into a world coated in frosty white.

His boots crunched across the crusted snow as he walked over to the school. He unlocked the door and hurried to build a fire in the stove so the room would be warm by the time the students arrived.

Satisfied with his efforts, he returned to the teacher's house and changed his clothes from a pair of old canvas pants and a worn woolen shirt into one of the suits he wore for work. He struggled with the buttons and barely managed to execute a sloppy tie. He doubted the students would be overly critical. If anything, some of the older ones would tease him for not dressing like a farmer.

Tom ate two of the cinnamon rolls his mother had packed for him and finished off his meal with a glass of milk, grateful for the help and care of his parents. He washed the dishes, gathered a stack of books and the lesson plans he'd made with Alex's help, then headed to the schoolhouse.

He hung his coat on a hook near the door, adjusted the sling on his arm, and strode down the aisle to the desk at the front of the room.

Alex had given him a booklet she'd kept from when she first received her teaching certification. Tom spent the previous evening pouring over the details offered for successfully mastering a classroom.

Among the many pages of wisdom, he'd studied a list of dos and don'ts all teachers should adhere to:

Do not lose your head or your temper.

Do not appear meek to your students.

Do enter the classroom with a purposeful gait and gaze lifted with a steady eye.

Do decide exactly what you will and will not allow in your classroom.

Do make your standards perfectly clear from the start.

Do appear to take it for granted that you will get what you want from the students.

Do state your plans in a clear manner and under no circumstances change your mind.

Do not allow a wayward child to escape punishment from kindness of heart.

Do not threaten vaguely or offer general declarations.

Do not grumble or nag.

Do not make exceptions to your rules, once established.

Do not allow a child to argue about a punishment.

Tom decided some of the rules were good, others questionable. If possible, he hoped to avoid meting out punishment. As a substitute teacher who would be gone after Christmas, he didn't feel it was his place to come into Alex's classroom and change anything. He wouldn't tolerate disrespect or disruption, but beyond those things, he wanted the children to be free to express their thoughts and ideas.

He grinned, ruminating over the students he'd be teaching. Among the liveliest were Percy Bruner and Erin Dodd. Throw little Maura Granger into the mix, and the classroom would be far from boring.

The sound of children's laughter drew his gaze out a side window. Students arrived, setting their slates and lunches on the step as they rushed to get in a few minutes of play before he rang the bell signaling the beginning of classes for the day.

He opened the notebook with his lesson plans and picked up a piece of chalk. After several starts and stops, he stared at the blackboard, wondering how he'd force his left hand to write legibly enough the children could read it. Boots stamping on the steps outside pulled his attention to the door.

Lila Granger breezed inside with a bright smile and the wafting scent of lilacs. If he'd been given to fanciful thoughts, Tom would have said she carried sunshine like a mantle across her shoulders and springtime in her step.

"Good morning, Miss Granger," he said, in his most polite tone.

"Good morning, Mr. Grove. Luke asked me to see if you needed help writing anything on the blackboard when I walked Maura to school this morning. My fingers are yours if you need them." She tugged off a fur-lined leather glove the color of emeralds and waggled her delicate hand at him as she walked up the aisle between the desks.

The desire to grasp her hand in his and pull her close enough to kiss made him take a step back, away from temptation. Instead, he smiled and nodded. "Your assistance would be greatly appreciated, Miss Granger. I was just pondering the best way to go about scribbling on the board with my left hand."

She tugged off her other glove and shoved them into her coat pocket. Hastily, she unbuttoned her coat and draped it over his chair then took the piece of chalk from his hand.

Tom tried not to stare at the green plaid woolen dress she wore that matched her gloves or the fine shape of her figure when she removed her coat.

"Where shall we begin?" she glanced at him over her shoulder.

Unaware he'd been intently staring at her, Tom turned and lifted the notebook he'd left open on his desk.

"If you'd be so kind, I'd like to put these spelling words on the board," he said, stepping beside her and holding out the notebook in his left hand.

"Your wish is my command." Lila grinned and began printing the words on the board. "Did you get settled into the teacher's house? Luke said you planned to stay there until Christmas."

"I did. My folks helped me yesterday," Tom said. Of all the women he'd met, why did the presence of the one standing next to him with a smudge of chalk dust on the curve of her exquisite cheek render him incapable of keeping his thoughts straight?

He drew in a deep breath to clear his mind and nearly choked on the soft scent of lilacs enveloping him. Unable to focus on the spelling words she wrote on the blackboard, his gaze roved over the waves of her dark hair. Pinned beneath the brim of a black hat, trimmed with green and navy blue plumes and a plump cabbage rose the color of plums, one wayward tendril lazily trailed along the slim column of her neck.

Tom wanted, in the worst way, to reach out and finger that silky strand. In need of distance from the entrancing woman, or perhaps to stand a few minutes in the bracing cold air, he subtly moved away from her.

Oblivious to his distracted state, Lila wrote the last word and looked at Tom. "Anything else?" she asked.

It was on the tip of his tongue to tell her no and that her help wouldn't be required in the future, but necessity won over the turmoil churning inside him. "If you wouldn't mind writing these arithmetic assignments, I'd be most appreciative." Tom turned the page and showed her the list of numbers.

"Certainly."

Tom cleared his throat, doing his best to look anywhere other than the fabric straining across her bodice as she reached up to write one of the math problems on the blackboard. "So, are you here for an extended time or will you return to New York soon?"

He'd asked his parents a few questions about the Granger family and manipulated the conversation around to finding out Lila arrived in town a few months ago, her parents were deceased, and she'd been a big help to Luke and Filly after the arrival of their son.

Lila continued posting the math problems. "I'll most likely return to New York at the end of January. My fiancé will be back then. He's been gone for a year, studying at the University of Oxford. Emerson is so smart. He plans to…"

Stunned by the revelation Lila was engaged to wed, Tom took another step away from her. He had no business entertaining any ideas about the intriguing girl in the first place. Considering her betrothed state, he absolutely had no right to hold any thoughts about her.

What was he thinking?

Clearly, he hadn't been.

Annoyed with himself, he moved further away.

"Oh, can you bring the notebook closer?" she asked, striving to see the next math problem.

"Sorry," Tom muttered, holding the notebook out while he remained an arms-length away. Suddenly, the classroom felt very small and incredibly confining.

He didn't care if he had to pay Percy a nickel every day to come write the lessons on the board, he couldn't spend more time around Lila Granger. With every nerve ending attuned to each move she made, every sense activated by her presence, spending any additional time alone with her would be pure stupidity.

"All finished," she said, setting down the chalk and pulling a handkerchief from her pocket to wipe away the dust lingering on her hands.

"Thank you," Tom said, setting the notebook on his desk, doing his best to ignore the bright light twinkling in eyes the color of the silvery leaves on his mother's lamb's ears plants.

When Lila turned to him with more chalk dust on her cheek, Tom gave no thought to reaching out and brushing it away.

At her startled look, he dropped his hand. "Chalk."

"Oh, thank you," she said, smiling once again. Her graze traveled around the classroom then landed back on him. "Do you need assistance with anything before I leave?"

"No, Miss Granger, but I do appreciate your help this morning."

"My pleasure," she said, reaching for her coat. Tom did his best to help her slip it on one-handed.

"Thank you, kind sir. I best be on my way. Filly and Abby will keep me busy until lunch running errands this morning."

"Then I won't detain you," Tom said, smiling down at her, wishing the consuming attraction he felt would immediately dissipate. He followed her down the aisle between the rows of desks to the door, admiring the way her skirts swished as she walked.

Once again capturing his wayward thoughts, he sighed inwardly, mentally lecturing himself on proper comportment.

At the door, Lila turned back to him. "If you need anything written on the blackboard this afternoon, I can do it when I check on Maura at lunch."

"That won't be necessary, Miss Granger. You've already done more than enough." Tom wondered if she had any idea of what, exactly, she'd done to him. In his unsettled state, the students would likely stage a revolt and take over the classroom before they got through the morning prayer.

"Enjoy the morning, Mr. Grove." Her hand lingered on the knob as she gave him a long, observant glance. She stepped in front of him and reached up, adjusting his tie. "We can't have you greeting the students on your first day with your tie half undone." Skillfully tying a knot, she stepped back and surveyed her work. "There, that's much better. Now you look entirely respectable."

Tom smirked. "Does that mean I only looked partially respectable before?"

Flustered, she opened the door and stepped outside. Cold air engulfed him as he continued staring at her.

"I didn't... that wasn't... oh, I'll see you later, Mr. Grove. Goodbye."

With that, she hurried down the steps, stopped to give Maura Granger a kiss on her upturned face, hugged Erin Dodd, then bustled off toward the heart of town.

Tom watched her until she disappeared around a corner. He picked up the hand bell located just inside the door and rang it loudly, summoning the students to class.

Chapter Five

"You are a first-rate ninny, Lila Angelique Granger," Lila muttered in disgust as she marched away from the school.

For reasons she couldn't understand and refused to explore, something about Tom Grove jarred her interest. Maybe it was the kindness she read in his face. Perhaps it was the way his soul seemed to glimmer in his warm blue eyes.

It most certainly couldn't be the woodsy smell of him or how handsome he appeared when she stepped into the classroom. Even with his tie all a mess and one of his shirt buttons about to work its way out of the buttonhole, he held a rugged appeal unlike the men she'd known in New York. Although he exhibited fine manners and was well spoken, she sensed an underlying restlessness, a hint of outdoors and freedom in him she'd not noticed in the men who had attempted to court her.

Vividly aware of him the entire time she wrote the spelling words and math problems on the blackboard, the moment he'd brushed the chalk dust from her cheek, her knees began to quake.

The slight touch of his fingers against her skin sent something skittering from the point of contact to every extremity. She wasn't attracted to the man. The very notion was utterly ridiculous.

After all, she was engaged to Emerson. She would marry him as soon as she returned to New York and confirmed his ability to make her stomach swirl with emotion every bit as much as Tom had done to her that morning.

Unnerved by the notion she already referred to Mr. Grove as Tom in her thoughts, she lambasted herself all the way back to Granger House.

As the chilly winter air nipped around her, she couldn't help but think about how appealing Tom looked as he tipped up his chin and allowed her to fix his tie.

Perhaps all she felt for him was pity. The man *was* practically incapacitated with his arm in a sling. The cast looked dreadfully heavy and had to be a source of much discomfort.

Yes, sympathy for his condition had to be the reason for her unbridled interest in the man. That would explain why she'd noticed his square chin, full bottom lip, and long dark lashes that rimmed his expressive eyes.

"Stop it, you addlepated loon," Lila grumbled, causing Bart to raise his head in question as she stomped up the back steps.

"Not you, Bart, old boy. I am the one in trouble today. Big trouble." Lila dropped down to her knees on the porch, heedless to the cold or wet puddles of snow melting around the dog's warm body. "I think I need to begin this day anew and set my focus on

Emerson. He's smart and witty, wonderful and kind. Indeed, I should concentrate on keeping him foremost in my mind."

The door swung open and Filly glanced down at her. "Are you talking to Bart again? I heard a voice and wondered if someone accompanied you home."

Lila grinned and surged to her feet, hustling inside. "Bart's a good listener," she said, whipping off her coat and hat, leaving them on hooks by the door. "What would you like me to help with this morning?"

"Would you mind keeping an eye on Cullen while I finish the laundry?" Filly asked as she peeked at her sleeping son in the cradle near the table.

Lila looked around Filly and smiled at the baby slumbering with one little fist above his head and his lips pursed, as though he wanted to suck on something. "I can do the laundry," she offered.

"No. I'll finish it. I just have one load left to do and I don't think you want to wash your cousin's drawers and socks." Filly grinned at Lila as the two of them walked to the laundry room door.

Lila gave Filly a saucy look. "You're right. The last thing I want to do is that load of laundry. I could begin fixing lunch or work on the pile of ironing."

"We're having leftover stew for lunch, there isn't anything dry enough to iron, and the house is clean. Why don't you read in the kitchen? Or you could take Cullen into the library, if you like." Filly picked up a pair of Luke's dirty socks.

"I'll find something to occupy myself in the kitchen." She backed up a few steps. "Are you sure you don't need help?"

"I'm sure, but thank you for offering. If you keep an eye on the baby, that's all I ask."

"Very well." Lila hurried to her bedroom and gathered her writing case. She returned to the kitchen and took out several sheets of thick monogrammed stationery, an inkwell, and her pen.

Determined to set her mind on her fiancé, she wrote him an informative letter, sharing about the delicious Thanksgiving dinner Filly prepared, how Alex performed several magic tricks, and plans for the holiday season. Ginny and Blake would host their annual skating party, the school's carnival promised to provide much amusement, and Lila had volunteered to help with the children's Christmas program at church.

She tapped the end of the pen against her chin, mulling over what else to write. The more time she spent away from Emerson, the harder it was to feel a connection to him. As she gazed out the kitchen window, she tried to envision what he looked like the day she'd gone to the pier to see him off. Instead of his vibrant cobalt eyes and blond head, she envisioned soft blue eyes full of emotion, depth, and warmth, and a short-cropped head of brown hair.

Annoyed her thoughts once again circled around to Tom Grove, Lila quickly finished the letter and sealed it in an envelope. She addressed it and slipped it into her coat pocket to mail when she went to check on Maura right before lunch.

She put away her writing things in her room and returned to the kitchen to find Cullen waving his little fists in the air.

The baby rarely cried. Ruefully, Lila smiled. Most likely, the little one had no need to cry since someone rushed to meet his every need as quickly as possible.

"Well, Cullen, are you hungry or does that diaper need to be changed?" Lila asked, lifting the infant into her arms.

She cuddled him close and kissed his cheek. Like Maura, he had a tiny little dimple in his chin, greatly resembling the one Luke sported. His pale hair was so soft, Lila couldn't help but gently brush her hand over his head and inhale his wonderful baby scent.

"What do you think, Cullen Lucas? Hmm? Is it time for your mama to finish with the laundry and feed you?" Lila talked to the baby in a quiet singsong voice. The baby watched her face as she spoke and sucked on his fist. She carried him down the short hall to the laundry room. "Shall we see if your mama is finished washing your daddy's smelly ol' socks?"

Filly glanced up as she ran the last sock through the mangler that squeezed all the moisture out of the wet laundry. "Is he awake already?" She tossed the sock in a basket with others then wiped her hands on her apron before taking the baby from Lila. "I suppose he's hungry, too."

"He is just like his father," Lila teased, lifting the basket and carrying it to the room next door. The large space over the boiler in the basement stayed warm and made the perfect place to dry clothes in the cold winter months. While Filly nursed the baby and changed his diaper, Lila hung up the laundry to dry, took down the sheets that had already dried, and folded them into a stack for Mrs. Kellogg to iron when she came the following morning.

When she finished, Lila returned to the kitchen and glanced at the clock. She had plenty of time before she needed to check on Maura. Her footsteps carried her to the parlor. She sat down at the piano, playing an assortment of popular, uplifting pieces.

"I love hearing you play," Filly said as she strode in the room with the baby. She took a seat in a rocking chair near the fire and set it into motion while Lila continued to segue from one song to another. She sang along to some tunes and merely played others.

At the sight of Cullen's eyes drooping in slumber, she switched from boisterous songs to soothing, calm tones. She sang a lullaby as Filly rocked the baby and soon he slept.

"I'll put him down in here where it's warm and quiet," Filly said, rising to her feet. Lila whisked off to the kitchen and returned with the cradle, setting it down just close enough to the fire to absorb the warmth it offered.

After gently tucking the baby into the cradle, Filly and Lila returned to the kitchen. "I think I'll whip up some cornbread to go with the stew and I suppose I should make some cookies. Luke seems to think the cookie jar is replenished by magic, but not even Alex could make that happen."

Lila laughed and slipped her arms into the sleeves of her coat then wrapped a scarf around her neck. "That would be quite a trick, considering how quickly yours empties." She tugged on her gloves and picked up her reticule. "Do you need anything from the Bruner's store while I'm out collecting Maura?"

"No, but thank you for asking." Filly creamed sugar and butter together for cookies. "Oh, would you mind inviting Tom for supper tonight? I'm sure he'll be tired after his first day of teaching. He'll have quite a time trying to cook with his arm in a sling."

"Of course," Lila said, her voice slightly clipped.

Surprised, Filly cast an odd look her way.

Lila ignored it and breezed out the door. The last thing she wanted was to sit across the dinner table from Tom Grove. She'd been unable to get him off her mind all morning. Attempts to convince herself pity drove her interest fell flat. She couldn't explain what about him, exactly, fascinated her, but something did.

Resolved to shoving her curiosity about the man aside, she rushed to the post office and mailed her letter to Emerson then hurried to the school. She reached the steps as the door opened and children spilled outside, eager to run off the energy they'd bottled up all morning.

Erin waved as she ran past Lila with two of her friends, making a beeline for the swings Blake and Luke had hung in some of the big trees.

Concerned Maura had raced past her unseen, Lila quickly gazed around the faces of students, but the little girl wasn't there.

Lila briskly marched up the steps and inside the schoolhouse. Tom Grove held Maura's coat while the little girl chattered nonstop, shoving her arms into the sleeves.

"Do you know my doggie, Mr. Grove? Bart's a good doggie, but Aunt Ginny calls him a slobbering bafoon." The little pixie smiled up at him. "Erin showed me a picture of a bafoon in a book. Bart's not a monkey. Why does Aunt Ginny call him a monkey?"

Lila pressed her hand against her mouth to keep from laughing as Tom struggled to help Maura button her coat. "Did your aunt call him a baboon or a buffoon? A baboon is a monkey, but a buffoon is someone silly, who amuses others with jokes."

"Oh," the little girl said, appearing thoughtful. "I understand. Bart's a buffoon." Maura clapped her hands together and spun in a circle chanting. "Bart's a buffoon, a funny foon."

Tom's eyes rolled upward as he bit back a smile. He held out his hand to Maura and she took it. "Did you bring your lunch, Maura?"

"No. Lila will bring it."

"And here I am," Lila said, making her presence known. Maura released Tom's hand and raced over to Lila, giving her a tight hug around the waist.

Tom's gaze snapped to Lila's and he offered her a hesitant smile. "Hello, Miss Granger."

"Mr. Grove," Lila said, cordially tipping her head his direction. "How did the morning lessons go? Did you have any problems?"

"No. Quite to my surprise, the students were all well behaved and settled right down to the business of learning with very little problem." He winked at Maura. "With the exception of a few little chatterboxes."

"Maura, were you talking during class again?" Lila asked, helping the child tug on her mittens.

"Only while we worked on maths." Maura shrugged as though that explained everything.

"You have to be quiet during class or your daddy said you have to stay home."

A little lip puckered out and moisture gathered in the pale green eyes. "I 'member, Lila. Please, I want to come to schools. I don't want to stay home."

Tom knelt down and placed his hand on Maura's back. "You did fine, Maura. Perhaps tomorrow you can make it all morning without forgetting to be quiet during class."

"I'll try, Mr. Grove." The little girl sniffled and threw her arms around his neck. "Thank you for teacheding me."

Tom hugged her back. "You're welcome. Now, you best go with Miss Granger."

Lila bent down and smiled at Maura. "Why don't you run along outside a moment, honey bunny? I'll be right there."

Maura scampered outside with Tom and Lila watching. She ran over to where Erin played with her friends.

"I hope she wasn't a disruption to you or the other students," Lila said, glancing up at Tom.

He offered her a reassuring look. "She was fine, Miss Granger. For one so young, she does incredibly well. Are you taking her home for lunch?"

"Yes. She won't be back this afternoon. Filly thinks whole days are still too much for her even though Maura would argue otherwise."

"She is a lively little thing. Between her and Erin Dodd, I'm not sure which one is full of more mischief."

Lila laughed. "I do believe it's a tie." She took a step outside then turned back. "Filly asked me to invite you for supper. We eat at six."

Without giving him time to say he appreciated the offer but wouldn't join them, Lila flounced down the steps and called to Maura. The little girl ran over and Lila took her hand, leading her home.

Tom watched them go before returning inside the schoolhouse and shutting the door. Like it or not, he'd be spending the evening at the same dining table as the lovely Lila Granger.

Much to his dismay, Tom realized how much he indeed liked the idea.

Chapter Six

"You're joshing us," Luke said, staring in disbelief at Tom as they gathered around the large dining room table at Granger House. In addition to Tom, Filly invited Dora and Greg, Alex and Arlan, and Blake and Ginny to join them for the meal.

Tom wiped his mouth on his napkin and returned it to his lap. "No, sir, I'm not. I was standing right there, across from the police chief's desk, when a beautiful gypsy woman stormed into the room. She had a colorful scarf tied around her hair and her clothes fairly dripped with jewels. She even had a sparkling bracelet around her arm, here," Tom said, motioning to his upper arm. "Big round circles of silver hung from her ears and the rings on her fingers flashed in the sunlight streaming in the office window. She marched right up to the mayor and spoke rapidly in a language none of us understood. When she finished, she turned and spat on the floor, lifted her hands heavenward and uttered something else we couldn't understand. The police chief decided it had to be a curse for tossing her brother in jail for picking pockets."

Transfixed, Lila listened to Tom's story. "What happened?"

"When he left that day, the police chief's horse bucked him off a block away from the police station. He ended up staying home with a broken leg for several weeks." Tom glared at his broken arm. "Maybe some of the curse rubbed off on me for standing too close when she was there."

Alex playfully grinned. "Now, you're being ridiculous."

"You would know, my gypsy wife," Arlan said, offering Alex an indulgent smile.

"I'm not Romanian, Arlan. How many times must I tell you just because I may look like a gypsy, or even acted like a gypsy traveling from town to town in my magic wagon, I was not raised by gypsies?"

Arlan chuckled. "I know, dear lady, but I find it most amusing to see your reaction each time I mention it."

"Humph!" Alex huffed in feigned annoyance, and then turned back to Tom. "It sounds as though your work is certainly interesting."

He nodded his head as he swallowed the bite of tender roast beef. "It is, Alex. I'm so glad you all encouraged me to move to Portland and pursue a career in writing. I've learned so much working at the newspaper and look forward to getting back to it."

"Maybe next time the press is down, you'll make sure it can't come back to life before you stick your arm inside it," Luke suggested, pointing toward the cast on Tom's arm.

"Definitely." Tom tossed an unobtrusive glance at Lila as she sat across the table from him. She looked entirely lovely in a crimson-colored gown that made her cheeks appear as though they'd been touched with pink blossoms.

Distracted by her lilac fragrance and the mirthful light in her eyes, he wondered how someone so full of laughter and fun was related to uptight Dora Granger. However, the woman had mellowed considerably in recent years. The arrival of her grandchildren seemed to have a profound effect on her former snobbish attitude. Perhaps she was too busy doting on Maura and Cullen to be critical of others.

Tom shifted his attention from the entrancing young woman across from him to Greg Granger. "Did I hear that you and Mrs. Granger recently returned from a trip to New York, sir?"

"That's right, Tom," Greg said, accepting the breadbasket Luke held out to him and helping himself to another piece of Filly's light bread. "I had some business to attend to, but it's always nice to return home to Hardman."

Tom nodded. "Were you able to take in the automobile show at Madison Square Garden while you were there?"

Greg's eyes lit with excitement. "Dora didn't wish to attend, but I went with two business associates. The event lasted several days and featured more than a hundred different vehicles. For the outrageous sum of fifty cents, anyone could attend the 'horseless horse show,' as they called it."

"Didn't you say they had a wooden ramp to show off hill-climbing capabilities?" Luke asked, looking to his father.

"They certainly did, son. It was quite something to watch as those cars tootled right up the hill. A few took on the challenge with more gusto than others." Greg grinned. "Ransom Eli exhibited a prototype for a new car called a runabout. He seems determined to be a leader in the automotive industry with his Oldsmobile."

"What do you think of automobiles, Mr. Granger?" Tom asked, interested in the topic. He'd seen any number of motorized vehicles in Portland, and ridden in several, but he had yet to decide to purchase one. It was an expensive investment and one he wasn't convinced was necessary.

"Oh, they are quite grand, although I prefer a dependable horse to those machines. The show included an assortment of engines, powered by electricity, steam and internal explosion using fuel. Those gasoline powered engines are a rather noisy lot, and smelly, too. I'm not sure they'll have much of a future."

Luke grinned. "From what I've read, gasoline is inexpensive to produce and the cars that run on them have more power. I wouldn't discount them quite yet."

"They are terribly smelly," Lila wrinkled her nose. "One of my friends has an American Morrison electric car. He claims to have driven it almost one hundred and eighty miles on a single charge. Isn't that something?"

"It certainly is," Tom agreed. "I'm with Luke, though. I think the gasoline motors hold merit."

Lila smiled. "You sound like my friend, Willie. He built a gasoline-powered auto in early summer. He called it a ghost because it could go so fast. Why, he actually was arrested for speeding!"

The group laughed and Luke smirked at Lila. "Willie has always been enthralled with speed and winning."

"I believe his wife would agree. The poor dear said Willie is obsessed with making his autos faster and better, racing all over the place like there was no tomorrow." Lila looked over at Tom. "Although, I think it would be fun to ride in one of his racing autos."

"Until the bugs slapped you in the face," Ginny said, drawing another round of laughs from the group. "I, for one, would be happy with a Columbia electric auto. Why, you see them all over New York."

"You do," Lila agreed. "In fact, it seems many cabs are Columbia autos these days." She looked back at Tom. "Are there many autos in Portland?"

"There are, and getting to be more all the time." He cast Luke a sly glance. "When is the town's esteemed banker going to bring the first auto to town?"

Luke shook his head. "Unless you are referring to Arlan, I have no plans to purchase one of those silly things. I much prefer my horses."

"Me, too," Blake said, raising a glass in toast. "To our four-legged friends. They faithfully carry us from place to place without worries of punctured tires, exploding motors, or frequent break downs."

After everyone joined in the toast, the conversation continued in a lighthearted manner. Tom enjoyed being among these people he considered friends. They made him feel at home.

Even though the Granger family was accustomed to grandeur and luxury, they didn't put on airs. Rather, it was easy to forget their wealth when Luke bounced Maura on his knee and Dora cuddled Cullen while Alex, Lila, and Ginny helped Filly with the dishes.

Everyone gathered in the parlor and Tom found himself on a settee next to Lila. Derisively, he contemplated if something or someone conspired to put them together. Although everyone appeared innocent, he couldn't help but wonder if there wasn't something afoot among the scheming women gathered around him.

As he studied his friends, he quickly dismissed the notion that any of them wanted to torment him with Lila's beguiling presence. They all knew of her fiancé. Some of them even knew the man personally. He couldn't imagine any of them wanting to do anything that might disrupt her future happiness.

A gentle nudge to his side made him glance over at Lila. "Want to look?" she asked, holding out a stereoscope. A box of photo cards sat on her lap.

"Sure," Tom said, taking the handle of the stereoscope in his hand and looking at the images as Lila changed the cards. Some were hand painted, others colored with the slightly brown hue of most photographs. The cards took him on a trip from New York, to New

Jersey, Chicago, Philadelphia, Boston, and across the prairies of the mid-west.

When she lifted the last card, Tom handed the stereoscope back to her. "Thank you. I haven't looked through one of those in years."

"Oh, you'll have to be sure to stop by after Christmas," she whispered, covertly glancing at Luke as he laughed at a joke Blake shared. "I ordered a new box of slides for Luke for Christmas."

"I'm sure he'll love them. It's almost like taking a trip to look at the images." Tom leaned toward Lila as he spoke, keeping his voice low as he unconsciously breathed in her scent. For a crazy moment, he wondered what would happen if he ran his hand over her fragrant hair. Although she wore it fashionably swept up on her head, the firelight gleamed on the dark tresses. His fingers itched to see if it would feel as silky as it appeared.

Mindful of his thoughts, he abruptly rose to his feet, desperate to remove himself from the temptation Lila provided.

"Thank you all for a lovely evening, but I have papers to grade." He inched toward the door as all eyes looked at him.

Lila stood and squeezed his left hand. "It was so nice of you to join us this evening, Mr. Grove."

"Thank you for the invitation. I didn't mind getting out of making myself dinner and an invitation to dine at Granger House is one I'd never turn down." Tom ignored the jolt shooting up his arm from Lila's innocent touch as he continued moving toward the door. He nodded to his hosts. "Thank you for a delicious meal and a pleasant evening."

Filly joined Luke at the door, handing Tom's coat to her husband. Luke held it while Tom slipped his good arm inside the sleeve and allowed the other side to drape around his shoulder, covering his casted arm in the sling.

"You're welcome to come anytime, Tom. Our door is always open. If you ever want to join us for a meal, just come on over," Luke offered, opening the front door.

"Yes, Tom. Please feel free to join us any evening. We'd love to have you," Filly said, patting him on the shoulder.

"Thank you. You might be sorry you extended that open invitation."

The couple laughed. "I doubt that. Have a good evening," Luke said, waving as Tom hurried down the steps and out to the boardwalk.

He kept a brisk pace, chilled by the cold winter air on his journey back to the little house by the school. In truth, he'd finished grading the papers before he joined the Granger family for dinner. The excuse of having work to do conveniently allowed him to escape Lila's presence before he did or said something he shouldn't. Like kiss those inviting lips and get lost in her captivating eyes.

During his work at the newspaper, he'd learned to study people's eyes to get a glimpse of their character, to see into the depths of their heart. Some people had such cold, calculating gazes. He'd interviewed victims of atrocities who had lifeless eyes, as though no hope remained in them.

Many children held curious, fascinated looks in their inquisitive peepers.

Occasionally, women looked at him with interest or longing. Peers might glance at him with judgment, sizing him up as competition, or with admiration for a job well done.

But Lila's eyes, those deep gray orbs full of fun and enthusiasm, kindness and sass, made him wish he could stare into them for hours.

And that was precisely why he needed to avoid the woman. Blake had asked her about Emerson. From what Tom gathered of the conversation, Blake's parents invited the man to their home for a long weekend. Recently, he'd written to Lila about how much he enjoyed visiting the Earl and Countess of Roxbury.

Tom still had a hard time picturing easy-going Blake Stratton as a viscount. The man was a talented carpenter and bred some of the strongest, fastest horses in the region, but if he chose, he could live a titled life in England with his parents.

A smile crossed Tom's face as he thought of Ginny Granger Stratton presiding over some fancy English tea. The woman would fit right in, but Blake would most likely be outdoors looking over the horses of the guests.

He'd just inserted the key into the lock on the door when a hand reached out and thumped him on his shoulder.

Tom spun around and stared at Fred Decker.

"Fred! What are you doing skulking around in the dark?" Tom asked, grinning at someone who had once been a school chum. He unlocked the door and motioned the young man to follow him inside.

"I was on my way home from work and noticed you walking through town. I heard you were taking over duties for Miss Alex for a while. Thought I'd say howdy." Fred took the match from Tom and lit the wick on the lantern sitting on the kitchen table. Without being asked, he added wood to the stove in the kitchen then looked around. The last time he'd been in the little house was when his father had beaten him senseless. He ran away from home and hid in an old mine about a mile from the school. Alex Guthry found him and made him accompany her back to the teacher's house. She'd fetched the doctor and kept quiet about his whereabouts until his father was hauled off to jail on a variety of charges.

Before then, Fred had given her and many other people in town an unending supply of grief. From that day forward, though, he'd changed his life around. He decided to do his best never to turn into his father.

"Where are you working these days? I thought you'd gone off to work in Heppner for the railroad." Tom motioned for Fred to have a seat at the table then pushed the teakettle to a hot spot on the stove.

"I worked for the railroad for about a year, but Mother wasn't doing well, so I came back to keep an eye on her. I've been working for Douglas at the livery and doing some odd jobs here and there." Fred took a cookie from the tin Tom held out to him with a grateful nod.

"I was sorry to hear about your mother's condition. Is she doing better?" Tom asked, taking down two mugs from the small cupboard and setting them on the table.

"She is doing a little better. I can't get her to leave the house, but she's regained most of the mobility in her hand, although her face definitely looks different since she had a stroke."

Tom didn't know what to say, so he made two cups of tea and handed one to Fred. "Do you like working at the livery with Mr. McIntosh?"

"I do enjoy it." Fred took a sip of the tea and grinned. "Banging hot metal on an anvil helps me work through any lingering aggression."

Tom smirked. "I'm sure it does. Have you seen John or Ralph? How about…"

The two young men visited for an hour before Fred glanced at the clock on the wall and stood. "Thanks for letting me come in, Tom. It's nice to have you home, even if it is just for a few weeks. Do you think you'll enjoy teaching?"

"Yeah, I do. Today was challenging, but fun, too." Tom walked Fred to the door.

Fred tugged on his coat and pulled a hat down on his head. "That's because you were always teacher's pet."

"That's not true. Percy and Anna were right up there, too."

Fred laughed. "Still are, from what I hear. What do you suppose that nice little Jenkins girl sees in a boy like Percy?"

"Whatever it is, it's lasted since they were only six. It wouldn't surprise me in the least if the two of them grow up and get married." Tom opened the door.

Fred nodded in agreement. "I don't think it would surprise anyone if they did. Have a good night, Tom. If you need help with anything while you're here, let me know."

"I appreciate that, Fred. Thanks for stopping by. Give your mother my regards."

Fred waved a hand and jogged off in the direction of town.

There was a time when Tom hated the very thought of seeing Fred. The boy had been full of demons none of them knew about or understood. Now, though, he was glad they could once again be friends.

After banking the fire in the stove and sliding between the cool sheets of the bed, Tom let his thoughts wander. Much to his dismay, they tripped right over a vision of Lila, laughing at something Filly said at dinner.

Tightly squeezing his eyes shut, he hoped that would squeeze all thoughts of her right out of his mind.

Chapter Seven

Cold air blew up the aisle, barely reaching Tom's desk, accompanied by the sound of the school door quietly closing.

He glanced up from the spelling tests he graded and smiled at Lila as she removed her coat and tiptoed to an empty chair at the back of the room.

In the week he'd been teaching school, she dutifully came each morning and wrote assignments on the blackboard for him. As had become the habit, she'd fix his tie and straighten his collar, leaving him unsettled before the day hardly began.

She returned at noon, to either bring Maura her lunch or take the child home. If Maura stayed for afternoon classes, Lila returned just before classes released for the day to walk the little one home.

Although she quietly sat at the back, her presence distracted Tom to the point he could hardly think straight.

Lost in thoughts of the lovely woman, he didn't notice Percy Bruner waving his hand in the air from his seat.

"Mr. Grove?" Percy finally spoke, drawing Tom's attention.

"Yes, Percy?" His forced his gaze away from Lila and over to the lively redheaded boy.

"You promised to do a magic trick before we all left today if we worked hard this afternoon. I think we all did a bang-up job, didn't we?" Percy grinned, looking mischievous and sincere all at the same time.

Tom smiled. "That you did. Are all of you finished with your arithmetic assignments?" His gaze roved over the students, noting they all nodded their heads. "Very well, then. Percy, would you and Anna collect the assignments and set them here on my desk while I prepare to do an amazing feat of phantasmagorical wonder."

The students began buzzing about what sort of trick he might do. Most all of them knew he'd trained with Alex and was privy to many of her illusions.

While Percy and Anna gathered the assignments, Tom took a box of crayons out of his desk drawer and withdrew eight of the twelve colors.

"Are you all ready to be spellbound with a fantastical example of illusionary marvel?" Tom's voice took on a theatrical tone as he moved to stand in front of his desk.

The children clapped and cheered right along with Lila. Tom winked at her before turning his attention back to his students.

"I need four volunteers," Tom said, watching as every child shot a hand up in the air. He shook his head. "Oh, I can't choose. Miss Granger, would you select four students?"

Lila spent enough time around the class to know the students who were often shy, so she chose them.

"Come on up here, students," Tom encouraged, inviting the four students up to his desk. "I'm going to turn around and hold these crayons behind my back. When I say your name, I want you to choose one, but keep it hidden in your hands until I ask you to show the class. Any questions?"

The four volunteers shook their heads.

Tom turned and faced the blackboard while holding out the crayons behind him in his extended left hand. He rotated the crayons around, so he had no way of knowing the positions of any of them.

"Milo, you choose the first crayon. Remember, don't let anyone see it." Tom felt one of the crayons slide out of his hand. "Next will be Sarah, then Alice, and Billy."

When all four students held crayons clasped in their hands, Tom continued to hold his hand behind his back. "Percy, please take the remaining crayons from my hand." The boy did, standing off to the side out of Tom's view. Tom glanced down at his empty hand then lifted his head. "Milo, show the class the color of your crayon. Is it blue?"

"Yes, sir!" Milo said, showing the class the blue crayon he held.

Tom called on Sarah. "Sarah, is your crayon yellow?"

"Yep!" The little girl held up her crayon for her classmates to see.

The children grew more animated.

"Alice, it's your turn. Is your crayon green?"

"It is, Mr. Grove!" The child excitedly waved the crayon above her head.

Their enthusiastic responses pulsed against Tom's back like a palpable force, making him smile. "And Billy, do you hold a red crayon?"

The boy nodded his head, causing Lila to laugh. "He's nodding his head, Mr. Grove. It is, indeed, red."

Tom turned around and executed a bow with a flourish of his left hand. "If you return the crayons to my desk, you may all be excused for the day."

"Thanks, Mr. Grove!"

"That was wonderful, Mr. Grove!"

"Can we have more magics tomorrow, Mr. Grove?"

The children's animated comments drifted around him. "If I did magic every day it wouldn't be special.

You'll just have to keep coming every day to see when I do another trick. Have a nice evening, students."

Lila hurried to bundle Maura into her coat and hat, sending the little girl outside to play with her friends.

Tom held the crayon box with his casted hand while attempting to stuff in the crayons. Lila took pity on his efforts and did the job for him. "How did you know which crayon each child took?"

He smirked at her. "The first magic lesson Alex taught me was that a good magician never gives away his secrets."

Lila rolled her eyes and made a silly face. "That's fine for your students, but I must know."

"You must?" he asked, enjoying her playfulness. It was hard to imagine someone who looked like such a fine, well-heeled lady making such a funny face. In fact, Lila could have been out for a stroll on some fashionable New York avenue in the outfit she wore. The deep purple of the gown brought out the loveliest highlights in her dark hair and made her grey eyes take on a fascinating hue. He'd yet to see her wear the same gown twice, but of the jewel-toned ensembles she'd worn, the purple dress was his new favorite.

"I must." She clasped his hand in hers and gave him a pleading look. Her bottom lip crept out as she affected a pout. "Please? Won't you tell me?"

Tom battled the overwhelming desire to kiss her delectable bottom lip. Instead, he pulled his hand from hers, painfully aware of the sizzling current shooting up his arm from the contact. "It's quite simple," he said, lifting his hand so she could see his closely trimmed fingernails.

At first, she didn't appear to understand what he showed her, then she noticed the hint of wax under his nails. "Oh, you are a fake and a cheater!" She took his hand in hers again, studying his fingers, discovering the colors were in the order in which the children took the crayons.

"The trick is that you carefully scrape just a bit of the crayon as they are pulling it out of your hand. I started with my index finger for Milo, and so on." Tom gave her a solemn stare. "But you are sworn to secrecy, Miss Granger. No one can know about this, is that clear?"

"Yes, sir!" Lila stood at attention and executed a salute that made him laugh.

"I'm serious, you loon," Tom said, grinning at her tomfoolery. "When Alex first started showing me how to do magic tricks, she threatened to sell me to the gypsies if I ever told anyone how she does her tricks."

"Maybe the woman who cursed the police chief will come claim you, now that you showed me how to do the magic crayon trick," Lila teased. She wiped off the blackboard while Tom gathered his papers and stuffed them into a leather satchel.

"You better hope not. Otherwise, Luke will cajole you into taking over teaching duties for Alex again." Tom closed the satchel and handed her a handkerchief to brush the chalk dust from her hands.

She took it with a grateful nod then returned it to him. "Oh, I hope not. I've got enough to do now that I've promised Chauncy and Abby to help with the Christmas program."

"The Christmas program?"

"Yes. At church. Abby has more than she can handle right now and Ginny is rather indisposed. Since she and Blake usually oversee the program, Pastor Dodd asked if I would help." Lila walked to the back of the classroom and lifted her coat from a hook.

"I see," Tom said, wondering what Chauncy was up to, since he'd also asked Tom if he'd help with the Christmas program. He kept his thoughts to himself as he banked the stove and followed Lila outside.

"You know, Miss Granger, I feel I owe you a debt for all your assistance here in the classroom. Would you at least allow me to take you to dinner at the restaurant?" Tom wondered where the words that tumbled out of his mouth came from. He didn't need to spend any more time in the alluring woman's presence. She drove him daft as it was. That truth was evident in the fact he'd just asked her to dinner.

"That sounds lovely. I can't tonight, but perhaps tomorrow?" she asked, turning to him with her wide gray eyes.

It would be so easy to bend down and kiss her, but Tom resisted the urge. "Tomorrow it is. I'll call for you at five-thirty, if that suits you."

"I look forward to it," Lila said, motioning for Maura and Erin to join her. "Have a nice evening, Mr. Grove."

"I will, Miss Granger." He watched her take the hands of the little girls in hers and head toward the boardwalk. "Remember what I said about gypsies."

She glanced back over her shoulder at him and laughed. "I won't forget."

Tom sighed and walked over to the teacher's house. He opened the door, stoked the stove, and made a pot of coffee. An hour later, he finished grading assignments for his students and set the papers back in his satchel. He prepared an easy to cook dinner comprised of a slice of fried ham with eggs and toasted two pieces of bread from the loaf his mother gave him.

As he ate, he did his best to jot down his lesson plans for the following day with his left hand. Once he finished washing and drying the dishes, he found himself bored and restless. Slipping on his coat, he tugged on a hat, wrapped a scarf around his neck and ventured outside, deciding to go for a walk.

He hoped the cold, bracing air would clear his head and chase away thoughts of lovely Lila Granger.

Just that morning, she'd happily prattled on and on about receiving a letter from Emerson. It was apparent she looked forward to seeing him again when they both returned to New York.

Tom snorted, thinking of how ridiculous it was for Lila to wed the man. The woman surely hadn't given due consideration to the absurd change it would bring to her name. Lila Lylan. The name made it sound as though someone stuttered.

Lila Grove had a much better ring to it, in his opinion.

Frustrated with how his every thought circled back around to Lila, Tom strode down a side street then turned and walked along the main thoroughfare of town. He admired the greenery and festive bows some businesses had already hung in their windows to herald the approaching Christmas holiday. He wondered if Filly would bedeck Granger House with oodles of garlands as she had in the past. Perhaps he'd have a chance to see the inside of the house, too.

He didn't want to wear out his welcome at their home, but Luke and Filly had both reiterated their invitation for him to join them anytime for supper.

Perhaps he'd take them up on it a few times.

Alex and Arlan insisted he join them for dinner the previous evening. He'd enjoyed visiting with them both. After dinner, he and Alex thoroughly trounced Arlan in a game of cards. Alex had asked him about the students, offered suggestions for some individual attention, and encouraged him to let her know if he needed help with anything.

Tom breathed in the crisp, clear air and turned his gaze up to take in the blanket of stars above him.

When he was in Portland, he kept so busy, he often forgot to admire the beauty around him. And the air there certainly wasn't as clean and refreshing as it was in Hardman.

Tom hadn't realized how much he missed the small town where he'd grown up. For the most part, the people were friendly and welcoming. Hardman felt like home.

His thoughts drifted to his parents' home. He'd enjoyed spending the weekend with them, helping his father with a few projects in the barn. His mother made chicken and dumplings for supper Saturday. It was one of Tom's favorite meals. For dessert, she baked a chocolate pie, also one of his favorites.

None of them mentioned the upcoming arrival of a baby. However, while he and his father talked about farming practices and new inventions, his mother's knitting needles flashed in the firelight as she worked on a small blanket made of buttery yellow yarn.

Happy for his folks, he also realized the baby would drastically alter their family dynamic. Uncertain where he would fit into it, especially when he spent so much time gone, he hoped they could all make a smooth transition from a family of three to four.

The thought of having a younger brother or sister who grew up not knowing him caused Tom to pause in his walk. He hadn't given any thought to not returning to the city to work, but if he remained in Portland for too many years, he'd be a complete stranger to his younger sibling. He didn't want to be someone the child barely recognized or hardly knew.

"You look like you're thinking heavy thoughts," a soft voice spoke from beside him.

Tom whirled around and looked down into Lila's smiling face. "What are you doing out here in the cold?"

"I just needed a little quiet and some fresh air. Dora and Greg came over for dinner, along with Blake and Ginny. Ginny and Luke spent the entire time arguing over one thing or another while Dora kept insisting they behave. If it wasn't so comical, it might get annoying."

Tom grinned. "I've noticed Luke and Ginny like to bicker, just for the sake of opposing one another."

"Oh, they do," Lila agreed. "Filly said they'll both be old and gray, shaking their canes at one another and shouting into each other's ear trumpets, trying to get in the last word."

Laughter rolled out of Tom. "I could picture that." He held out his left arm to Lila. "May I escort you back to Granger House, since it appears you were headed that direction."

"You may, kind sir," Lila said, looping her arm around his.

Together, they meandered down the boardwalk. Neither felt the need to speak as they ambled along. Rather, they soaked up the companionable silence as they both feasted on the site of the twinkling stars overhead.

"It's so peaceful here," Lila whispered, as though speaking any louder would somehow disrupt the calm atmosphere.

"It is," Tom said in a deep, rumbling voice. "Mama always says a little peace is balm for the soul."

"Your mother is a smart woman, and such a lovely one, too." Lila grinned at him. "If I didn't know she was your mother, I'd never believe her old enough to have a grown son."

"She and Dad married young. Mama was nineteen when I was born." Tom expelled a long breath. "If you can keep a secret, I'll tell you something else about them."

Lila gazed up at him with a sparkle in her eyes. "I promise I won't tell a soul." She wrapped both hands around his arm and gave it an encouraging squeeze. "I love secrets. What is it?"

Tom glanced around to ensure they were alone, strolling in the frosty air beneath the stars. Assured they were the only ones out and about at that moment, he bent down until his mouth hovered above her ear. "They're going to have a baby."

Lila squealed and enthusiastically shook his arm then glanced around wide-eyed to make sure no one heard. Tom hurried her down the boardwalk and around the corner of the newspaper office into the shadows.

"That's so wonderful, Tom! When is the baby due?" Lila gave him a hug then stepped back.

"Early summer, or so my mother said. Both of my parents are excited about it. Mama's waited a long time to have another baby."

"I should say so. Oh, you must be so happy for them, and yet…" Lila gave him an observant glance. "I'm sure it will be challenging to adjust to the changes after being an only child for so long."

"It's not like I'm at home anyway." Tom shrugged. "I am very happy for them, even if they've been acting like a couple of moony teens since I've been home."

She laughed and patted his arm as they strolled back onto the boardwalk. "I think it's sweet the way they appear to be so in love. I've concluded there is something strange in the air that has caused a sudden swell in the population around here."

Tom waggled an eyebrow at her. "Did any gypsy wagons pass through town recently?"

Lila giggled and bumped against him. "Not that anyone knows of. Although, that might explain a few things."

He leaned closer to her ear again. "I think there's something in the water, so you best be careful, Miss Granger."

She gave him a scathing look then burst into another round of giggles. "After sharing that secret with me, I believe you better just call me Lila."

He nodded his head. "Then it's only fair if you call me Tom, at least when I'm not standing in front of a classroom of students."

"Agreed." Lila stopped as they reached Granger House. "Thank you for walking me home and making me laugh, Tom. I appreciate it."

A smile quirked the corners of his mouth upward. "You are an easy one to make laugh, Lila. I'll see you tomorrow."

"Good night." She walked around to the back door.

He heard her say something to Luke's dog before she disappeared inside.

With a lighter heart and mood, Tom whistled as he made his way back to his house.

Chapter Eight

Tom rushed out of the house at a quarter past five and made his way to the mercantile. Aleta Bruner smiled at him as he hurried inside.

"Evening, Tom. How are things going over at the school?" she asked, standing behind the register at the front counter.

"Very well, I think. Although, I suppose Percy and Alice might have differing opinions on the matter," Tom said, grinning at the store owner as he browsed the confectionary selections. He chose a small box with three chocolates and walked over to the counter.

"According to my two rascals, they miss Alex teaching, but have decided if she can't be there, you fill the position quite nicely. Alice is still talking about you guessing what color crayon she held in her hand. How did you do that?" Aleta asked as she accepted the change for the candy.

Tom grinned. "A magician never tells his secrets."

Aleta laughed. "I've heard that from Alex many times. Have a nice evening, Tom."

"You, as well, Mrs. Bruner."

Tom strode down the street to Granger House, his long legs eating up the distance in no time. Uncertain whether he should go to the front door or the back, he decided to go around to the kitchen door. Most likely, it was where he'd find Lila.

He stopped long enough to rub a hand over Bart's head as the dog stood and wagged his tail in greeting at the top of the back steps.

"Are the ladies inside, Bart?" Tom asked, giving the dog a final scratch on his back before reaching up to tap on the door.

It swung open and Lila smiled at him in greeting. "You're right on time," she said, stepping back and pulling the door open wider.

"I wouldn't dare keep you waiting," he teased. He removed his hat and nodded to Filly. She held the baby on one arm and stirred something on the stove with her other hand.

Maura ran into the room with a doll in her hands and beamed at Tom. "Hi, Mr. Grove!"

"Good evening, Maura. Is that your dolly?" he asked, hunkering down to smile at the child.

"Yes, this is Bubbie." Maura held out the rag doll to him.

Tom balanced his hat on his knee and accepted the doll, studying the brown yarn hair and embroidered facial features. "She seems like a very nice doll."

"She's wonnerful!" Maura proclaimed, taking the doll from Tom and squeezing it against her chest. Swiftly, her attention shifted from the doll to her teacher. "Why are you here? Did you come for supper?"

"No, Maura. I came to take Miss Lila out for dinner."

"Oh!" Maura tossed her doll on a chair and raced over to the pegs by the door, reaching for her coat. "I'll go."

"No, you won't, little busybody," Filly said, setting Cullen into his cradle then swooping Maura into her arms. "I need you to stay here and help me with dinner. Your daddy will be in from doing chores any minute and be ready to eat. A big girl like you can help set the table, don't you think?"

"Okay!" Maura clapped her hands together and squirmed in her mother's arms. Filly set her down and they watched as Maura raced over to a drawer and took out a fistful of forks.

"You two better go while she's occupied," Filly said, quietly nudging Lila toward the door. "Enjoy your meal."

"I'm sure we will," Lila said, quickly slipping on her coat with Tom's help. "We won't be gone long."

"Take all the time you like. No need to rush back." Filly gave Tom an encouraging look as he opened the door and Lila breezed outside. "It's not like you have any engagements to attend to."

Uncertain whether he should be amused or concerned by Filly's behavior, Tom gave the dog another pat on the head then cupped Lila's elbow in his hand, escorting her down the steps and out to the boardwalk.

They strolled through town and turned down the side street to the restaurant. Clouds hid the stars and Tom wondered if it might snow again. The air held a certain bite to it that almost guaranteed a storm.

At the restaurant, he held the door while Lila hurried inside out of the cold. "Oh, it is freezing outside," she said, rubbing her hands on the arms of her coat sleeves as they stood at the entry waiting to be seated.

Tom stepped closer behind her, hoping to block the frigid air blowing around them. When he did, Lila's fragrance filled his senses and addled his thoughts.

Before he could act on any of the inappropriate impulses flooding his brain, a waitress motioned for them to follow her to a table.

Tom helped Lila remove her coat, admiring her rich burgundy gown. The color made him think of cranberries and Christmas.

He smiled as he draped her coat over the chair next to him and removed his own. "That's a lovely gown, Lila. You look like a dish of delicious cranberries."

She gaped at him then glanced down at the expensive dress, embellished with jet beads and a black satin sash at the waist. "That's the first time anyone has compared my attire to food, particularly one of such a festive nature. I'm not sure if I should be insulted or amused."

"Definitely amused," Tom said, winking at her.

They ordered their meals and discussed the students, the upcoming Christmas carnival, and the Christmas program at church.

Tom cleared his throat. "I don't know if Chauncy told you, but he also asked me to help with the program. Is that okay with you?"

Befuddled, Lila gaped at him. "Why on earth wouldn't it be okay with me, Tom Grove? In fact, it's fantastic. You know all the children quite well from school. Who better to help with the program?"

Relieved, he leaned back in his chair and relaxed. "I'm glad you don't mind."

"I don't mind at all. Truthfully, I'm pleased. I can handle the music part of the program with my eyes closed, but the rest of it seemed a daunting task to undertake on my own."

"We'll do it together," Tom said, reaching across the table and squeezing her hand with his.

Lila tossed him a saucy grin. "I like the sound of that. Now, tell me the truth. Do Percy and Anna always play Mary and Joseph?"

Tom nodded. "Since they were six. Percy begs and pleads to reprise their roles every year. I think that boy is going to insist on portraying Joseph until he's too old to be in the play."

"At least he's consistent," Lila said, taking the last bite of her roasted chicken.

"Would you care for some dessert?" Tom asked, watching her dab at her lips with a napkin. He wondered what she'd do if he slid around the table into the chair next to hers and wrapped his arm around her shoulder.

Most likely, she'd slap him silly and never speak to him again.

The thought of doing something to damage their friendship kept him in his seat. Acutely aware he had no romantic future with Lila, he hoped they could at least maintain the friendship that had developed between them over the course of the last week.

If Lila had been available and Tom hadn't been leaving right after the holidays, he would have poured every ounce of his energy into courting the woman. She was everything he could ever want in a wife: articulate, amusing, witty, fun, kind, and intelligent. Then there was her outward beauty. She had to be one of the loveliest women he'd ever seen.

But no matter how much he might wish otherwise, dreaming of a future with the woman was a waste of time.

She dabbed at her lips again. "No dessert for me, Tom, but you go ahead if you like."

He inhaled another whiff of her entrancing fragrance. "Why do you smell like lilacs?" The question burst out of him before he could reel it back.

Lila grinned and tipped her head to the side, holding a teacup with both hands. "It's my favorite perfume. I always wear it. It reminds me of springtime, and happy days, and my mother. She wore it, too."

"Well, it's a lovely scent," Tom said, his voice quiet as he held her gaze. "It suits you, Miss Lila Lilac."

She laughed and raised an eyebrow. "Really? You're going to call me Lila Lilac?"

Tom nodded, charming her with his smile. "Why not? In a few months, you'll be Lila Lylan. Might as well add a lilac in there, too. Mrs. Lila Lilac Lylan. It's got quite a ring to it."

Astounded, she stared at him.

The name did not have a ring to it. It was ridiculous. Furthermore, hearing Tom call her Lila Lylan made her realize how horrible it sounded. Did she really want to spend her life as Lila Lylan? It would twist anyone's tongue in a knot.

How had she not given any thought to her last name changing to Lylan? Oh, it was dreadful. Lila Lylan. Tom was right. Lilac could only make it sound better.

A traitorous part of her head suggested Lila Grove had a much nicer sound to it than Lila Lylan.

Disgusted with herself for even thinking such a thing, she wondered what Emerson would think if she followed the lead of some of her suffragist friends and kept her own last name. There wasn't any law that said she had to change her name to her husband's. The notion of Emerson allowing her to continue to go by Granger seemed quite unlikely. The man was a traditionalist from the top of his head right down to his costly-covered toes.

She'd worry about the problem with her name later. For now, she intended to continue enjoying her dinner with Tom.

He was full of fun stories and took great delight in teasing her. At school, he seemed focused on providing a good example to the children and remaining serious and studious for the most part. However, when he read to the students or performed a magic trick, he seemed more like an overgrown child.

As she gazed across the table at him, though, there was no confusing the good-looking man with a boy.

Tom was wonderful and kind, and one of the most interesting people Lila had ever met.

She'd be sad when the holidays were over and he returned to Portland. Not long after that, she would return to New York.

Thoughts of never seeing Tom again left her heart heavy. How could she want to be in two places at the same time so badly? Actually, she wanted to be in three. She loved living in Hardman with her family. And she wished she could go to Portland with Tom and see all the sights there he'd described. But her heart was in New York, or at least it would be when Emerson returned.

For now, she would focus on enjoying the friendship Tom so easily offered, and relishing the holiday season in Hardman.

"Does your family have any special Christmas traditions?" Lila asked, abruptly changing the subject. A distraction from her thoughts was sorely needed.

Tom studied her for a moment before responding. "They do. We always attend the Christmas Eve service at church, of course. Mama and Dad used to wait until after we got home from the service to decorate our Christmas tree, but when I was old enough to help, we usually did that a few days before Christmas so we could enjoy it longer."

He appeared thoughtful as he recalled the traditions his parents followed every year. "They always allowed me to open one special gift on Christmas Eve while we drank hot chocolate and ate slices of this wonderful cake Mama only makes during the holidays. The gift was always something small, like a piece of candy, or a handful of nuts, but it was fun to look forward to receiving it. Christmas morning, we'd open presents, eat a leisurely breakfast, then I'd go out to chore with Dad while Mama started preparing Christmas dinner."

Lila smiled. "Was it always just the three of you?"

He nodded. "Grandpa Grove lived with us until he passed away when I was seven. He was a farmer, too, but he encouraged me to tell stories. Grandpa used to sit on the porch with me and whittle, listening to the silly tales I'd make up."

"That's wonderful, Tom," Lila said. She reached across the table and settled her hand over his. "We all need someone like that who encourages our dreams."

"We do," he agreed, holding her gaze.

She loved looking into Tom's eyes. Nearly bottomless in their depths, they appeared so full of sincere warmth and genuine care. His eyes might not have been the most striking shade of blue, but she found them appealing just the same.

Mindful her hand lingered on his, she pulled it back and placed it on her lap.

Tom pretended not to notice as he lifted a cup of coffee and took a drink. "What about you, Lila? Did your family have many traditions?"

"Oh, yes," she said, her eyes glowing with the precious memories of her childhood. "Our tree always went up the week before Christmas. It was a grand thing, majestically presiding over the entry foyer. One year, Father allowed me to choose the tree and when the deliveryman brought it, they had to cut four feet off the bottom just to keep from brushing the upstairs ceiling. It must have been more than twenty-feet tall."

Tom's eyes widened as he imagined the sight. "I bet it was beautiful."

"It was," Lila agreed. "We also had a smaller tree in the drawing room where we'd gather on Christmas Eve. Sometimes my parents would throw a party that afternoon that stretched into the evening. Then we'd all go to church for the services before returning home. Mother would play the piano and we'd sing carols until midnight. There were always oodles of gifts, but those were just things. It was the time spent with my parents that meant the most to me."

"And you didn't have any siblings, either?"

Lila shook her head. "No. I was an only child, spoiled rotten and treated like a pampered little princess."

He smirked. "That explains so much."

She glowered at him before breaking into another smile. "I'm sure I was positively awful in my younger years. Ask Luke if you want the truth. One day, I guess I just grew up and realized that everyone is special in God's eyes, and wealth or station makes no difference to Him."

Pleased by her words, Tom reached out and clasped the hand she'd placed back on the table. "That's a wonderful way to view life, Lila."

They remained silent for a few minutes, although Tom continued to hold Lila's hand in his. Finally, she pulled away and glanced at the clock on the wall.

"Oh, I didn't realize it was so late," she started to stand, but before she could push back her chair, Tom was beside her, pulling it out for her. Impressed by his manners, she smiled at him over her shoulder. He did his best to hold her coat with one hand while she slipped it on then pulled on his own. After leaving money on the table for their meals, he guided her outside.

The temperature had dropped considerably while they ate. Big, fluffy snowflakes floated from the sky, looking like bits of cotton on a dark velvet background.

"Gorgeous, isn't it?" she asked, tipping back her head and looking upward.

"Gorgeous," Tom repeated, although his gaze lingered on her instead of the softly falling snow.

Unsettled, yet oddly thrilled by the look on his face, she ambled down the street.

"Are you in a rush to return home?" Tom asked, keeping step beside her.

"Well, it is late, and you most likely have papers to grade and lessons to plan," she said, unwilling to confess she wanted to spend more time with him.

Tom shrugged. "I can get to the papers later, but I thought you might like to see something. If you'd rather go straight home…" The hint of an exciting opportunity hung between them as they approached Main Street.

Lila stopped and tipped her head to one side. "What do you want to show me?" she asked. She attempted to gauge whether there was really something or if Tom just wanted to put off telling her good night.

"I can't explain it. You have to see it." He bent his knees until he looked her square in the face. "Home or adventure?"

A smile wreathed her face and mischief twinkled in her eyes. "Adventure, of course!"

Tom chuckled and took her hand in his. "Come on, then, Lila Lilac."

She allowed him to lead her to the school, but instead of heading to it or his house there, Tom took her down a trail she hadn't noticed before. It led them into the trees. Suddenly, he stopped and looked down at her feet.

"Are your shoes suitable for walking up a hill?"

She lifted her skirts just enough he could see she wore warm winter boots.

Tom nodded approvingly. "Sensible and practical. You might just be the most perfect girl I've ever encountered."

"Please remember that when I do something silly or stupid, which will eventually happen." She tossed him a cheeky grin.

He smiled and pulled her a little closer. "I'll remember, Lila Lilac."

She rolled her eyes at the teasing nickname as she followed him along a path through the trees. Although it was hard to see, she could tell by the incline they climbed upward. The exertion combined with the arctic air blowing around them made it hard for her to breathe, but she didn't complain. Instead, she held tightly to Tom's hand and wondered where in the world he took her.

When she'd nearly given up on ever seeing anything beyond the shadowy shapes of trees liberally frosted with snow, they topped the hill. Tom turned around and pointed to the town of Hardman below. Lights glowed as though someone had painted them in pale smudges of yellow against a dark background.

"Oh, Tom," Lila whispered. Hesitant to speak in a normal tone, she didn't want to disturb the peaceful silence surrounding them. Up high, with nothing but darkness around them, the snowflakes falling around them appeared even bigger. If she didn't know better, she would have said they almost sparkled with something magical.

"What do you think?" Tom asked, continuing to hold her hand.

"I think it's one of the most wonderful things I've ever seen," Lila gushed. "I wish Ginny was up here with her paints to capture the splendor of it all."

Tom snorted. "Now that would be something to get Ginny up here in her condition. You might have to wait until next year to try that."

Lila grinned. "If she decided she wanted to come, I have no doubt Blake and Luke would figure out some way to get her up here."

"Most likely," Tom agreed. "I don't know how many other people have visited this spot, but I've always liked to come here when I needed a quiet place to think."

"Wasn't it quiet at home?" she asked, turning to look into his face.

"It was, but my parents didn't give me a lot of time to sit quietly and ponder life. As their only child, I sometimes got more attention than I wanted or needed."

Lila nodded her head. "I know exactly what you mean."

Without thinking about her actions, Lila moved in front of Tom. She leaned back against him, against his strength. His hand settled on her waist and she didn't protest or move when he stepped closer behind her. The heat of his body enveloped her, leaving her languid and content, even with snow swirling around them.

Several long moments passed with neither of them moving or speaking before Tom expelled a heavy sigh. "I better get you home before your toes freeze or Luke thinks you've been kidnapped."

"My toes are quite warm, it's my nose that's being nipped without mercy." Lila hid her shock when Tom unwound the scarf he wore and draped it around her neck, wrapping the length around a few times until her nose and mouth were covered in the soft wool.

"Better?" he asked, taking her hand in his again.

She nodded, inhaling the woodsy scent that clung to the scarf, an aroma that smelled masculine and inviting — and so like Tom Grove.

Silent as he led her down the hill and back into town, she tried to make sense of her tumultuous feelings.

It didn't take long to stroll along Main Street and reach Granger House. Tom walked her up the front porch steps to the door.

"I see Filly has started her annual decking of the halls," he said, pointing to garlands and ribbons draped across the porch rails.

"Luke hauled several trunks of decorations down from the attic this morning. He would adamantly refuse to admit it, but he loves Christmas every bit as much as Filly."

Tom laughed and backed up a step. "I better let you get inside. Thank you for having dinner with me, Lila Lilac, and for all your help at the school. It's greatly appreciated."

She smiled at him, consumed by the wildest wish that he'd kiss her. Distraught by her thoughts, she opened the front door. "Thank you for dinner, and for sharing your special spot with me, Tom."

"Good night."

Lila hurried inside the house and closed the door then breathed in Tom's scent once again. If she weren't careful, Emerson would return home to find her thoroughly smitten with another man.

Chapter Nine

Tom grinned at Lila over the heads of the children clamoring around her, eager to receive their assigned parts for the Christmas program at the church. Chauncy stopped by long enough to give them the information from previous programs and show Lila where to find the costumes Abby had made over the years. An assortment of props Blake made and Ginny painted were also available.

Without time to sort through it all before the children arrived for the first practice, Lila suggested they return on a day when they had more time to figure out costumes and backdrops.

"Did you save Joseph and Mary for me and Anna?" Percy Bruner asked, impatiently looking at Lila. Tom hid a grin as the boy reached back and tugged Anna beside him.

"Joseph and Mary? Are they in the play?" Lila teased, drawing a worried glance from the boy. "I thought I heard you two wanted to be shepherds."

Percy appeared stricken and Anna's face paled.

"Quit teasing him so," Tom said, nudging Lila with his arm. He grinned at the freckle-faced boy. "Of course you and Anna will play the roles of Joseph and Mary. By now, you two have the lines completely memorized."

"Will Filly and Luke let Cullen play baby Jesus?" Anna asked in a quiet, hesitant voice.

"Filly implied a willingness to do it, if we promise to keep all the animals away from the manger." Lila glanced at Tom. "She mentioned something about a half-crazed sheep destroying the manger one year."

Tom nodded. "A few years back, one of the sheep got away from the shepherds and smashed the manger. Fortunately, they were using a doll that year."

"It wasn't very fortunate for Anna's doll," Percy said, frowning at the two adults. "It clean busted the head in half."

The girl placed a gentle hand on his arm. "I'd much rather have a broken doll than an injured baby."

"Agreed," Lila said, turning back to Percy. "Perhaps you boys can figure out a better place for the animals to gather, far away from the manger. Or, maybe we could have some of the younger students pretend to be the animals and forego live animals in the play."

"That's not a bad idea," Tom said. The live animals had been challenging to keep in control in the past, not to mention the messes they made in the church. "What if we add a donkey, cow, sheep, and camel to the play? That would give four more children the opportunity to participate."

Lila smiled. "All we'd need are costumes. I'm sure we can come up with something suitable."

"Perhaps Alex would help. Since she's at home, she might like something to keep her hands busy even if she isn't feeling well enough to teach," Tom suggested. He motioned for students lingering by the door to join the rest of them at the front of the church.

Lila beamed and clasped her hands together. "That's a splendid idea. I'll stop on my way home and speak with her."

"Mith Gwangah, can I be a theep?" asked an adorable little sprout missing his two front teeth.

"You certainly may, Andy." Lila bent down as she spoke and tapped the end of his nose with her finger, making him smile.

"I can baaa good." The boy demonstrated his skill in pretending to be a sheep.

Lila laughed. "You certainly can."

After assigning parts and discussing expectations for the children participating in the play, Lila gave the children cookies she and Filly baked that morning. She helped the younger children on with their coats and mittens before they all raced outside and headed home.

Tom straightened the papers Chauncy had given them and tucked them inside a leather satchel. He held Lila's coat for her, grateful to have more mobility in his broken arm. The doctor had told him just that morning he could leave off the sling and begin using his hand. He wasn't supposed to lift anything or do any activities that caused discomfort, but he had held a pencil with it and graded assignments while the students worked on their math lessons. His arm ached after about ten minutes, but he knew each day he'd gain more use.

Lila held out the cookie tin to him once he'd slipped on his coat. He helped himself and took a bite of the soft sugar cookie.

"Did you make these?"

She nodded. "I did. Filly made the cinnamon cookies."

"These are about the best sugar cookies I've ever had," Tom said, finishing the cookie in another bite. He opened the church door and held it for Lila as she stepped outside. "Feel free to bring them to any of our practices."

Her head tilted to the left as she grinned. "Maybe next time I'll bring carrot sticks. What do you think of that?"

"I think you'll have a church full of disappointed little children and one very disappointed big boy." Tom held out his arm to her as they stepped onto the boardwalk.

She wrapped both hands around his arm and strolled with him toward Arlan and Alex Guthry's home. "Perhaps the big boy should eat more vegetables and set a good example for the youngsters."

Tom scowled at her. "I'll have you know, Miss Granger, I eat plenty of fruit and vegetables at meal times. However, when we say there will be treats at the program practices that means it must be a treat. I promise you, the children will not view carrots as something special. They aren't rabbits, after all." He wrinkled his nose and pulled back his lips to expose his front teeth.

Lila laughed and rolled her eyes. "Very well, then. Sugar-laden treats it will be."

He tipped his head toward the mercantile as they walked past it. "I'm happy to take turns providing snacks. I'll pick up something for our next practice."

She started to argue, but didn't want to offend him. "That would be fine. I've heard the children are quite partial to peppermint sticks."

"That they are. I bought some for the class last week and thought I might have a mutiny on my hands."

Her laughter rang around them, drawing interested glances from others out on the street who heard the delightful sound.

Tom turned down a side street and directed her to the Guthry home. He tapped on the door. It opened almost immediately. Alex's smile widened when she saw who stood on her front step. She pulled the door open wider and stepped back. "Come in, come in. What brings you two to my door today?"

Tom removed his hat and held it in his right hand while helping Lila remove her coat with his left.

"We have a favor to ask," Tom said, following Alex into her parlor. She motioned for them to have a seat on the sofa while she settled into a chair close to the fire.

"Ask away," Alex said, looking from him to Lila and back again.

"Rather than have live animals at the Christmas program this year, we decided to allow some of the younger children to play the parts." Tom removed his coat and sat beside Lila. "I suggested that you might be willing to help with the costumes. If you aren't interested, Alex, don't feel as though you must agree."

"Although we'd be so happy if you would," Lila added with a saucy look that made Alex laugh.

The woman threw her hands up in the air. "How can I say no? Truthfully, I wouldn't mind a project to work on. I've read every book in the house at least twice, finished making all my Christmas gifts, and have nearly driven poor Arlan mad trying to find things to occupy my mind. Even if my body refuses to cooperate in my desire to be out and about, I could certainly make a costume or two."

"Are you feeling any better?" Lila asked, concerned by Alex's pale face.

"I'm starting to. Doc said the sickness should pass in a few more weeks. I, for one, can't wait until it is gone completely." Alex glanced over at Tom. "I'm sure you aren't interested in such matters. Forgive me for discussing it."

He shook his head. "On the contrary, I hate to see you under the weather and hope you are feeling more like yourself very soon. You have to be well before school reconvenes after the holidays or the children will be left without a teacher."

"I plan to be better by then." Alex leaned back in her chair. "Tell me about these costumes. What do you need me to do?"

"Well, we added a cow, sheep, donkey, and camel. Would you be able to make one or two of them?" Lila asked. She would have volunteered to make them, but they were far beyond her sewing capabilities. Abby Dodd certainly didn't have time and neither did Filly. Ginny and Dora could barely thread a needle, so they wouldn't be any help.

"I think I could make the donkey and I'd like to try the camel. Can you find someone to make the other two costumes you need?" Alex asked.

"I'm sure Mama will make one," Tom said, hoping his mother wouldn't mind helping.

"Wonderful. How is your mother doing?" Alex gave him a look that made him wonder if she knew the Grove family would be welcoming an addition around the same time her baby was due.

"She's doing very well."

Alex nodded. "Excellent. Tell her to stop by for tea sometime when she's in town. I'd love to have a good visit with her. It's been far too long."

"I'll do that, Alex." Tom glanced at the clock and rose to his feet. "I best escort Miss Lila home and then get busy grading assignments and preparing for class tomorrow."

"It's a never-ending cycle, isn't it?" Alex asked.

"How do you suffer through this drudgery day after day?" Tom teased. All three occupants of the room knew both Alex and Tom enjoyed teaching.

"It's a struggle," she said with a big smile. "What ages are the camel and donkey? I'd like a better idea of what size to make the costumes."

"Billy Tomkins is playing the camel and Molly Smith is the donkey," Lila said. "Billy begged to play the camel and spent most of the time at practice walking around on all fours with his little rump in the air."

Alex laughed. "I can picture that. Give me a week or so to see what I can figure out."

"As long as we have them for Christmas Eve, there's no rush." Tom rose and held out his hand to Lila.

She took it and stood, aware of Alex eyeing them speculatively. Uncertain of her own feelings, she certainly didn't need anyone questioning what, exactly, transpired between her and Tom.

Although she tried to convince herself they were nothing but friends, she'd caught him studying her a few times with a look in his eyes that went beyond friendship.

In addition, he meant more to her than a mere friend. The fact that he did left her convicted and disconcerted. She was an engaged woman with absolutely no business letting another man turn her head. No matter how fun and kind and entirely appealing she found him, it was still wholly unacceptable.

Unnerved by the direction of her thoughts, Lila hurried to slip on the coat Tom held for her then gave Alex a warm hug.

Alex returned it and shot Lila a knowing wink before looking to Tom. "You do know Christmas Eve is a little more than two weeks away."

"I do know that, ma'am. And if I didn't, the children remind me daily of the approaching holiday."

"I'm sure they do," Alex said, opening the door as Tom shrugged on his coat. "It's nice to see you out of the sling. I assume that means your arm is healing."

"Yes, thank goodness. Doc said I can start using my hand, but to be careful about my arm."

Alex narrowed her gaze. "Knowing you, he probably should have made you wear that sling for another week or so."

"No, thank you. What a botheration!" Tom grinned as he settled his hat on his head, then cupped Lila's elbow as they made their way down the steps. "Thanks, again, for helping, Alex. We truly do appreciate it."

"You are most welcome." She waved then closed her door.

"Do you really think your mother will help with costumes?" Lila asked as Tom walked with her toward Granger House.

"I'm sure she will. I'll ask her tomorrow when I go home for the weekend." Tom guided her around a puddle. Although it remained cold with snow on the ground, there were a few spots where the sun shone all day that had melted enough to make messes on the streets.

"Are you enjoying the time you spend with your parents?" Lila wished almost daily she could spend even one more day with her parents. Their sudden deaths had left her so alone and bereft.

"I am," Tom said, tipping his hat to a group of women exiting Abby Dodd's dress shop. Both he and Lila waved through the window to the harried dressmaker then continued on their way. "We had a bit of a rough start, but things are fine now."

Lila shot him a questioning gaze, but he didn't share any further detail. From what she'd observed, Tom adored his parents and seemed genuinely pleased at the prospect of finally having a sibling, though he rarely mentioned anything about anticipating the baby's arrival.

"I think it's nice you spend your weekends at the farm with them. I'm sure they appreciate the opportunity to see you, since you don't make it back to Hardman frequently, or so I've heard."

Tom gave her a long, studying glance. "What else have you heard about me? Perhaps I need to find whoever it is that is spreading rumors about me and put a stop to it."

Lila laughed. "I'll wish you much luck with that. Everyone talks about you being such a fine student since Alex took over teaching and how proud they are of your successes in Portland. Even Mr. Daily at the newspaper brags about how you used to write articles for him."

Caught off guard, Tom didn't know what to say.

She glanced over at him and grinned. "I've also heard how you once trapped a skunk in the outhouse and failed to tell the teacher. You must really have disliked him."

"He wasn't a very nice man or a good teacher. We were all glad when he left. Then we got a new teacher who was afraid of us older boys. She had a terrible time handling the classes and she was rather short-tempered with the younger students. Arlan courted her for a very brief time, until Alex arrived in town and that was that. Alex took over teaching when the position opened and by then Arlan had fallen for her charms."

"I don't think Arlan is the only one who fell for Alex's charms. Ginny said all you boys practically followed her around like puppies on a leash."

Incredulous, Tom glared at her. "Ginny talks too much."

Lila laughed. "She does, but she means well. Besides, if it wasn't for Ginny's loose lips, how would I find out all the news about town, both past and present?"

"I'm sure I don't know. Unlike some people, I have better things to do than engage in idle gossip and hearsay." He lifted an eyebrow and gave her a look that made her giggle.

"That's why you're sadly uninformed about the most exciting happenings in town," she teased, walking around to the back door at Granger House.

Bart bounded down the steps and leaned against Tom, seeking attention. He hunkered down and gave the dog several good scratches along his back and behind his ears before gently thumping his side. "Be a good boy and stay out of trouble."

Lila watched the dog saunter off toward his house in a far corner of the yard. He spent most of his time near the kitchen door, but sometimes he curled up on the bed of old blankets in his house and slept.

"Thank you for walking me home, Tom. I'll see you at school tomorrow." She hurried up the porch steps. Before she opened the door, she stepped back down the top two, until she could reach Tom. She thumped his back with her gloved hand and repeated the phrase he'd used on the dog. "Be a good boy and stay out of trouble."

Tom chuckled. "You are too full of sass and nonsense for your own good, Miss Granger."

"I know," she said, taking the steps in one leap and sailing inside the house.

No one was in the kitchen, so Lila removed her outerwear and washed her hands, humming as she peeked in the oven and inhaled the scent of roasting beef.

Although she couldn't explain it and would steadfastly deny it, being with Tom Grove made her happier than she'd ever been in her life.

Chapter Ten

"I could have walked out to the farm," Tom said as he locked the door to the house and followed his dad over to his waiting wagon.

"Your mother sent me into town to pick up a few things at the mercantile, so it was no trouble to stop." James dropped Tom's bag in the back of the wagon then swung up to the seat.

Tom climbed up and settled beside his father. "Did you and Mama have a good week?"

"We did." James clucked to the horses and guided them out to the road. "I finished repairing the stalls in the barn and your mother stripped all the wallpaper off the spare bedroom walls."

A curious look settled on Tom's face. "Didn't she just decorate that room how she'd always wanted it a few years ago?"

James nodded. "She did, but she wants to turn it into a room for the baby."

"I see." Tom worried that his mother was giving up something she loved just to keep his old room exactly as he'd left it. Well, not exactly. It was definitely cleaner than he'd kept it when he lived at home.

A frown rode James' brow as he looked to his son. "Look, Tom, I know the whole thing about your mother and I expecting a baby in the spring has come as quite a shock to you, but I don't want you to feel like that's going to change how we feel about you. We care..."

Tom interrupted his father. "I'm happy for you both, Dad. Truly." He grinned. "In fact, I rather like the idea of finally being a big brother. If it's a boy, maybe I can take him hunting or out riding when I come to visit. Or, if Mama gets her way and the baby is a girl, I can treat her like a little princess."

James smiled and thumped Tom on the back. "You're something else, son. Do you know that?"

"What that something is would be the question." Tom offered his dad a cocky smile before turning serious again. "I was just thinking about Mama redoing the bedroom she worked so hard to decorate. If she wants to redo my bedroom for the baby, I don't mind."

James gaped at him. "But that's your room, son, for as long as you want it. I hope you'll plan to still visit us, even after the baby arrives."

"That gives me a reason to come home more frequently, don't you think?"

"It most certainly does, son." James sat a little straighter and snapped the reins on the horses, inordinately pleased with the fine young man sitting beside him.

It was nearly dark when they arrived home. Tom climbed down from the wagon to help with chores, but his father shooed him toward the house. "Go on in, Tom. I don't want you doing anything to hurt that arm of yours. Besides, you need to change out of your nice clothes before you set foot in the barn."

Tom glanced down at the suit he wore beneath his black wool coat and realized he'd forgotten to change after he released school for the day. In fact, as he and his father drove out to the farm, it seemed like the happy days of his youth when his father would sometimes give him a ride after school so he didn't have to make the long trek home in the cold and snow.

"I'll go change and come back out." He lifted his bag from the wagon and started toward the house.

"Just stay in the house, son. I did some of the chores before I headed into town. It won't take long to finish. No need in both of us freezing out here." James backed the wagon beneath the shelter of a building where he kept the farm equipment out of the weather.

Tom hurried up the back steps and inside the warmth of the kitchen. The scent of apples and pork filled the air, making his stomach growl.

His mother glanced up from where she set plates on the table with a smile. "Hi, sweetheart! Did you have a good week at school?"

Tom felt like he was twelve instead of twenty-one as he removed his coat and hat, hanging them by the back door. He stepped over to the table and gave his mother a hug. "I did have a good week. Those little rascals I teach, though, get more unruly the closer we get to Christmas. They keep talking about the carnival, programs at church, and, most importantly, what Saint Nicholas will bring them."

"That was always one of your favorite topics," Junie teased, patting Tom's scruffy cheek. Since he'd been unable to shave, he'd allowed his beard to grow the past few weeks. It itched like crazy. That morning, he'd decided it would be worth every penny it cost to go to the barber and get a shave. As soon as classes released Monday afternoon, he planned to head directly there, unless he could manage to do it himself without slicing open his neck.

Junie took a step back and studied him, as though she hadn't seen him before. Her hand slid to the base of her throat and tears glistened in her eyes. "Oh, Tom, when did you grow into such a tall, handsome man? I keep thinking I'll turn around and find you pulling worms or snowballs out of your pockets. Yet, here you are teaching little boys every bit as ornery as you ever were."

"Aw, Mama, you knew all along I was going to grow up someday. When that day comes, I'll let you know." He wrapped his arms around her and smiled against the pile of wheat-colored hair on top of her head.

She laughed, as he knew she would, and sniffled as she squeezed him tightly. "If I had a dozen children, you'd still be special to me, Thomas James Grove, because you make me laugh and lighten my heart."

"Now, Mama, don't tell fibs. If you had a dozen children, more than likely at least a few would be girls and you'd have forgotten all about me in light of ribbons and lace and little girl stuff." Tom kissed the top of her head and let her go. He snitched a cookie from the jar on the counter and took a big bite.

As he expected, his mother smacked his arm and gave him a dark look. "I've told you a million times not to eat a cookie right before supper. You'll spoil your appetite."

He finished the cookie and brushed the crumbs from his hands. "And I've told you a million and one times, there is no possible way one little ol' cookie will keep me from eating my share of food. Besides, I'm a growing boy. I need all the sustenance I can get."

Junie shook her head at him and lifted the spoon she used to stir a pan of fried apples, seasoned with cinnamon, sweetened with a liberal helping of sugar, and cooked in a generous spoon of butter.

Tom breathed in the spice-laden aroma and closed his eyes. It reminded him of wonderful autumn days spent at home as a boy when his mother would pop a big bowl of buttery popcorn. They'd eat it on the front porch while the fruity fragrance from their small orchard would drift to the house on the evening breeze.

"I'll run upstairs and change. Dad refused to let me help in the barn, so if there's anything you'd like me to do, just put me to work."

Tom rushed up the stairs with his bag and soon clattered back down to the kitchen dressed in a pair of worn canvas work pants and a soft flannel shirt. Now that he could at least use his right hand, it made shoving buttons through their holes a much easier task.

"Pork roast, fried apples, fluffy biscuits, and..." he sniffed the air again, wrinkling his brow in question. "What is that smell?"

Junie waggled her spoon at him. "That's cauliflower. Aleta had a fresh shipment the other day and I couldn't resist buying a few heads. Fresh produce tastes so good in the winter."

"If you say so," Tom said. The dubious expression on his face caused his mother to shoot him an indulgent look.

While she dished up the food, he poured glasses of milk and set them on the table. His father stamped his feet at the back step and entered the kitchen, bringing in a draft of cold air.

"Brr. I'm glad to be done with the chores for the evening. It is cold out there and the temperature keeps dropping." James hung his coat and hat on hooks by the door then washed his hands at the sink. "I wouldn't be surprised if it snows again this weekend."

Junie held out a carving knife and fork to him and motioned to the pork roast resting on a platter. With expert strokes, James carved it and set it on the table.

"Will you give thanks for us, son?" James asked, once they all were seated.

Tom shared a short but heartfelt prayer then snapped the napkin next to his plate in the air and draped it with ceremony across his lap, making Junie smile once again.

"What's gotten into you two?" James asked, eyeing his son and wife with suspicion as he helped himself to a serving of the succulent pork.

"Nothing out of the ordinary," Junie said, winking at Tom as she passed him the fried apples.

When he attempted to pass the cauliflower without taking any, she added a spoonful to his plate.

"Mama, you know I don't like that," he whined.

James laughed and pointed his fork at his son's plate. "Eat up, Tom, or no dessert for you. I know for a fact you don't want to miss out on tonight's offering."

Tom craned his neck, trying to see what his mother had made, but he didn't catch a glimpse of anything sweet. "What did you make, Mama?"

She lifted an eyebrow and gave him a motherly glare. "I'm not telling until you clean your plate."

"Yes, ma'am," Tom said, doing his best to sound like a scolded, repentant child. Secretly, he was amused his parents thought they could still tell him what to do and expect him to obey. He'd eat the blasted cauliflower, not because he wanted to, but because it would make his mother happy.

Later, when his mother served him a large slice of chocolate cake with freshly whipped cream and a cup of her good coffee, he decided the three bites of cauliflower he'd eaten were worth it to get dessert.

"This looks great, Mama. Thank you." He took a bite of the cake and moaned in pleasure. "Mmm. That is so good. No one makes chocolate cake quite like yours."

"Do you eat out a lot in the city?" Junie sat at the table with a small serving of the cake.

"Not too often. It can get expensive. I eat more than my share of sandwiches, though. I don't have a lot of time for cooking and even less talent at it, although I do make a mean pan of scrambled eggs."

James grinned. "So you've copied the one thing I can make that is edible."

"That I did, Dad." Tom took another bite of the cake then looked to his mother. "Dad mentioned you scraped the wallpaper in the spare bedroom this week. If you like, I can help you work on the room tomorrow."

"That's good of you to offer, honey. I won't refuse the help. I think I should have waited until spring to take on such a big project, but I want to have the room ready long before it is needed for our little one." Her hand dropped down to her belly and she rubbed it gently.

Tom observed her movements. "Have you thought of any names?"

Junie glanced at James and he nodded. "Well, we've been thinking about Jamie. That way, it wouldn't matter if it was a boy or a girl."

"Jamie Grove." Tom tested out the name, liking the way it sounded. "I think that will do quite nicely."

"We're glad you approve," James said, with a hint of sarcasm.

Tom smirked at his father. "Then again, Hortense and Herkimer are nice, too."

Junie slapped her napkin over her mouth to keep from spewing out the drink of tea she'd just taken.

James roared with laughter and Tom chuckled. He shot his parents a puckish grin. "Maybe you'll have twins and can use both those names."

"Bite your tongue," Junie said, when she regained the ability to speak. "My lands, Tom, but you are full of foolishness tonight. You seem happier than when you first arrived in town. What's put such a big smile on your face?"

James smirked. "I don't think it's what, but whom."

Tom scowled at his dad and took a big bite of cake so he wouldn't have to respond.

Junie's eyebrows rose so high they nearly reached her hairline. "Have you met a girl, Tom? Here in Hardman?"

He could almost see the wheels spinning in her head. If he met a local girl and fell in love, then he wouldn't leave again. Sadly, he had to crush his mother's dreams.

"We're just friends, Mama. That's all."

Junie pinned him with a pointed stare. "And who is this friend, sweetheart? The one you obviously don't like and aren't smitten over?"

Exasperated, Tom sighed. "It's Lila Granger. Everyone knows she's engaged to be wed as soon as she returns to New York and that's that."

James and Junie exchanged a look Tom couldn't decipher. The fact that he couldn't annoyed him every bit as much as their secretive system of communication. If he ever wed, he planned to dedicate particular time and effort into perfecting a similar means of expressing his thoughts to his wife. It would certainly come in handy for leaving their offspring perplexed and agitated.

"Before you start plotting and planning, let me make it perfectly clear — Lila and I are just friends. Only friends. I'll be heading back to Portland after the new year arrives and she'll leave at the end of January to return to New York to marry her true love."

"Who said her fiancé is her true love?" Junie asked.

Confused, Tom glared at her. "He'd have to be or she wouldn't agree to marry him, would she?"

Junie shrugged. "Girls agree to wed for any number of reasons that have nothing to do with true love. Didn't Lila lose both her parents last year?"

"Yes. She said Mr. Lylan proposed not long after their passing because he was heading overseas to study for a year. He's due back in the middle of January."

Junie gave him a disgruntled look. "You mean to tell me he had the poor taste to propose when she was deep in grief over losing her parents, just to assure she'd be waiting for him when he returned?"

"That is my understanding of the matter," Tom said, sipping his coffee, gratified by his mother's response. He thought it rude of Emerson to propose then head off for his year of studies at Oxford. Perhaps his dislike of the man, because he held Lila's heart, adversely colored his opinion on the matter.

"That does seem in poor taste," James commented, then appeared thoughtful. "What did you say his name is?"

"Emerson Lylan." Tom fairly spat out the words.

Amused, James couldn't hold back his laughter.

"What is so funny?" Tom asked, further irritated with his father.

"The name," James said, trying to curtail his mirth. "Lila Lylan. You can't let that girl marry him for the name alone. It sounds like someone is trying not to trip over their tongue. Lila Lylan. Oh, that's too much!"

Tom couldn't help but smile. "I thought the same thing myself." A soul-deep sigh rolled out of him. "But what can I do? She's already promised to him."

Junie grinned. "Promised to him is a long way from married to that man. He's across the ocean and you, my dear, sweet boy, are right here in Hardman. Romance blossoms in town during the holidays. If you put your mind to it, you could certainly woo one beautiful, lively young woman who looks at you with a great deal of affection."

Tom's head snapped up at his mother's words. "Does she really?"

"Yes, honey, she does. I noticed it quite plainly at church last Sunday." Junie sat up straight in her chair. "If it was me, I'd certainly give a fine young man like you a second look. Lila's given you more than that."

"You should tell him," James said, reaching out to squeeze Junie's shoulder.

Puzzled, Tom looked from his mother to his father. "Tell me what? If it's a bigger surprise than your little bundle of joy's upcoming arrival, I'm not sure I'm up for it."

Junie shook her head. "No. It's nothing that dramatic and blessed." She took her husband's hand in hers and held it on her lap. "You see, Tom, before I met your father, I was engaged to marry another."

"You were?" Tom's eyes widened as he stared at his mother, trying to picture her as young and carefree as Lila. He could almost envision it.

"I was. You know I grew up in Shaniko. What you don't know is that I was working the counter in my father's store one afternoon when a dashing young farmer walked inside. He had the warmest blue eyes and the most engaging smile. He was on his way home after delivering a load of wool for a neighbor." Junie smiled at James. "One of the local boys asked me to marry him a few months before that. He'd gone off to Portland to study to become an attorney. Like Lila's young man, he proposed a few days before he left. Caught up in the excitement of being engaged, especially when I was so young, I readily agreed. However, I wasn't in love with that boy. I was in love with the notion of being in love, but not Edward. I lost my heart to your father the moment he looked at me and said hello."

"How did you two court if Dad was here on the farm and Mama was in Shaniko?" Tom asked.

James grinned and kissed his wife's cheek. "She married me the next morning and came home with me."

Tom's jaw dropped and he gaped at his parents. "No kidding? You two married complete strangers?"

Junie smiled. "We might not have known everything about each other when we wed, but we knew enough to realize we were in love, even after just a few hours. I wrote Edward a letter, breaking our engagement, packed my things, hugged my mom and dad goodbye, and left with James. I've never, not even for one day, regretted my decision to follow my heart." She reached across the table and squeezed Tom's hand. "That's what you need to do, honey. Follow your heart, wherever it may lead. Even if it takes you right to Lila's door. If you love her, tell her. Don't let a silly thing like an absent fiancé keep you from finding happiness."

Tom sat back, attempting to digest his parents' love story and the idea he still had a chance with Lila. If he worked up the courage to tell her how he really felt, would she spurn him? Laugh in his face?

Or finally allow him the pleasure of tasting those sweet, sweet lips of hers.

"Oh!" Junie gasped, and placed both hands on her tummy. James looked at her with concern, until she smiled and lifted his hand, placing it on her stomach. "Can you feel that?" she asked, gazing adoringly at her husband. "I think the baby moved."

James remained perfectly still, fingers splayed over her belly. A grin broke out on his face and he beamed. "He's going to be a lively little fellow."

Junie frowned. "He might be a she, so none of that nonsense." She turned her gaze to Tom. "Do you want to feel it?"

Not ready for that sort of experience, Tom shook his head. "Maybe another time." He softened his refusal with a teasing grin. "You might as well just call the baby Jamie, Dad. If that's the name Mama likes, then that's the name it will be."

"That it will, son."

Chapter Eleven

"Mr. Grove! Please wait!"

Tom and his parents stopped and turned as Dora Granger hurried their direction after church on Sunday.

The woman smiled as she approached, wearing one of the ugliest hat's Tom had ever seen. Shaped like a tricorn, the pale yellow felt swooped upward in the back almost a foot in height. A swath of creamy, airy fabric dripped over the brim while a flower as big as a dinner plate bobbed at the very top of the crown. A bejeweled clasp glittered from the hat's front in the morning sunlight.

"Hello, Mrs. Granger. That is quite a hat," Junie said, subtly elbowing Tom in the side.

He fought back an urge to laugh. He and his mother so often found the same things amusing, like Dora Granger's penchant for the most attention-grabbing hats anyone in the county had ever seen.

Dora reached up and brushed the brim of the hat. "It is something, isn't it? When Mr. Granger and I were in New York last month, we were strolling along the avenue past some of my favorite shops when I saw this one and just had to have it."

"It's unlike anything I've ever seen," Junie said, with more diplomacy than Tom could have mastered.

He bumped his mother on purpose, knowing she was on the verge of laughing, too.

Oblivious to their amusement over her millinery selections, Dora smiled at the trio. "Mr. Granger and I would be so pleased if you would accept our invitation for lunch today. A few other guests will also attend. It would be an honor to have you join us at our table."

"Oh, Mrs. Granger, that's so kind of you to invite us," Junie said, casting a quick glance at James. He offered a slight nod of agreement. "We'd love to come."

"Splendid!" Dora clapped her hands together, making Tom think of the enthusiasm her daughter often exhibited. In truth, Dora and Ginny looked more like sisters than mother and daughter. Petite, blonde, and possessed of a take-charge attitude, the two women shared many similarities beyond their appearances. "Please come over to the house as soon as you finish visiting with members of the congregation."

Dora smiled at Tom and his parents then flounced off toward her husband as he spoke with their son and son-in-law.

"Well, that's something," James commented as they slowly ambled over to their wagon. "We've known the Grangers for years, and that's the first time Dora has invited us to dine with them."

"Perhaps the thought just never crossed her mind before," Junie said, accepting James' help in climbing into the wagon. Tom climbed up on one side of her while his father swung up on the other side.

"Maybe the spirit of the season has infected even her," James mused.

"Whatever the reason, I'm looking forward to seeing inside the house. The only times I've been in it are during the Christmas carnival," Tom said. "It's so packed full of people then, you can barely turn around."

"I agree, honey. It will be fun to see the house," Junie said as James guided the horses away from the church and down the street. Dora and Greg Granger lived just a few blocks from the mercantile, so it didn't take long to reach their home.

James had just set the brake on the wagon when Luke stopped behind him in his sleigh. The jingling harness sounded like holiday bells in the snappy winter air.

"Hello!" Filly called, waving to them as she stepped out of the sleigh holding a blanket-bundled baby Cullen.

Lila accepted Luke's hand and stepped down, then offered Tom a small, friendly wave.

In the time it took James to help Junie from the wagon and the three of them to approach the front walk of the impressive home, Blake and Ginny, the Dodd family, and Alex and Arlan Guthry arrived.

"My gracious, this looks like a regular party," Junie whispered. Nervous, she reached up to check her hair.

"You look lovely, June-bug." James offered her a private smile that Tom ignored as they walked toward the others.

"How nice of you to join us!" Ginny said, reaching out a hand to Junie in welcome. "Mother said she planned to invite you. I'm so glad you didn't have other plans."

Tom held back a comment. As had become their habit, he and his parents would have fixed lunch at the cramped teacher's house and visited for a few hours before his folks returned to the farm. None of them minded the interruption to their plans.

As they all filed toward the front door, Tom gravitated toward Lila until he fell into step beside her.

"Did you have a nice weekend with your parents?" she asked in a quiet voice as they moved down the walk and up the porch steps.

"I did have a nice time with them. I helped my mother prepare the walls in the spare bedroom for a new coat of paint yesterday morning. Most of the afternoon, I worked with Dad in the barn. It was good to spend time with them both." Tom motioned for Lila to precede him inside the house.

Since he was the last one in, he closed the door behind him then turned to help Lila out of her coat.

He had to work to keep his mouth from dangling open as she stepped away from the covering and smiled at him.

The silvery gown she wore featured an elaborate panel of lace down the front, embroidered with sprays of lilacs. Tom had no idea about fabrics or fashions, but the dress fulfilled his ideal of the perfect gown for the dazzling girl. The soft gray hue complimented her sparkling eyes and the lilacs made it seem as though she carried the fragrant bouquets with her.

A deep breath filled his nose with her delightful scent, further validating his belief that Lila was like a burst of springtime on a bleak winter day.

Sitting two rows behind her at church, he hadn't been able to tell what she wore. If he'd seen her gown before Chauncy began delivering that morning's sermon, Tom would have been hard-pressed to pay any attention. Just the sight of her gleaming dark hair gathered up beneath the brim of her smart little hat had created enough of a diversion.

"You look so beautiful, Lila Lilac." Tom offered her a lopsided, teasing grin.

She laughed and took his hand in hers once he hung up both of their coats on the hall tree by the door.

"If anyone else dared call me that, they'd get both their ears boxed," she said, leading him to the spacious front room where everyone gathered.

"Oh, Lila! That gown is beautiful," Junie said, sliding closer to James and making room for Lila to sit next to her on one of the sofas. Tom took a seat on a chair nearby.

"Thank you, Mrs. Grove," Lila said, smiling at the woman.

Junie grinned. "Please, call me Junie." When Lila nodded in agreement, she tipped her head toward Tom. "Thank you for helping my son at the school. He said he didn't know what he would have done without you there to write assignments on the blackboard and help with some of the duties his arm prevents him from seeing to."

"It's my pleasure." Lila glanced over at Tom. "I've greatly enjoyed the opportunity to expand my education, too."

"You have?" Junie asked, somewhat baffled by Lila's comment. The girl was obviously well educated.

"Certainly. I've learned that Tom is a terrible tease parading around as a mild-mannered school teacher who really works for a big city newspaper. He hordes his magic secrets like they were gold bars, and he has a horrid habit of feigning innocence when he's made a particularly wicked comment."

Junie laughed. "I see you do know him well."

A servant's appearance at the door announcing the meal was ready kept Lila from saying anything further to make red creep up Tom's neck.

She wrapped her arm around his as they made their way to the formal dining room. He held her chair then took a seat beside her while his parents sat across the table, next to Alex and Arlan.

Lively conversation flowed around the table. After the meal, the men wandered down the hall to Greg's library while the women gathered in the ladies' parlor.

Undeniably feminine, the parlor was Lila's least favorite room in the house. It seemed overrun with bric-a-brac and extravagant touches. Filly and Ginny also seemed to prefer to sit in the large front room or any of the other gathering rooms to this one.

Erin and Maura curled up on a rug by the fire with a pile of picture books to keep them occupied while Filly sat in the rocking chair, cuddling Cullen.

Lila noticed Junie Grove's amusement as she listened to Dora discuss New York with Alex, who had grown up there.

Bored and wishing she could escape, Lila quietly rose to her feet and sidled out the door. She started to back down the hall and collided with a solid form.

Spinning around, she stared at Tom as he held his fingers to his lips, indicating she should remain silent.

With a brief nod, she led the way to the front door where they pulled on their coats and slipped outside undetected.

"What are you doing sneaking out?" Tom asked, smiling at Lila as they wandered down the steps.

"Dora was prattling on and on about the shops and restaurants in New York as though there isn't any place quite as grand." Lila sighed then glanced over at Tom. "Don't get me wrong. I adore her, but honestly, if I could choose anywhere in the world to live, I'd pick Hardman over New York any day."

"Then why don't you stay here?" Tom asked, opening the gate at the end of the walk so they could step out on the boardwalk. "Why do you have to return to New York?"

"Because Emerson's life is in New York. There isn't a thing he could do here in town for work and he'd never adjust to life in such a small place. He loves big cities and noise, and all of the bustle."

Tom took Lila's hand and wrapped it around his arm, leaving his fingers resting on top of hers. "What about you? Do you like the bustle and noise and crowds and crime?"

Lila shook her head. "No. Not at all. I like the quiet and peace and friendliness of living here." She studied Tom a moment. "I could ask you the same question. Do you like living in the city?"

"No. Not at all. After the third or fourth murder I wrote about for the newspaper, any delusions I held about living in a big city dissipated. But, like your fiancé, I have to live in the city if I want to do the work I enjoy."

"What about the newspaper here? Couldn't you work for Mr. Daily?" Lila asked as they meandered down the street.

"Not full-time. He already has a staff of regular employees working for him and part-time work wouldn't pay my bills or build my writing career."

She shrugged. "But you could work for your father part-time on the farm. With your family expecting a little one right before the busy summer season, I'm sure your father would value any time you could spend there."

Tom frowned. "I know he would, but I want to write for a living, not farm."

Lila waved at a couple across the street. "Have you ever considered writing for magazines or submitting articles to national publications? It might supplement your income to the degree you could afford to live in a smaller town. One like Hardman."

Tom stopped and looked down at her. "If I didn't know better, I'd think you were trying to convince me to move back to Hardman. Why do you care where I live? You'll be leaving in another month or so, anyway."

"Perhaps, but I know you seem very happy here, among your family and friends. I happened to have a conversation with Fred Decker at the mercantile the other day, and he told me how much your friendship means to him."

"Fred had a rough time for a while, but he seems to have outgrown many of his troubles."

"What about you?" Lila asked, continuing to amble aimlessly down the street.

"What about me?" Tom glanced down at her again.

"Have you outgrown your troubles or grown into them?"

Tom grinned. "I suppose that depends on who you ask."

Disturbed by the direction the conversation had gone, he realized they'd merely circled the block. Erin Dodd's little sled leaned against the inside of Greg and Dora's fence where Chauncy had left it after pulling his daughter to their house after church.

Tom reached over the pickets and grabbed it, setting it down on the edge of the street. "Come on, Lila Lilac. Let's have some fun."

She planted her feet and crossed her arms over her chest. "I don't know what you have planned, but I'm not sure I want a part of it."

"Of course you do," he said, grabbing her arm and propelling her forward. "Get on and I'll give you a ride."

The sensible, decorous side of Lila ordered her to march back in the house and sit with the women. The fun-loving part of her, though, cheered for her to hop on the sled and enjoy an afternoon in the winter sunshine with a handsome man who clearly enjoyed her company.

She glanced once toward Dora and Greg's house then lifted her skirts and plopped down on the sled, folding her legs beneath her.

Carefully, Tom tucked in her trailing skirts then took the leather strap of the sled in his left hand and gave it a tug.

Lila giggled as he pulled the sled down the street. Before either of them gave a conscious thought to their destination, he took her out to a small hill at the edge of town. At the top, he stopped and moved the sled into position. With a dramatic bow, he placed the leather strap in her hand then gave the sled a mighty shove.

Amid much excited squealing, she sailed down the hill. When the sled upended in a snowbank at the bottom, she threw herself back in the snow and stared up at the winter sky, full of contentment.

The sound of crunching snow and Tom calling her name drew her attention to him as he raced down the hill.

"Are you well, Lila? Did you break anything?" Worry laced his tone as he hurried toward her.

Rather than shout that she was fine, she closed her eyes and remained unmoving, wondering what he would do.

His warmth encircled her as he dropped to his knees next to her and bent down, gently tapping her cheek with his left hand. "Lila, honey? Can you hear me? Lila?"

The endearment he used made sweet, oozy warmth settle in her stomach while heat flooded through her entire body. Strange feelings, ones she'd never experienced, filled her until every part of her seemed keenly attuned to Tom.

"Lila? Please be okay? Please?" He bent close and pressed his cheek to hers, slipping his arm beneath her and lifting her head and shoulders from the snow.

As his scent tickled her nose with a pleasing aroma, she delighted in the experience of being wrapped in his arms. Even with his heavy cast pressed against her back, she couldn't think of anywhere she'd ever been that seemed more like home.

"Lila?" His voice sounded more concerned as though he bordered on panic.

Unable to continue her ruse, she popped open her eyes and grinned at him. "I'm fine, Tom. I was just teasing you."

"You shouldn't... that's not..." He pulled back long enough to look deep in her eyes. Whatever he searched for he must have found because he wasted no time in pressing his lips to hers, plundering her mouth with barely restrained passion.

Lila had no idea how it happened, but her arms wrapped around his neck and she pulled him closer as their kiss deepened.

Finally, Tom lifted his head. "I'm sorry, Lila. That shouldn't have happened."

Abruptly coming to her senses, she sat up and blinked her eyes. "No, it shouldn't have, but I'm the one at fault if anyone shoulders the blame."

"I didn't mean to... that's to say I didn't plan on... It's just that..."

Lila placed her gloved finger over his lips. "It's fine, Tom. Honest. Let's just pretend it didn't happen."

"Agreed." He leaned back and looked around, taking in the expanse of pristine snow. "Since you're already all covered in snow, we might as well make a few angels while we're here."

"Oh, that's a lovely idea," Lila said, flopping back and waving her arms and legs.

Tom took a spot beside her. When he finished, he rolled to one side and found himself positioned over her.

A battle raged between doing what was right and what seemed impossibly wonderful. He trailed his fingers over her smooth cheek, tucking an errant strand of silky hair back behind her ear while his gaze focused on her just-kissed lips.

Lila watched the war in his heart through the windows in his eyes. She almost reached up to pull him down to her again. He tasted like peppermint and coffee, and something decadent she had no idea how to define. His lips had been so warm against hers, and she rather liked the idea of finding them there again.

Then she thought of Emerson, her fiancé. Ardor immediately cooled at what he would say if he found out she'd been cavorting in the snow with another man.

Before Tom could kiss her again, she grinned and made a silly face. "Want to help me drag this sled back up the hill? I'd like to give it another go."

Tom released a long sigh then rolled over and stood. He reached a hand down to her with a smile. "Come on, Lila Lilac. Let's see if you can make it down to the fork in the road."

Together, yet keeping a safe distance apart, they walked back up the hill.

The moment the front door clicked shut, five women hurried to press their noses to the window glass and crane their necks to see if Tom and Lila went for a walk together.

Uncertain what transpired, Junie Grove looked at Dora, Filly, Ginny, Alex and Abby as though they'd lost their minds.

Filly noticed her on the settee and motioned her to the window. "Come over, Junie. We're spying on your son."

Junie rose to her feet and joined them at the window. Tom and Lila walked around the corner and disappeared from sight.

The women all turned around and returned to their seats.

Junie looked from Filly to Ginny then Dora. "May I inquire why you are spying on my son and Lila?"

"Of course," Ginny said as she settled in a chair and adjusted a pillow behind her back. "We want Lila to stay here and we've all noticed she favors Tom."

Junie smiled. "He's quite fond of her, too. However, I understand she's engaged to someone in New York."

"Oh, bosh," Dora said, waving her hand dismissively to the side. "Emerson is a fine young man, handsome and wealthy, intelligent and kind. We just don't think he's the right man for our Lila."

Ginny grinned. "I thought she'd never get bored of your purely horrid conversation with Alex, mother. Honestly, I thought I might have to volunteer to sing or something to send her running outside."

Junie smiled, inordinately pleased with this group of women. While she had a passing acquaintance with them, she realized now they could all become good friends, especially when they were all determined to encourage Lila to fall in love with Tom.

Luke poked his head in the room and glanced around. "Did it work?" he asked, stepping inside when he didn't see Lila among the women.

Filly nodded. "Yes! We watched them stroll down the street together."

A sigh rolled out of Luke as he rubbed a hand across the back of his neck. "Thank goodness. If Arlan, Dad and I had to talk about balancing bank books another moment, I thought I might run outside myself."

The women laughed. Luke peeked at his son, sleeping in Filly's arms, kissed the top of her head and wandered back down the hall to join the other men.

Filly noticed Junie admiring Cullen and stood, walking over to where she sat. "Would you like to hold him?"

"Oh, may I?" Junie asked. She'd so desperately wanted to hold the baby, to practice for when she had her own to hold once again, but she didn't feel it was proper to ask.

"Of course." Filly settled the baby boy in her arms and took a seat beside her. "Cullen is used to being passed around among the adults, so it doesn't disturb him in the least to hand him off to someone."

"He's such a good baby, Filly. I've hardly heard him raise any sort of fuss."

Filly studied the sweet little face of her son. "He is a good boy, although I'm sure if he's anything like his father, he'll keep us both on our toes when he's older."

Junie laughed softly. "Boys are like that."

"They certainly are." Filly leaned back and relaxed. "You must be so proud of Tom. He's been such a blessing to all of us, stepping in to teach until Alex feels well again."

"Tom is special," Junie agreed, enthralled with the baby she held. He was so tiny and perfect. "He's going to make some lucky girl a marvelous husband."

"I think so, too. I rather hope that lucky girl will be our Lila. She's one of a kind." Filly gave Junie a long, observant glance. Her voice dropped to a whisper when she spoke. "Please don't think me rude for asking, Junie, but I can't help but notice you are positively glowing. I don't think it's just because Tom is home for Christmas."

Junie blushed and shook her head, leaning closer to Filly. "No. James and I are quite excited by the news we are expecting our own little bundle of joy."

Sheer determination was all that kept Filly from excitedly blurting something the others might hear. She beamed as she wrapped an arm around Junie's shoulders and gave her a hug. "Oh, that's the most wonderful news! I'm so happy for you both."

"We couldn't be happier." Junie smiled at the lovely woman. "At first, we weren't sure how Tom would adjust to the idea. After all, he's old enough to have his own children. I'm sure the last thing he expected was to come home and find his parents planning for a new baby, especially when we'd given up on that dream a long, long time ago."

"But he's happy about the news?" Filly asked, unable to imagine Tom being anything except supportive of his parents.

"Oh, yes. Just the other night, he was teasing that we should have twins and name them Hortense and Herkimer."

Filly giggled. "Those are perfectly horrid names. You should have heard some of the names that were suggested for Cullen." She tipped her head toward Dora where she and Ginny engaged in a conversation about the women's right to vote.

"So the invitation to lunch today was to throw Tom and Lila together?" Junie asked, impressed the Granger family would go to such effort to play matchmakers.

"Only partially. We really did want to spend time with you and James, too. It seems we all are so busy all the time, we forget how important it is to make new friends." Filly gave Junie an imploring look. "I certainly hope we'll continue being friends."

"I'd like that very much, Filly." Junie slowly rocked the baby in her arms back and forth. "Especially if our combined efforts can bring Tom and Lila together."

"Exactly! Now, here's what we had planned for the coming week..."

Chapter Twelve

"Filly?" Lila called as she breezed into the kitchen, expecting to find the woman there. Cullen slept in his cradle, but Filly was nowhere in sight.

Lila noticed a half-empty cup of tea and a book on the table. She stepped over and lifted the book, amused her cousin chose to read love poems in the few moments of free time she had during her busy day.

"Oh, are you getting ready to go out?" Filly asked as she stepped into the kitchen with an armload of neatly folded dishtowels.

"I am," Lila said, waggling the book Filly's direction. "I wouldn't have pegged you as an admirer of such writings."

Filly shrugged. "Sometimes they're fun to read. Do you like poetry?"

Lila set the book on the table and lifted her coat from the rack by the door, slipping her arms into the sleeves. "I do. I'll even confess that Dickinson is one of my favorites."

Filly stored the dishtowels in a cupboard then gave Lila a casual glance. "You might enjoy Tom's poetry. Alex has a few of them at the school, although my favorite is one he wrote for the Christmas carnival auction the first year we held the event. Ginny painted a scene and Alex wrote it in a beautiful script, but the words were all from his heart."

Lila feigned indifference to hearing Tom's name. In truth, she'd thought of little else but him since he'd kissed her Sunday afternoon.

In her twenty-two years, Lila had been kissed several times — chaste pecks to her cheeks and a few impertinent brushes against her lips. Of course, she exchanged a few kisses with Emerson after they agreed to wed. However, his kisses didn't make her toes tingle and insides heat.

No. Those reactions belonged to Tom alone. Even the thought of his kisses left her limbs languid. Despite her head telling her how wrong it was to encourage him, Lila found herself wanting to kiss him again.

If Emerson kissed a girl in England as passionately as she had kissed Tom, she would be furious with him. The betrayal would be unforgiveable.

Wouldn't it?

Although she attempted to work up some semblance of annoyance at the very idea of him kissing another, she couldn't quite manage it. Not when she longed, with every breath she took, to kiss Tom again.

Determined to put him from her mind, at least for five minutes, she yanked on her gloves and picked up her reticule, abruptly changing the subject. "Do you need anything from the mercantile?"

"I don't, Lila, but thank you for asking." Filly snatched a basket from a high shelf and quickly wrapped a loaf of bread. She placed it inside then added a tin full of cookies she'd baked that morning. "Would you mind taking this to Tom when you retrieve Maura? I'm surprised she wanted to stay all day, since she was dragging around this morning."

Lila nodded. "I appreciated Luke checking on her so I could spend the morning helping Abby. If she doesn't deliver that baby before Christmas, I'll eat Dora's new hat."

Filly burst into giggles. "You better hope Abby has the baby early, then. That hat is a monstrosity. I can't imagine it would taste any better than it looks."

Lila opened the door and sailed outside with a cheeky grin.

Bart barked and waggled his back end as she stopped to scratch his ears. "Would you like to come along, Bart? Huh? Would you like to go with me to get Maura?"

The dog barked twice and raced down the walk, as though he understood what she said. He looked back at her and barked again, encouraging her to walk faster.

Lila laughed. "I'm coming you crazy canine." She whistled to the dog and he ran back to her, planting himself at her side as they made their way into town and to the school.

No children ran around outside, so she assumed classes had not yet been dismissed for the day.

"Stay, Bart. You stay right here," she commanded, pointing to a spot nearby. She walked on silent feet up the steps and quietly went inside.

Tom sat at the front of the class reading while the children intently listened. No one paid her any mind as she settled onto a chair at the back of the room and removed her coat.

Engaged in the interesting tale, Lila grinned when Tom looked up and noticed her. He glanced at the clock, placed a slip of paper in the book to mark his place and snapped it closed.

"I'm sorry, class, but I've already kept you ten minutes later than I should have." He stood and smiled. "The story will still be here tomorrow, but it's time for you all to go home."

"But Tom... er, I mean Mr. Grove, can't you at least finish the chapter. It was getting really good," Percy Bruner pleaded.

Tom shook his head. "No. I promise to allow extra time for reading tomorrow, though. Your parents will wonder what's happened if I don't send you all home right away."

"Aw, shoot. They won't care," Percy said, but he stood and gathered his things then hurried to get his coat and Anna's from the back of the room. Lila waved at the children and spoke to several as they filed by on their way outside.

Erin and Maura both ran over to her, eager to tell her all about their day. Interested, she listened to their excited chatter as she helped them on with their coats and mittens. She sent them outside to play for a few minutes.

In no hurry to leave, Lila wandered up the outside aisle and studied the variety of projects hanging on the walls. She stopped in front of a framed image of stars twinkling above a landscape of snow with a sweet poem that touched her heart.

"T. Grove" and the date was printed in the bottom corner.

"Reading my early, childish works?" Tom asked from behind her.

Lila spun around, clutching the basket in front of her as she stared at him. She'd been so absorbed in the words, she hadn't heard his approach.

"It's a lovely poem, Tom. Even in its simplicity, there is beauty and depth. It's clear it was written from the heart and that's what makes it special."

Pleased by her words, he smiled. "Other than escorting Maura and Erin home, what brings you by today?"

Since Sunday afternoon's kisses, Lila had carefully avoided Tom. She left Maura outside the past two mornings and managed to escape checking on her at noon by hiding at Abby's shop. She helped the woman by sewing and pressing the straight seams while Abby

134

worked on the more intricate stitching. When it came time to fetch Maura and Erin from school, she'd waited outside for them rather than go into the school.

She'd been there so often, the children didn't even blink when she arrived.

However, with Tom's arm healing, he no longer needed her to write assignments on the blackboard or help him with little things around the classroom. She had no excuse to see him, other than she desperately wanted to.

She held out the basket of bread and cookies. "Filly sent these for you."

"That was kind of her," Tom said, taking the basket and setting it on a nearby desk before moving closer to Lila. "Are you going to Ginny and Blake's skating party this Saturday?"

"Of course. Everyone is going, aren't they? I thought I heard Aleta say something about closing the store for a few hours so even she and George could attend." Lila wondered what Tom would do if she rose up on her tiptoes and kissed him. Those thoughts would get her into serious trouble... so she gave them even more consideration.

Tom gave her a long look. "Most everyone in town closes their business for a few hours. It's an enjoyable day, with plenty of hot beverages and delicious things to eat. Arlan said the band is planning to play if the temperature isn't too cold."

"Oh, that will be fun," Lila said, backing toward the chair where she left her coat. Tom kept pace with her until they both stood in the corner. He lifted her coat and held it as she slid her arms into the sleeves. His hands lingered on her shoulders a moment longer than necessary. Distracted, she glanced at the cast on his arm. "Will you be able to skate?"

"I plan on it, whether I should or not."

His boyish grin did the strangest things to her heart, making it feel like melted butter.

Resolved to ignoring the attraction pulsing between them, Lila heard Bart bark. She'd forgotten all about bringing the dog with her.

"I forgot about Bart. I had better go. He's been patient long enough." She tugged on her gloves and nodded at Tom as he held open the door for her. Bart struggled to walk with Maura attempting to ride him while Erin pranced alongside the dog, calling out encouragement.

"Maura, get off the dog! He's not a pony!" Lila rushed down the steps and lifted the girl in her arms, tickling the little imp.

"Bart doesn't mind," Erin said, hugging the faithful dog around his neck and earning a slobbery lick to her face. The child wrinkled her nose as she giggled.

"Regardless, you don't want to hurt him doing something like that. Bart isn't as young and spry as he used to be, so you must be careful," Lila warned, setting Maura down and taking her hand then motioning for Erin to take her other. She glanced back at Tom and smiled. "Enjoy your evening, Mr. Grove."

"I will, Miss Granger. And I believe it's my turn to bring treats to the children's practice tomorrow."

Somehow, practice for the children's program had also completely slipped her mind. "Thank you," she called, and hurried away with the two little girls and the dog trotting beside them.

If she didn't stop obsessing over Tom, she'd soon forget her own name.

Chapter Thirteen

The cookies Tom brought for practice from the bakery were a big hit with the children, if the box of crumbs was any indication.

"The little gluttons didn't leave any," he groused as he picked up the empty container and shook it.

Lila laughed as she gathered up the script and assorted papers from the play, stuffing them into a bag. "What do you expect? I've already learned if you want to get in on the treats, you best hide one before the children arrive." She hurried to put on her coat before Tom could help her, determined to keep him at arm's length.

He stepped in front of her and gave her an imploring look. "Did you hide anything today?"

Efforts at remaining expressionless failed her and she giggled as she took two cookies from her coat pocket. She handed one to him then bit into the other.

"You're nearly as sneaky and devious as those hooligans I've been teaching."

Playfully, Lila smacked his left arm. "I'd be thoroughly insulted, sir, if that wasn't true."

Tom chuckled and ate his cookie as he gathered his things. He'd just pulled on his coat when the church door opened and his mother breezed inside followed by his father.

"What are you two doing in town?" Tom asked, kissing his mother's cheek.

"I worked on the sheep costume today and I thought it turned out well, so I wanted to see what you two think," Junie said. She looked at Tom then winked at Lila. "Mostly, I wanted to see what you thought because Tom's opinion about costumes doesn't particularly matter."

Lila laughed while Tom feigned insult. James thumped him on the back as Junie pulled a costume out of the cloth bag she carried.

"Will this do?" Junie asked, holding it up for Lila's inspection.

"Oh, my gracious!" Lila's eyes twinkled as she took the sheep costume and did an excited little jig where she stood. "It's perfect, Junie! It's absolutely adorable! How on earth did you make it?"

"One of our neighbors brought us some wool he'd used in a display. Since it was so clean and fluffy, I thought it would work well for the costume." Junie looked to Tom. "You remember Mr. Galloway, don't you son?"

"Yes, Mama."

"He took several of his sheep to the World's Fair in Paris. It closed last month, so he's only been back a short while. Anyway, he had some wool left from demonstrating how to trim wool and whatnot, so he asked if I'd like it. Of course, I said I would."

Tom studied the costume that did, in fact, look like a sheep with wool carefully stitched onto a fabric outfit. His mother had even created a hood with ears. "You did a good job, Mama. Thank you."

"Good job?" Lila scowled at Tom. "It's amazing, that's what this is." She grabbed Junie's hand. "Will you come with me to show Alex? She's working on the other two costumes."

"I'd be happy to," Junie said, following her toward the door. She looked back at James and Tom. "Let's eat at the restaurant. I'll meet you there in forty-five minutes."

"That'll be fine, June-bug," James said. He turned to Tom and thumped his back again. "Galloway was telling me they had more than fifty-million visitors at the fair. Can you imagine that many people?"

"It's hard to fathom, isn't it?" Tom asked, lifting his leather bag and walking with his father toward the door. "Did Mr. Galloway talk about other exhibits at the fair?"

"He mentioned Art Nouveau something or other being popular. There was a big refracting telescope, and a palace of electricity. The first Olympic games held outside of Greece took place there." James waited while Tom shut the church door. They strolled down the steps before he continued. "While your mother was fixing tea in the kitchen, he told me all about one of the exhibits having a bunch of women, a harem he called them, doing strange dances wearing hardly any clothes at all."

Tom's eyebrows shot upward in shocked surprise.

James chuckled. "I got the idea that was Galloway's favorite part of the whole thing."

Tom smirked. "Most likely, Dad."

The two men ambled toward the school so Tom could leave his satchel at his house before they met Junie at the restaurant. He hoped Lila would join them since Luke had stopped to get Maura after the program practice, leaving Lila free to do as she pleased the remainder of the evening.

"How are things going with the students?" James asked as they walked past the school to Tom's temporary home.

"Great. They're all such good students, and so bright. They've been working hard on projects for the Christmas carnival. Somehow, they talked me into reading to them the last thirty minutes each day. Yesterday, they didn't even notice when I read past time to release them."

"You always did have a good reading voice, son." James waited while Tom unlocked the door and pushed it open. He set his bag on the floor by the table and motioned to the stove. "Would you like me to make some coffee?"

"No need for that. We'll be at the restaurant soon enough." The two of them removed their coats and draped them over one of the chairs. James took a seat at the table while Tom stoked the stove then washed his hands.

"How do you like helping with the Christmas program at church?" James asked.

Tom took a seat across from his father. "I've been enjoying it. As much as it pains me to admit it, I'm almost glad I broke my arm because it forced me to come home. I think I needed to spend some time away from the city."

"I'm glad to hear that, son. Pretty Lila Granger couldn't have anything to do with how much you're enjoying your time at home, now, could she?"

Heat burned up Tom's neck and reddened his ears. "Why would you ask that?" He fidgeted with the saltcellar he'd left on the table.

"Because you look at her like I look at your mama. You might fool her and you may even fool yourself, but it's obvious you care about her, son. Have you given any more thought to what your mother and I told you about our courtship lasting less than a day?"

"I have, Dad," Tom said. He sighed and ran his hand through his hair. "As much as I'd like to court Lila, she's quite taken with Emerson. Besides, it doesn't seem right to horn in when I know she's spoken for. I wouldn't like it if someone did that to me."

James snorted and gave his son a pointed look. "If you'd asked Lila to wed, you sure wouldn't have ventured off to some fancy university overseas. Even if you had gone, you'd have made sure she went along as your wife." The older man shook his head. "It seems to me if Emerson was that interested in making sure Lila didn't get away, he wouldn't have left that door of opportunity open."

Tom studied his father for a long moment then broke into a wide grin. "I'm glad you're on my side, Dad. I'd sure hate to have you conspiring against me."

James chuckled. "I'm not conspiring against anyone. But if Mr. Lylan wanted to make certain Lila would be sitting at home, awaiting his return, he should have exchanged nuptials with her before he left New York City. As far as I'm concerned, she's fair game."

Tom smirked. "You talk about her like she's some wild animal I'm out to hunt down."

"You've got her in your sites, so just pull the trigger, son." James grinned at him. "What's the worst that could happen? She might tell you she isn't interested. On the other hand," the man leaned back in his chair with a smug look, "she might just tell you yes. You'll never know if you don't put a little effort into winning her affections."

"I know, Dad, it's just..." Tom stared at the floor rather than meet his father's probing gaze.

"Just what, Tom?" James continued looking at him until Tom finally glanced up. "What's holding you back? And don't give me any twaddle about her being engaged. If you really wanted to marry that girl, the two of you would have already stood at the church with Pastor Dodd officiating."

Tom traced an invisible pattern on top of the table with the index finger of his left hand. "Lila isn't like other girls I've known, Dad. She's a Granger and comes from old money, and lots of it. She grew up in a mansion with servants to cater to her every need. Do you really think she'd give all that up to marry someone like me? A farm boy trying to make his way in the newspaper business?"

James smiled. "I think if she loved you, really loved you, Miss Lila Granger wouldn't give a flying fig if you had two dollars or a million to your name. She doesn't strike me as the type of girl to think money was a measure of a man's worth."

"No, she's not like that," Tom said. He sighed and glimpsed the time, rising to his feet. "We better go or Mama will beat us to the restaurant."

"And that would never do." James shrugged into his coat while Tom pulled on his. Together, they walked through the crisp evening air to the restaurant. They turned the corner from Main Street and smiled as Junie and Lila approached from the opposite direction.

Junie kissed James' cheek and looped her arm around his as they met in front of the restaurant.

"I'm starving," she said, smiling as Tom opened the door and held it for them to enter.

"Me, too," Lila said, winking at Tom as she sailed inside. As she moved past him, he inhaled the scent of lilacs. The delightful fragrance, so out of place in the frosty December air, made him smile as he stepped inside and followed her to the table where the waitress seated his parents.

Quickly pulling out her chair, he helped her remove her coat. Once she was seated, he removed his own and sat beside her.

"Did Alex like the costume?" Tom asked, looking at his mother.

Junie nodded. "Oh, she did. You should see the camel costume she's creating. It is wonderful."

Lila wiggled excitedly beside him. "I wish I was one of the children so I could wear one of the costumes. They are just amazing."

Tom pictured Lila as a child, with big gray eyes full of mischief and excitement, a head full of dark, unruly curls, and an enchanting smile.

He picked up his menu to hide the amusement created by a vision of her as a willful child. The way he pictured her as a little girl wasn't much different than she appeared as an adult. He'd never seen a grown woman who looked so unabashedly ready for a fun adventure. Her positive outlook and venturesome spirit were among the many things he admired about her.

The conversation he'd shared with his father played through his thoughts as they ordered their meals. His dad was right in that he'd never know what Lila's response to his interest in courting her might be if he didn't try to woo her.

Determined to make an effort, he lifted his left arm and draped it across the back of her chair. Other than give him a quick glance and a smile, she continued her conversation with Junie about things she'd enjoyed most in New York during the holidays.

Aware of his sly maneuver, James lifted an eyebrow and gave him an approving nod.

Once the waitress appeared with their meals, the conversation moved to local happenings. When there was a lull between topics, Tom wiped his mouth on a napkin and grinned at his parents.

"Did you hear about the ghost at the White House?" Tom asked.

"A ghost?" Junie gave him a dubious look. "I didn't hear about that."

"I read an article in the Heppner newspaper that the President and Mrs. McKinley were startled when a great crash sounded in the East Room on a recent evening. The room had been closed up since that afternoon, so several staff members conjectured what might have caused the disturbance. Everything from a collapsing wall to an exploded bomb was suggested."

Lila stared at him, eyes wide with interest. Tom could have kissed her but refrained, even when she blinked and leaned toward him. "What happened, Tom?" she asked in a light, breathy voice.

Unsettled by the sound of it, he cleared his throat. "A handful of attendants went to investigate and discovered a life-sized portrait of Abraham Lincoln on the floor. The frame, a ten by fifteen foot affair of gilded moulding, was badly damaged, but the canvas was salvageable. The article said a new frame will be constructed."

Tom leaned back in his chair and grinned. "The painting was hanging on a wall with likenesses of George and Martha Washington and Thomas Jefferson. Although some speculated work on a new stairway to the president's office loosened the plaster and caused the cornice where the picture hung to give way, I think it was Jefferson's ghost. He probably gave ol' Abe's painting a shove and off the wall it went."

Lila giggled when Tom stuck out his left arm, as though he gave someone a hearty push.

"I highly doubt Jefferson would have done such a thing. Perhaps it was Mrs. Washington's ghost," Lila teased.

"It couldn't be George," James said, grinning at them both. "Our nation's founding father wouldn't stoop to that type of thing."

"You all are wrong. If there was a ghost acting ornery, it was most likely Zachary Taylor. Old Rough and Ready was probably reliving his days of battle, brandishing a sword throughout the place as he battled imaginary foes, and knocked the painting off by accident," Junie said. Her conversational tone and the sincere expression on her face made Lila give her a second look to gage if she was serious or joking.

A little dimple popped out in Junie's cheek and she laughed, drawing the rest of them into her mirth.

When the meal ended, James insisted on paying. Outside the restaurant, the cold air nearly stole their breath away. James settled an arm around Junie and tipped his hat to Lila. "Thank you for joining us this evening, Miss Granger. It was a pleasure to dine with you."

"Thank you, kind sir," Lila said. She politely nodded her head while a happy smile filled her face. "The pleasure was all mine." Impulsively, she gave Junie a warm hug. "Thank you for making the sheep costume. I can't wait to see what you come up with for the cow."

"I'll bring it in to show you as soon as I have it finished," Junie said, returning her hug then giving one to Tom. "Make sure you walk Lila home, honey. It's far too cold and dark for a girl to be out on her own."

"I was planning on it, Mama. You and Dad had better head home, too. It'll only get colder and with you being..." He caught himself before he referred to her pregnancy. "With your delicate condition, you shouldn't get chilled."

James thumped him on the back. "I'll be sure to keep her warm, son. Now you two go on."

Tom rolled his eyes, but took Lila's elbow in his hand and started toward Main Street. He glanced back and grinned at his parents. "See you both later."

They waved and James made a face that caused Tom to work to hold back a laugh.

"I like your parents. They are bunches of fun," Lila said, smiling up at him. "All through dinner, I was trying to decide if you took after one of them more than the other."

Tom glanced down at her and raised an eyebrow in question. "And? What did you conclude?"

"Well, you look quite a bit like your father. He's very handsome for a man his age, so I assume you will be as well." She leaned back, as though she studied him. "But you have your mother's smile, her sense of humor, and penchant for fun."

Tom nodded. "That's about right." He observed her for a long moment. "Which of your parents are you like?"

Lila shrugged. "I think a combination of them both. I closely resemble my mother, but my zest for life and positive outlook are from my father. Greg reminds me of him in many ways."

"Mr. Granger is amusing. When they first came back to town, I expected him to be rather stodgy and look down his nose at people like me, but he's always so friendly and kind. I suppose that's where Luke and Ginny get it from."

A wry smile touched her features. "It certainly isn't from Dora, although she has changed considerably in the last several years. I think each grandbaby that arrives softens her heart even more."

"Well, perhaps Filly and Luke better plan on having another half dozen," Tom teased as they strolled through town. He noticed Lila shiver and moved so his arm settled around her shoulders, holding her close to his side.

Rather than protest, as he expected her to do, she sighed in relief as his warmth enveloped her. Emboldened by the slight progress he made toward winning her affections, he stopped at the gate to Granger House and smiled down at her.

"Miss Lila Granger, if I asked nicely, would you allow me the pleasure of accompanying you to the skating party at Blake and Ginny's home this Saturday? I know you're going anyway, but it would be a great honor if I could escort you."

Clearly caught off guard by his question, Lila appeared to frantically work to formulate a reply.

Tom wished he hadn't asked. He'd rather have Lila's friendship than nothing at all. He backed a step away from her and dipped his head. "I'm sorry, Lila. Forget I asked. I just thought…"

She settled her hand on his left arm and gently squeezed. "No, Tom. It's fine. I'd very much like to go with you. However, it will save you a long trip into town and back out if I meet you there. I'm sure we'll go out

146

early since Filly is helping with the refreshments and Luke is assisting Blake. Why don't you arrive half an hour early? No doubt, you'll be put to work if you do, but that way we can visit that much longer."

A wide grin settled on his face as Tom's eyes sparkled with joy. "I'll be there, Lila. Have a nice evening."

"Good night, Tom." She offered him a quick wave then hurried up the walk and disappeared inside the house.

Tom watched until the door shut then turned and hurried back to his home. He didn't care what he had to do, he wouldn't stop until he won Lila's heart.

Chapter Fourteen

Impatient to leave, Lila stood at the back door with a basket of doughnuts in one hand and another of cookies in her other.

The fourth time she glanced at the clock in as many minutes, Luke chuckled as he waited beside her. "In a hurry to go somewhere, Lila?" he asked.

She scowled at her cousin and feigned indifference. "I just don't want to be late."

Another chuckle rolled out of Luke. "You don't want to be late or you want to be sure you're early and have plenty of time to see a certain young man?"

Indignant, Lila huffed. "Not that it is any of your concern, but I asked Tom to meet us at Blake and Ginny's place thirty minutes early. It would be terribly rude to keep him waiting."

Luke smirked. "Terribly rude, indeed." He reached out and tweaked her nose. "You, my lovely little cousin, are smitten with Tom Grove. Why don't you just admit it?"

Aghast, she gaped at Luke. "I'm no such thing! Did you forget I'm an engaged woman, practically wed to Emerson, at least I will be once he returns to New York."

"I haven't forgotten, but I thought you may have." Luke studied her a moment. "You aren't married to Emerson, Lila, so it's okay if you have feelings for Tom.

Honestly, if Emerson was that worried about holding on to you, he wouldn't have ever let you go while he traipsed all over England."

She stiffened. "He's hardly traipsing all over, as you put it. Emerson has been diligently studying at the university. I'm sure he's worked very hard in his academic pursuits."

"I'm sure," Luke agreed. "That still doesn't change the fact that Tom makes your eyes sparkle or that you just seem to blossom when he's around. Emerson won't be back for another month or so. Why not give yourself time to explore things with Tom? What if you miss out on the opportunity to know a very special kind of love because you're clinging to one that's familiar?"

Rather than offer a sharp retort, she snapped her mouth closed and considered his words as Filly sailed into the kitchen with Cullen on one arm and Maura skipping behind her.

"I thought I'd never get these two wrangled into their coats," the woman said, smiling at Luke and Lila. "Shall we go?"

"We shall, wife," Luke said, taking Cullen from Filly and opening the back door. "The sooner, the better. Lila is quite anxious to arrive at Blake and Ginny's."

Filly grinned at her. "I take it Tom is coming?"

Lila nodded and scurried out the door without making any further comment.

The dog followed them out to the waiting sleigh and barked once. "You stay here, Bart, and keep an eye on things," Luke said, handing the baby to Filly once she settled onto the seat. He gave the dog a good scratch on his head and pointed toward the back step. "Go on, boy."

Bart woofed then trotted off in the direction of the back porch.

Luke swung Maura into the air and kissed her little cheek then set her down between Filly and Lila.

The child giggled and squirmed, drawing smiles from her mother and Lila.

"Did Blake finish making the benches he was working on for today?" Lila asked as Luke guided the sleigh through town and headed out toward the Stratton place.

"He did. Dora contributed several cushions to pad them for the elderly folks who'll be using them," Filly said. "We took out a bunch of pillows for the children to use as padding."

Lila gave her a strange look. "Padding? For what?"

"Tia and Adam came up with the idea of tying pillows around the little ones' waists, so when they fall backward, they land on the pillows and it softens their fall." ·

Lila grinned. "That's brilliant! I wish someone had done that for me when I was learning to skate. I had so many bruises that I was black and blue for weeks."

"I gonna skate good!" Maura declared, looking at her mother then Lila.

"I'm sure you will, little miss," Lila said, tapping the child on her nose. "Who do you plan to skate with today?"

Maura tipped her head to the side, deep in thought. The child brightened as a smile filled her face. "Daddy!"

Luke chuckled from the front of the sleigh. "You certainly will skate with me, honey."

"Who else?" Lila asked, wrapping an arm around the little girl and pulling her closer to her side.

"Uncle Blake and Uncle Arlan and Uncle Chauncy..." Maura grinned up at Lila. "And Mr. Grove and maybe Billy."

"Billy?" Lila asked, knowing Maura liked the little boy who sat across the aisle from her at school. "He's a handsome lad."

Maura wrinkled her nose. "Billy pushed me on the swing yesterday."

Filly smiled at her daughter. "That was very kind of him, wasn't it?"

Maura nodded her head with such enthusiasm, her curls engaged in a frenzied dance around her little face.

Lila bit back a laugh. "How about Erin? Who will she skate with?"

Maura sighed and plopped her hands on her lap. "She's sad because Toby isn't here." She gazed at Lila with a solemn expression. "His mama and daddy couldn't come to visit because they gots a baby and it's too cold for babies to be on long trips.

"Yes, it is, but I bet Toby will come next year, don't you think?"

Maura shrugged. "Probly, if Toby doesn't get another baby. We gots Cullen and Erin's gonna get a new baby, too."

"She certainly is," Lila said, looking at Filly. There had been much speculation if Abby would make it to her due date. Her movements slowed every day and Lila had taken to visiting her more frequently to help all she could.

"Oh, look," Filly said, pointing to the wagons and sleighs already arriving at Blake and Ginny's place.

Luke stopped the sleigh near the door of the house and helped Filly out. He lifted Maura and set her down. Before she could run off, he cupped her chin in his hand. "You stay with your mother while I see to the horse, honey. I don't want you getting into mischief."

"Okay, Daddy," she said, traipsing after Filly into the house.

Luke drove the sleigh down to Blake's large barn. Lila pretended to watch him go while covertly looking around to see if Tom had arrived. She didn't see him in the handful of people milling around, so she hurried into the house where some of the older girls would take turns keeping watch over the babies and toddlers too young to be out in the cold.

Ginny smiled as she entered. "Hi, Lila. What a beautiful outfit. You'd be the belle of the ball if this wasn't a skating party."

Lila grinned and brushed a hand down the front of her deep purple velvet skirt. A matching jacket trimmed with mink fur, a fur muff, and lavender gloves completed her ensemble. "Thank you, Ginny. Mother had this made for me a few years ago when we planned to attend a big skating event the Vanluthen's hosted, but I caught a cold and wasn't able to attend."

"Well, it's gorgeous," Filly said. She settled Cullen into a cradle in the kitchen then lifted the lid on a pot on the stove. Fragrant, cinnamon-laced steam rose upward in an aromatic cloud, filling the kitchen with a delicious, mouth-watering scent. "Mmm, this cider smells so good, Ginny."

"Blake said we had to have hot cider this year. He thought if we made it in here, we could carry it out later when everyone is ready for a break from the skating." Ginny sat down at the table with a moan.

Lila placed a hand on her shoulder and gazed at her in concern. "Are you not feeling well?"

"I think I may have spent too much time on my feet the last few days getting everything ready for the party. My feet were so swollen this morning I couldn't get my shoes on, so I've been shuffling around in my house shoes." She held out a foot covered by a soft embroidered slipper.

"And how do you plan to put on your boots and frolic in the snow?" Filly asked as she slid a pan of rolls into the oven to warm.

"She doesn't," Blake said, stepping inside and grinning at his wife. "I don't care what she says, I think it best she stay inside today and rest with her feet up. If I have to tie her to the chair to keep her in here, I'm not above doing it."

With a complete lack of maturity, Ginny stuck out her tongue at Blake.

He laughed and kissed her cheek. "No fussing, love. You know I'm right."

"I might know it, but I don't have to like it," she said, leaning against him as he stood next to her chair.

"I'm sure some of the other women would be happy to stay in here with you." Filly brushed her hands on the apron she'd donned and tipped her head toward the window. "I don't think you'd get any argument out of Abby about staying indoors. And Alex might prefer to stay inside as well."

"And don't forget about Mrs..." Lila slapped a hand over her mouth, recalling not everyone knew about Junie Grove being in a family way.

"Mrs. who?" Ginny asked, staring at Lila.

Lila shook her head. "I forgot it's not something everyone knows."

Filly smiled and bumped Lila with her hip as she stepped beside her. "If you're talking about Junie Grove, we already know."

Lila sighed in relief. "Oh, good. It's such an exciting thing, isn't it?"

"It is," Filly agreed.

"I think it's wonderful they'll welcome a little one after all these years of waiting," Blake said, moving toward the door. He pointed a finger at Ginny. "And you, wife of mine, better not set foot outside this door or so help me, I'll pack you right back in here."

Before she could proclaim him a bossy, overbearing boor, he disappeared outside.

"I guess he told you," Lila said, offering her cousin a sassy smile.

"Oh, hush. Just wait until you are in my position and you won't find it to be nearly as funny." Ginny rubbed a hand over her belly. Lila watched it bounce as the baby kicked.

She envisioned herself round with a child and smiled. A picture of a beautiful baby with soulful blue eyes and thick brown hair filled her mind. A baby that looked like Tom Grove.

Dismayed by the direction of her thoughts, she took Maura's hand in hers. "Come on, honey bunny. Let's go see who has arrived."

"Bye, Mama," Maura said, waving at her mother as she and Lila hurried outside. Hand-in-hand, they strolled past the barn and along the path out to the pond where Blake had built a big bonfire and set up makeshift tables to hold the refreshments. Luke, Greg, and Tom set out benches while Dora placed cushions on the seats.

"Grandma!" Maura squealed, racing to Dora. The woman dropped the cushions on the closest bench and scooped the little girl in her arms, covering her face with kisses.

"How is my little sweetheart?" Dora asked, leaning back so she could look in Maura's face.

"I's good, Grandma! Did you bring skates? Will you skate with me? Daddy said he skate with me. Will Grandpa skate with me?" Maura patted her grandmother's cheeks with her mitten-covered hands.

"Of course, darling. We'll skate with you. Are your mother and brother in the house with Aunt Ginny?"

"Yep!" Maura squirmed to get down so Dora set her on her feet.

The older woman handed the child a few cushions. "You may help me put these on the benches, Maura."

"Okay, Grandma." Maura flopped cushions on two benches then waved to Erin Dodd and ran to greet her as she arrived with her father.

Lila watched Tom as he helped lift the benches, enthralled with the hint of muscle that played beneath the wool coat he wore. Although he could only use his left hand, he hurried to keep up with the other two men.

"Like what you see?" Alex Guthry teased as she and Arlan stepped beside her.

Lila blushed. "I was merely observing the placement of the benches."

Alex laughed. "If you say so. I thought perhaps you were observing the placer of the benches."

Lila glowered at the woman then pointed to the trumpet case Arlan carried. "Is the band really going to play?"

Arlan nodded. "We are, at least for a little while. Once my lips get cold, I'm quitting. I don't want them freezing to the trumpet."

Alex nudged him with her elbow. "I'd be happy to help keep them warm."

Arlan bent down and whispered something in her ear that made her smile while pink suffused her cheeks.

"Ladies," he said, tipping his hat to them both before he wandered over to the wooden platform where the band would perform.

"Have you been to the house?" Lila asked as she and Alex meandered to the refreshment table.

"No. We came straight out here. I thought I might be of some help in setting up the refreshments." Alex glanced around. "Where are Filly and Ginny?"

"In the house. Ginny's feet are terribly swollen. Blake forbade her to come outside, so she's pouting. Filly's making a few last minute contributions to the food." Lila waved to a group of new arrivals.

"I'll go check on them," Alex said, hurrying toward the house. Lila turned around and found her nose nearly pressed against the front of Tom's coat. His hands settled on her arms to steady her.

"Sorry, Lila. I didn't mean to sneak up on you."

She took a step back and smiled. "It's fine, Tom. How are you?"

"I'm good, but I'll be even better if you'll put on your skates and be my skating partner today." The imploring look on his face combined with his boyish smile left her incapable of refusing.

"I'd love to," she said, walking over to where Luke had left all their skates. She sat down on a bench and fastened her skates on her boots while Tom buckled on his. When they finished, he stood and held out a hand to her. "Shall we?"

"We shall," she said, placing her hand in his. Even through their gloves, a jolt traveled up her arm and spread down to her toes.

They made their way to the edge of the ice that Luke, Chauncy, and Blake had diligently cleared of snow earlier in the week. A few other couples and several children skated by, laughing and smiling.

"Come on, Lila Lilac." Tom grinned and led her onto the ice.

At first, they struggled to get in harmony with each other. Before they made it halfway around the pond, they found their rhythm and skated together as though they'd done it hundreds of times.

"This is nice," Lila commented as Tom settled his right hand on her waist and held her left hand in his.

"Very nice," he agreed.

She felt his gaze lingering on her but dared not look up at him. If she did, she'd end up tripping or something equally embarrassing.

The warmth of his breath caressed her neck and his voice rumbled in her ear. "You look beautiful, Lila. Like a lovely spring blossom dropped in the snow."

Pleased he found her attractive, she smiled. "Thank you, Tom. You look nice, too."

In fact, she couldn't imagine how he could be more appealing. Either he'd regained the ability to shave or had visited the barber, but his scruffy cheeks were clean shaven. The smooth, taut skin taunted her along with the slightly woodsy scent of his shaving soap. The blue scarf looped around his neck perfectly matched the blue of his eyes, making them stand out.

Recalling the fervent kisses they'd shared the day they went sledding, she wished he'd kiss her again. She'd never experienced anything like the sensations created when Tom held her close and pressed his lips to hers.

Lost in her thoughts of how badly she wanted to feel them moving on hers, she missed a step and they both went down on the ice in a tumble.

"Are you okay?" Tom asked, hurrying to disentangle himself from her skirts.

"I'm fine," she said, sitting upright and glancing at Tom in concern. He held his right arm against his chest, as though it hurt. "Did you hurt your arm when we fell?"

Ignoring her question, he got to his feet and held his hand out to her. She took it and stood, placing her free hand on his arm. "Tom, I'm so sorry. I didn't even think about the possibility of injuring your arm. Should we go back by the fire?"

"No. It'll take more than a little spill to keep me from skating with the prettiest girl here today." He smiled and returned his hand to her waist.

Lila caught his cringe of pain, but refrained from commenting on it. She would have been content sitting next to him on a bench watching the others. Instinctively, she knew Tom would chafe at the idea.

As they circled the pond, they skated past Dora and Greg. Maura clung to their hands, giggling as she slid her feet across the ice. A few of Tom's students waved and zoomed past them as they chased each other across the pond.

When the band began to play, Tom and Lila joined other couples waltzing across the ice, skates *swoosh-swooshing* in time to the music. Luke and Filly skated beside them. Lila scowled at her cousin when he waggled his eyebrows and tipped his head toward Tom.

"Something wrong?" Tom asked, noticing her frown as she watched Luke skate off with his wife.

"No. My dear cousin thinks he's far too clever for his own good, though."

Tom chuckled. "Luke is a clever fellow. After all, he did marry the best cook in the county before anyone else even knew who she was."

She grinned. "I concede he does have moments of brilliance, his marriage to Filly being one of the few."

The song ended and Tom guided Lila over to where his parents visited with some of their close friends.

"Oh, gracious, Lila, you look so beautiful," Junie gushed, giving her a warm hug. "That deep shade of amethyst suits you."

Lila smiled, pleased by Junie's kind words. "Thank you, Mrs. Grove. It's one of my favorite colors."

Junie slipped her arm around Lila's tiny waist and gave it a squeeze. "You must call me Junie, honey. Now, did Tom get you something to drink? Ginny and Filly made the best hot cider. Would you like a cup?"

"I would. Although the sun is shining, it's still unbelievably cold out today," Lila said, following Junie to the refreshment table. Tom accompanied them and handed both women a cup of cider before he took one for himself.

"Thank you, sweetheart," Junie said, patting her son's cheek. "The band makes the event even more festive, don't you think?"

"Oh, I agree," Lila said, sipping the hot beverage. "I love music of all types."

Junie gave Tom a sly look. "Did you hear that, son? She loves music."

"I heard, Mama." Tom wondered why his mother was acting so strangely. Perhaps her delicate condition was affecting her mind. "Lila hasn't made a secret of her joy in music. In fact, she hums and sings quite often, and she plays the piano with notable skill."

"You do?" Junie asked, turning to Lila. "Are you providing the music for the Christmas program?"

"For now, although Dora has promised to play the night of the program so I'll be able to better help direct the children," Lila said, unable to keep her toe from tapping as the band played a lively tune.

Junie took the cup from her hand then grabbed the one from Tom and motioned toward the ice. "Go on, you two. Don't waste your time standing here with me when you could be out there having fun."

Indulgently, Tom bowed then held out his arm to Lila. "Shall we?"

"We shall, kind sir," she said, executing a perfect curtsy. She took his arm and allowed him to lead her back to the pond.

They joined the other skaters circling around in time to the upbeat music. When the song ended and segued into one of a slower pace, Tom moved a little closer to Lila.

"This is nice," he said in a husky tone. His lips lingered close to her ear, making an involuntary shiver slide through her at the delightful warmth of his presence.

"Yes, it is," she whispered, afraid to turn her head lest her lips connect with his. If they did, the heat generated by their kiss would surely blast a hole through the ice.

Amused by her wild imagination, she grinned.

"What made you smile?" he asked, leaning closer to her again.

"You," she admitted, placing her hand on his as it rested on her waist. His fingers tightened slightly. She turned to catch a look of wanting in his expressive eyes.

"Lila Lilac, what in the world am I going to do with you?" he asked, his gaze locked to hers.

"What would you like to do?" she asked innocently.

Tom groaned and slowly guided her away from the skaters. They worked their way to the far end of the pond then followed the stream around a little bend that hid them from the view of others.

Assured of their privacy, Tom turned Lila around and wrapped her in his arms. "Do you really want an answer to your question, Lila?"

She looked up at him, studying his face. It wasn't a face as dazzling as Emerson's, but it was handsome, earnest, and full of sincere emotion.

Her conversation with Luke floated through her thoughts. Was she missing something truly special with Tom because of her obligation to Emerson? Would she regret it for a lifetime if she didn't allow herself the opportunity to investigate her feelings before making a decision?

Convinced she should explore what simmered between her and Tom, she reached up and bracketed his cheeks with her gloved hands. "I don't need a response to my question, Tom. I can see it in your eyes and I'd like to kiss you, too."

A rakish grin settled on his face and his eyes glowed with heat as he pulled her closer. "In that case, what are you waiting for?"

Their lips connected in a fiery burst of sparks that made her wonder if the ice and snow beneath them would immediately melt. Never had she imagined such wondrous, exhilarating, entirely unsettling feelings could exist.

She ignored the pounding beat of her heart, the wobble in her knees, and the unfamiliar heat filling her midsection. Instead, her sole thought was to remain locked in Tom's embrace as long as possible.

Overwhelmed with foreign, exciting sensations, she allowed him to plunder her mouth again and again, returning his kisses with equal ardor. Finally, when they both were breathless, Tom rested his forehead against hers and playfully kissed the tip of her nose.

"Lila," he said in a gravelly voice that made her toes threaten to curl inside her fur-lined boots.

Boldly, she reached up and pulled his head down, kissing him with all the passion he'd stirred in her.

"Tommy," she whispered, nuzzling his neck. He lifted her off her feet, holding her close and pressing kisses into the softness of her hair. The weight of his cast bumped against her back, but she didn't mind. Not when every dream she'd ever have of love suddenly blossomed within her.

After a particularly ardent exchange, Lila sucked air into her deprived lungs and realized her hat had sailed off, resting on a pile of snow.

"Lila, you have to know by now how much I…"

"Tom! Lila!" Luke's voice carried to them in the nippy December air. "Where in thunderation are you two?"

Tom sighed and released her, setting her back on her feet. She snatched up the hat and pinned it on her hair, hoping she didn't look like she'd been involved in a wanton exchange with the guilty-looking man beside her.

"We're over here, Luke," Tom called, placing his hand on her waist and guiding her back toward the pond. When he winked at her, she found encouragement in the teasing action.

Together, they rounded the bend as Luke skated toward them. He came to an abrupt stop in front of them, sending a spray of shaved ice into the air from the sharp blades strapped to his feet.

At the look on his face, Lila placed a hand on his arm in concern. "What's wrong, Luke? Is it one of the children? Did something happen to Filly? Abby hasn't gone into labor, has she?"

"No, nothing that drastic," Luke said, offering Tom a sympathetic look before glancing at Lila. "It's um..." His hand raked through his hair, leaving it in a disheveled state. "It's... well, you have a visitor, Lila."

Baffled, she stared at him. "A visitor? Who on earth would visit me clear out here? Other than the household staff, the only person who knows I'm here is..." Her countenance fell as her eyes widened in comprehension. "He's here?"

"Who's here?" Tom asked, thoroughly confused.

Lila took his hand in hers and gently squeezed it. "My fiancé. Emerson is here, is that right, Luke?"

Luke nodded his head. "He arrived a few moments ago, quite excited to see you."

"I suppose I better go, then. I'm so sorry, Tom." Lila wanted to tell Tom not to worry, that everything was fine. She'd enjoyed their kisses more than anything she'd ever experienced in her life. Unfortunately, with her fiancé waiting to see her, she couldn't. She gave him one long parting look then skated back to the gathering with Luke.

"Are you well, Lila?" Luke asked quietly as they neared the bank of the pond where people gathered around the newcomer.

"Not exactly," she whispered, glancing over her shoulder expecting to see Tom right behind her, but he was nowhere in sight. "Would you grant me a huge favor, Luke, and check on Tom? I fear I've bungled things with him quite badly."

"I'll do it, Lila. Do you need me to...?"

Before he could finish his question, Emerson caught sight of Lila and waved, rushing forward to sweep her into an exuberant hug.

"Lila, darling, oh, it's so good to see you," he said, kissing her cheek then holding her an arm's length away to gaze into her face. "You are even prettier than the image I carried these last long months in my heart."

"Emerson! This is such a surprise. What are you doing in Hardman? I thought you were spending the holidays with Blake's parents then returning to New York in January."

"I finished my classes early and couldn't wait to return to you, my love," Emerson gushed, hesitant to let Lila move beyond his reach. "I spent one night in New York with my parents then boarded the train to reach you as quickly as possible. I arrived in Heppner last evening and stayed at the hotel. This morning, I rented a horse and sleigh, and here I am! Oh, but it is so wonderful to see you again, Lila, dear."

Lila studied Emerson from the top of his golden head and bright blue eyes to the tips of his expensive boots. He wore a finely-cut woolen coat over a tailored suit that fit him to perfection. Handsome and charming, kind and witty, Emerson Lylan was everything a woman could possibly hope for in a husband.

Only Lila wasn't convinced she still wanted to marry him. Not after sharing such fervent kisses with Tom.

Emerson stared at her, as though he waited for her to say something, to express her joy in seeing him again.

Resigned to doing what was expected, she kissed his cheek and smiled. "It's nice to see you, Emerson. Have you met everyone? May I introduce…"

Chapter Fifteen

"You can't enter."

"I can, too!"

"I'll tell Ma if you do." Alice Bruner glared at her brother as they approached the school. Tom just happened to be walking over from the teacher's house and overhead their conversation.

"What are you not entering, Percy?" he asked, clapping a hand on the boy's shoulder.

"A contest at the store. Ma and Pop are giving away a camera as a prize. Everyone who spends a dollar at the store is entered in the drawing. I really want a camera, so I don't see why I can't enter." Percy frowned at his younger sister.

The little girl fisted her hands on her hips and got a look on her face that put Tom in mind of the child's mother. "You can't enter the contest, you big dummy, because it's our store! Maybe if you weren't so ornery, Saint Nicholas would bring you one for Christmas."

Percy smirked. "If I have to wait for Saint Nicholas to deliver what I want, I'll never get anything, little miss bossy britches."

Alice huffed. "Call me all the names you want, but you still can't enter the contest. Ma and Pop both said so."

Percy looked to Tom. "What do you think, teacher?"

"I think you should listen to your parents, Percy. It wouldn't be right for you to win one of their drawings. Have you expressed your interest in photography to them?"

"Nah." The boy scuffed his toe in the snow. "I figured they'd think it was silly."

"I don't think it's silly in the least," Tom said. "In fact, some very famous people are photographers like Matthew Brady and Edward S. Curtis. There's even a man in New York who started a service of sharing photographs with newspapers to accompany news articles."

Percy's eyes widened. "So you don't think it's stupid to like photographs?"

Tom shook his head and started up the school steps. "Not at all, Percy. In fact, I think it is quite an interesting career. If you'd like to know more about it, I could make a few contacts for you."

The boy grinned. "Thanks, Tom, er... I mean, Mr. Grove. That's swell."

Tom smiled. "Just behave yourself."

"Yes, sir." Percy took his sister's things and carried them inside before returning outside to play.

Tom stoked the fire he'd built in the stove then opened the book containing his lesson plans. He picked up a piece of chalk and began writing the morning's lessons on the blackboard behind his desk.

As he worked, his mind drifted to Lila. Since Emerson arrived on Saturday, he'd made a point to stay away from her. He sat behind her at church Sunday, watching Emerson attentively glued to her side.

Despite how much he wanted to hate the man, Emerson Lylan seemed like a perfectly respectable, entirely likeable person. Rather than put on airs, he had greeted everyone with genuine interest and friendly consideration.

In the past few days, Filly or Luke had escorted Maura to school and walked her home afterward. Tom assumed Lila spent every moment she could with Emerson.

He wondered when the announcement would come that they were returning to New York. The thought of never seeing Lila again made his heart ache with such force, he stopped writing spelling words and rubbed the offending spot.

The wise thing would have been to avoid the woman, just like his head told him to do. Instead, Tom had to go and fall head over heels in love with her. The ardent, involved kisses they'd shared Saturday at the skating party certainly made him think she held more than a passing fancy for him, too.

Alice's words of calling Percy a big dummy echoed in his ears as he continued working on posting that day's assignments. "Only a huge dummy would get into this kind of mess," he muttered to himself.

"What was that?" a familiar voice spoke from behind him, making him spin around. He gaped at Lila as she stood in the center aisle, watching him.

"I didn't hear you come in," he said, setting down the chalk and staring at her. "I thought you'd be occupied with Mr. Lylan."

"He went to Heppner today to see about some secretive business matter he insisted required his attention. He's convinced the telegraph office here isn't capable of sending a message, so he went to send it from the train depot." Lila fussed with her gloves, clearly uncomfortable.

She took a few steps toward him. The sway of her skirts, the rosy hue of her lips, and the alluring hint of her fragrance made Tom want to rush to her and pull her into his arms. Only he had no right to do that. No right to touch her. No reason to love her.

Except, his heart refused to acknowledge defeat.

Until Emerson put a ring on her finger, Tom decided to continue his efforts to win Lila.

Only a few feet away from him, she stopped and studied him for a long moment before she spoke. "I'm so sorry, Tom. I had no way of knowing Emerson would take a notion to travel out here. I certainly had no idea he had returned from his studies abroad. If I had, if I'd known..." she sighed and glanced away. "I'm sorry for any pain or problems I may have caused you, Tom. I truly didn't mean for things to get... for us to become..." She stopped, unable to continue as she dabbed at the tears spilling down her cheeks. "I just can't quite make sense of things."

Tom covered the distance between the two of them in a few long strides. His thumbs brushed away her tears then he wrapped his arms around her, holding her to his chest. "All is well, Lila Lilac. We both knew you belong to Emerson. He seems like a respectable fellow, one you can be proud of as a husband."

She sniffled and mumbled something he couldn't hear as she pressed her face against his chest.

Tom smiled to himself. If she came into his arms so willingly, made a point to come to the school the moment Emerson was elsewhere, perhaps all was not yet lost.

"Did you bring Maura to school this morning?" he asked, seeking some topic that would put them back on easy conversational footing.

"Yes," Lila said, sniffling again, then pulling a lacy handkerchief from her coat pocket and dabbing at her nose. She stepped back from Tom and gave him a watery smile. "You have to be the nicest, kindest, most wonderful man I've ever met, Tom Grove."

He bowed and offered her a rascally smile. "It gladdens my heart to hear you say that." With a quick glance at the clock, he knew he needed to ring the bell soon, but hated to send Lila away. His mind worked at a feverish pitch to create some reason for her to spend part of the day at the school. Although her presence always left him thoroughly distracted, he liked the idea of having her there. "Are you terribly busy today?" he asked.

She shook her head. "No more than usual. I was going to help Abby, but Chauncy forbade her from opening her shop today, insisting she rest at home with her feet up. Why? Do you need something?"

Your kisses. Your heart. Your love.

Tom tamped down the words lingering on the tip of his tongue and instead offered a plausible reason for her to be at the school. "The students are working so hard to finish their projects for the Christmas carnival auction, but there are some things beyond my limited talents. If you can spare the time, would you come this afternoon? A few girls have yet to finish their contributions and could greatly use help from someone who doesn't possess all thumbs."

Lila laughed and nodded her head. "I'd love to help. After school, we can go directly to the church for the program practice."

"Perfect." Tom managed not to cheer at her eager agreement to his devious plans to keep her close.

"What time should I return?" Lila asked, stuffing her handkerchief in her pocket and giving him a warm smile.

"Would one-thirty fit into your schedule?"

She grinned. "I'll be here." Slowly, she backed toward the door, holding his gaze. When she bumped into a desk, Tom bit back a grin. "Have a lovely morning, Tom."

"I plan to, Lila. See you later."

With another quick nod, she turned and disappeared out the door.

Cheered by the thought he might still have a chance with her, despite Emerson's presence, Tom whistled as he hurried to write the day's lessons on the blackboard.

After lunch, he felt as antsy as the children did while they awaited Lila's arrival. He mentioned that she planned to come and the students all cheered, excited at the prospect of spending time with the effervescent woman.

The hands on the clock crept slowly toward one-thirty. Although the students did their best to work on their lessons, he couldn't blame them for being preoccupied and restless. He knew exactly how they felt.

When the fourth child asked to be excused to the outhouse, he let Milo Jenkins go, but knew it was useless to insist the students work on their math equations.

"You know, class, just for today, I think it would be fine for you to put away your assignments." Tom smiled as the students turned eager faces to him.

"What are we going to do until Miss Granger arrives?" Percy asked.

"Do you think a magic trick would help pass the time?" Tom grinned and the children all cheered. "Settle down or we'll get those math problems back out."

Silence immediately descended over the students.

Tom looked around the room, studying the faces of each student. He stopped when he got to a shy little girl named Cindy. Rather than call her to the front of the room, Tom walked over to where she sat with another eight-year-old girl. Hunkering down, he smiled at her. "Cindy, do you think you'd like to help me with a magic trick?"

The little girl surreptitiously glanced around, to see who watched her reaction. She didn't lift her gaze to meet Tom's, but nodded her head.

"Excellent," Tom said, holding out his hand to her. She took it and slid off her seat, allowing him to lead her to the front of the class. Tom moved his desk chair from behind his desk to in front of it, then helped Cindy climb up on the chair.

"Can everyone see Cindy?" he asked, aware of the child ducking her head and pink staining her cheeks.

Although he'd never been shy, he knew it could be difficult to be the center of attention. He recalled the first morning Alex taught at the school. He and some of the other older boys had behaved badly. They returned from recess to find their desks moved to the four corners of the room and Tom's happened to be in one of the front corners. The whole time he sat there, he felt every eye in the classroom boring into his back. After that, he behaved himself and resumed his seat at the back of the room.

He smiled at the timid child again as he took a coin out of his pocket.

"Ladies and gentlemen," he said, using a voice one might hear from a carnival barker or a snake oil salesman. "Are you prepared to be dazzled and amazed by spellbinding acts of prestidigitation?"

The children clapped and cheered.

Tom waved his left hand in the air with a dramatic flair. "The lovely Miss Cindy will assist me today as I make a coin disappear."

"How you gonna do that?" one of the younger boys asked, rising on his knees on his seat to get a better view.

"Watch and see," Tom said. He flipped the coin into the air then rolled it between his fingers with such speed the children lost track of it. Finally, he turned back to Cindy. "Please hold out your hand, Cindy."

The child held her hand in front of her, palm up. Gently, Tom turned it over. He placed the coin on the back of her hand then gave her an encouraging look. "Do you know a magic word, Miss Cindy?"

The little girl nodded.

"Wonderful," Tom said, encouraging her. "When I count to three, you say the magic word. Ready?"

Another nod.

"Here we go. One. Two. Three!"

"Alakazam!" Cindy shouted excitedly.

Tom snapped his fingers and the coin disappeared. He snapped them again and made the coin reappear on her hand.

Cindy's mouth dropped open. In her excitement, she forgot about her shyness. She joined the rest of the class in clapping when Tom tossed the coin in the air again.

"Do another one, Mr. Grove! Please?" Erin Dodd begged. Several students echoed her request.

"One more," Tom said, more than willing to indulge the students. He helped Cindy down from the chair, bent to whisper in her ear, and awarded her with a peppermint stick. "You made a fine assistant, Cindy. Thank you."

The child scampered to her desk with a broad smile wreathing her face.

Tom bowed to the class then turned so they saw a side view of him. "For my next feat of extraordinary wonder, I shall levitate." He glanced over at the students. "Who knows what levitate means?"

"Isn't that like floating or something?" Percy asked.

Tom snapped his fingers and pointed at Percy. "That's exactly what it means. To float, by a supernatural power or means."

Excited, the children anxiously watched his every move. Slowly, he rose up on his toes. The way he positioned his body made it appear as though he floated a few inches off the floor.

He held the pose as Lila quietly entered the school and stood in the aisle, staring at him as he floated in front of the class.

With a saucy grin, she sauntered up the aisle, catching Tom's gaze as he saw her and came back down to the floor.

"That's quite a trick, Mr. Grove. Can you levitate the whole class?"

"No, Miss Granger, that is beyond my magical abilities. However, I think I can make something appear out of thin air, but I need a volunteer to spell levitate."

"Anna will do it," Percy said, nudging the girl sitting beside him. "Go on, Anna. You can spell anything."

Hesitant, Anne glanced at Tom. He smiled at her. "Go ahead, Anna."

She spelled the word, then looked to him.

"That's absolutely correct." He walked over to her desk, waved his fingers in the air, and made a peppermint stick appear, handing it to the girl.

"Thank you, Mr. Grove," she said, smiling broadly at her treat.

"You're welcome, Anna." Tom strode back to the front of the class. "Now, students, those of you who have not finished your projects for the Christmas carnival, please join Miss Granger at the back of the room. Those of you who have finished your projects, you may choose to read quietly or help with the projects."

A few students chose to read, but the majority jumped into the fun of helping their classmates with their projects. Lila soon had them singing a variety of Christmas songs and laughing as they worked. The time passed quickly and all but two of the projects were finished when Tom called an end to the work.

"Do you want to keep working or have reading time today?" he asked as he leaned against his desk.

"Reading time!" the children said in unison.

He grinned. "I thought that's what you'd say. Settle back into your seats and we'll read until it's time to release you for the day."

Lila took a seat at the back of the room. Tom gave her one quick glance before he started reading the story. When he finished for the day, the children all sat entranced by the story. They were so quiet, a pin could have dropped and echoed through the room.

"We'll finish the story tomorrow. Now, put on your coats and get out of here." He smiled as he waved toward the door. "Those of you who have practice for the Christmas program at church, Miss Granger and I will meet you there in fifteen minutes."

The children's voices rose to a playful roar as they scurried into their coats, grabbed their books and lunch pails, and raced outside. Lila helped Maura with her coat and mittens then told the little girl to play outside with Erin.

Once Maura ran down the steps, Lila hurried to the front of the room and picked up the book Tom had set on his desk. "What is this book?" she asked, glancing at the cover.

"*The Wonderful Wizard of Oz* by L. Frank Baum. It just came out this year," Tom said, hurrying to clean the blackboard. "I was fortunate to snag a copy that arrived at the newspaper office. The editor allowed me to keep it after I wrote the review. It's a wonderful story, especially for children."

"It's very intriguing," Lila agreed, opening the book to the place where Tom had inserted a bookmark. She began reading where he'd stopped for the day, but he snatched the book from her and tucked it in a desk drawer.

"No fair reading ahead. If you want to know what happens, join the students during story time tomorrow."

She gave him a look full of sass and spunk. "I'll be here, and you better not skimp on reading time tomorrow."

He laughed and gathered his papers, stuffing them into his leather satchel. "Shall we proceed to the church?"

"Yes. If we don't hurry, the little hooligans will eat all the cookies and get into who knows what sort of trouble." Lila hurried to slip on the coat Tom held for her then tugged on her gloves.

She rushed outside and called to Maura and Erin as she wrapped a scarf around her neck. "Time to go, girls."

Maura grabbed Lila's hand while Erin looked at Tom. He switched his satchel to his casted hand and held out the other to the child. She beamed and fell into step beside him, skipping as she walked.

"How is your mother, Erin?" Tom asked, mindful of the woman's condition. It seemed every time he turned around he bumped into an expectant or new mother. The more time he spent in town, the more convinced he was that something was definitely in the water.

"She's fine," Erin said, purposely sliding on a patch of ice while grasping his hand. "Daddy said she needs to get lots of rest but she does stuff when he isn't looking."

Tom grinned. "I can imagine. Your mother isn't one to idly sit around."

"My daddy said idle hands make for trouble. I 'spose that's why he and my mama always have plenty of chores for me to do."

Tom held back a snort of laughter, envisioning Erin with time on her hands to dream up more mischief than she already got into. Before he could respond to her comment, the child waved her hand over her head and raced down the boardwalk toward her father as he stood at the base of the church steps.

Maura tugged on Lila's hand, trying to hurry her along.

"Come on, Lila. I wanna see Uncle Chauncy!" Maura gave Lila a look that let her know she was impeding the child's desire for haste.

"Run ahead, then, honey bunny, but stay on the boardwalk." The second she released the child's hand, Maura raced ahead, wrapping her arms around Chauncy's knees. He picked up the child and gave her a hug then set her back on her feet next to his daughter. A gentle nudge pushed the children to go inside the church to wait.

When Tom and Lila reached Chauncy, he smiled at them both. "Afternoon."

"Nice to see you, pastor. What brings you to the practice today?" Tom asked, once again shifting the satchel in his hands so he could shake Chauncy's extended hand.

"Oh, I came home to check on Abby and just happened to be on my way to run a few errands when I saw you walking this way. Are the practices going well? Erin keeps us updated, but other than her thoughts on how marvelous the play and singing are going to be, is there anything else I need to know?"

Lila smiled at Chauncy. "We did tell you we're using children to play the animals instead of having live animals this year, didn't we?"

"Yes," Chauncy offered a relieved expression. "As fun as it was to have the live animals when I was a boy, it's a different matter when you're the pastor and have a cranky sheep or an annoyed donkey loose in the church. I fully support the decision to move away from live animals."

Tom smirked. "I heard a story about you and Luke turning mice free in the church during one Christmas Eve program. Do you think anyone might duplicate your efforts?"

Chauncy chuckled. "I certainly hope not. I don't think any of the boys in our congregation are nearly as ornery as Luke and I were at that age."

Lila giggled. "There aren't too many who are as ornery as you and Luke now."

"True," Chauncy good-naturedly agreed. "I best be on my way. You two have fun at practice."

Tom tipped his head to the pastor then escorted Lila inside. Children gathered around the front of the church where Lila had left a basket of cookies. Erin looked up at them and grinned. "Is it okay we had our treats?" she asked, the crumbs of a cookie clinging to her lip.

"Yes, it is," Lila said, brushing the crumbs from the child's face then tweaking her nose. "Did everyone get one?"

"Maybe even two," Percy Bruner said, hurriedly snatching another cookie from the basket.

"Let's get to work," Tom said. He set down his satchel then helped Lila remove her coat.

An hour later, they reminded the children to come back on Friday for another practice, the last they would have before the program Monday evening.

Tom walked Erin Dodd next door to the parsonage while Lila bundled Maura into her coat and gloves. He returned, shaking snow from his hat.

"It's snowing again?" Lila asked, noticing the coating of white on Tom's shoulders.

"It is. I hope all the children make it home before the storm kicks up," he said.

"All but the Jenkins kids live close to town. I'm sure they'll be fine."

Tom nodded. "I heard Percy mention something to Anna about taking her and the others home in his father's delivery wagon."

Lila appeared relieved as she picked up the empty cookie basket and took Maura's hand in hers.

"Time to go home, honey bunny."

"I's tired, Lila," Maura whined, dragging her little toes as Lila led her to the door.

"Oh, sweetheart, it isn't far home and then you can have a nice rest before we eat dinner. How does that sound?" Lila asked, bending down to look in Maura's angelic face.

"Good. I wanna go home and see Cully and Mama and Daddy." Maura's eyes fluttered shut but she popped them back open.

Tom shifted his satchel to his right hand and gathered Maura up on his left arm. "Would you mind if I carried you, Maura?"

"Thanks, Mr. Grove," she whispered. The child settled her head against his shoulder with an exhausted sigh.

Tom grinned and looked down at her then winked at Lila. Although he'd never had much opportunity to hold children, he'd experienced plenty in the last few weeks he'd been back in town. He rather liked the feel of tiny arms around his neck. He didn't even mind sticky fingers pulling on his hand or suit coat. And he especially enjoyed the childish sounds of laughter that rang around the school and the homes of his friends.

"Thank you for carrying her, Tom. It's so kind of you," Lila said, keeping step with him as they strode along the boardwalk to Granger House.

"Well, you can't expect this tired girl to trudge home in the snow." He smiled at Lila. "Besides, this gives me practice for when I have a little sister."

Lila's right eyebrow rose upward. "How do you know you'll get a sister? It could very well be a brother."

"Mark my words, the new addition at the Grove household will be a girl. Mama always wanted a daughter and I just know she'll finally get one. What in the world would she do with another boy, especially if he turned out to be like me?"

Lila smiled. "She'd likely be thrilled if she had another boy just like you, Tom Grove, but I don't think that's possible."

Baffled, he looked at her. "Why do you say that?"

"Because you are one of a kind, my friend."

Tom remained silent as they followed the walk around to the back door of Granger House. He stepped over the dog as Bart lounged across the top step of the back porch and followed Lila inside the fragrant warmth of the house.

Filly turned from the stove and stared at them as they trooped inside. "Is everything okay?" she asked, rushing over to Tom, holding out her arms for Maura.

Half asleep, the child shifted from Tom to her mother like a limp rag doll. "I's tired, Mama."

"Okay, baby." Filly kissed her forehead, mouthed "thank you" to Tom, and hurried from the room.

Tom helped Lila remove her coat, peeked at a sleeping Cullen in his cradle, then backed toward the door. "I'll see you later, Lila. Have a pleasant evening."

"Won't you stay for supper, Tom? We'd be happy to have you," she said, poking in a few loose hairpins after she removed her hat and hung it by the door.

"No, I really need to go. I'm glad you came by the school today, though, Lila. It was nice to see you again." He took another step toward the door.

"It was nice to see you, too. I may have to come back tomorrow, because I'm positively dying to know what happens in the story." Lila took a step closer to him.

If Tom didn't know better, he'd say she was as reluctant for him to go as he was to leave. Something shimmered in the silvery depths of her eyes, something that gave him hope all was not yet lost.

"About the other day, Tom, I wanted you to know…" Lila moved closer to him and placed her hand on his arm. "That is, I wanted to say how much…"

The door opened and Emerson strolled inside, brushing snow from his shoulders and knocking it off his hat. "My goodness, when it decides to snow out here, it doesn't hesitate at all, does it?" He looked up and noticed Lila standing near Tom. "Oh, hello." He stuck a hand out Tom's direction.

Tom took it and offered the man a polite nod. "Good evening, Mr. Lylan. Enjoy the warmth and company of Granger House."

"I intend to, Mr. Grove. Are you not staying for dinner? It seems as though Luke and Filly have as many visitors for meals as a boarding house."

Tom laughed. "No, I'm not staying, but you wouldn't be wrong in that assessment." He darted a quick glance at Lila then opened the door. "Good night."

As he walked home through the blowing snow, Tom contemplated how hard he'd have to work to make Lila completely forget she'd agreed to wed Emerson.

If the light shining in her eyes reflected what was in her heart, perhaps the battle wouldn't be all uphill.

Chapter Sixteen

"Tom! Tom Grove!"

Tom stopped and turned to watch Ed Daily hurry toward him as the man exited the newspaper office. Mr. Daily had owned the newspaper for as long as Tom could remember. In between school and working on the farm, Tom had written several articles for the paper before he left for Portland.

His mother had proudly cut each one out and saved it. As he recalled how naïve and young he'd been when he'd written those articles, he felt a little embarrassed. A career had to start somewhere. In truth, his had started with Mr. Daily and the Hardman newspaper.

"Evening, Mr. Daily. May I help you with something?" Tom asked as the man thumped him on the back.

"Possibly, Tom. Do you have plans for the evening?" Ed asked, keeping his beefy hand on Tom's shoulder.

"No, sir, other than grading a bunch of arithmetic assignments." Tom glanced over at the older man, wondering what schemes the man was up to. Ed Daily most often had an underlying motive for everything he did. Inviting a former employee to dinner out of the blue smacked of some purpose other than catching up on something as trivial as the weather, or how Tom liked teaching school.

"Perfect. Come home with me for dinner. I've got something I want to discuss with you." Ed turned a corner, still maintaining his hold on Tom, as though he feared it he let go, he might disappear.

"I wouldn't want to present an imposition to your wife, sir." Tom hesitated, but Ed nudged him onward.

"No imposition at all. I told her at lunch I may bring home a guest for dinner." Ed held open the gate to his yard and motioned Tom to precede him. "Over the years, she's grown accustomed to an extra mouth or two popping up at mealtimes."

Tom grinned. "She and Filly Granger would have that in common, then."

Ed laughed. "I imagine so. Ginny can't boil water without nearly burning down the house and Dora and Greg are frequent guests. With all the folks Luke invites home, Filly might as well open a restaurant." The man snapped his fingers and offered Tom a thoughtful look. "Now there is a grand idea. I wouldn't mind being able to order one of her delicious cream pies anytime I felt like indulging in a piece."

Tom, too, had enjoyed her cream pie on more than one occasion and heartily agreed with Ed, but kept his thoughts to himself.

Ed opened the front door and marched inside, divesting himself of his outerwear. "Bess, honey, we're home."

A small, plump woman with kind eyes and an indulgent smile breezed down the hall, wiping her hands on a voluminous apron.

"Hello, darling. You're right on time," she said, accepting a kiss from Ed on her cheek. She then turned to Tom and took both of his hands on hers, giving them a gentle squeeze.

"Tom Grove! How delightful to see you. Ed said he planned to talk you into coming for dinner. I'm so glad you could make it. Take off your coat and come on back to the kitchen."

"Yes, ma'am," Tom said, politely nodding to the woman. He removed his things and hung them on the hall tree then followed Ed to the kitchen.

"Unless we're throwing a shindig, we keep things pretty informal around here," Ed said, pointing to a table near a window set for three. "Have a seat, son."

Tom waited until Ed seated his wife before pulling out the chair across from her and sitting down. "Thank you for the kind invitation to have supper with you," he said, smiling at Mrs. Daily.

She laughed and patted her husband's cheek. "There's nothing kind about it. This one has something he wanted to discuss with you and decided the dinner table was the best place to do it."

Tom smiled and waited as Ed offered thanks for their meal. Once a full plate sat in front of him, he looked to Ed.

The man buttered a warm piece of bread and set it on his plate before he looked to his guest. "Well, Tom, you're probably anxious to know what I wanted to discuss."

"Yes, sir. Admittedly, I am curious."

Ed smiled at his wife and cleared his throat. "Well, Bess and I aren't getting any younger and I've been thinking it's time to begin planning my retirement. What I mean is that I want to find someone who will take over the newspaper and keep it going. I won't sell it to just anyone. It has to be a person who'll do a good job of running it and keep the community at the heart of it."

Tom stared at Ed, wondering what any of that had to do with him.

The older man leaned back in his chair. "I've followed your career in Portland, Tom. Read most every article you've written. I have to admit you do a first-rate job. That article you wrote about the woman who killed four husbands before she was caught gave me the willies."

Mrs. Daily shot her husband a scathing glare, as though she issued a silent warning about appropriate dinner topics.

Ed cleared his throat again. "Anyway, after following your career since you've been in Portland and seeing how you fit right back into the community upon your return to town for the holidays, I've concluded you would be my first choice."

"First choice, sir?" Tom asked, bewildered by the man's conversation. Did Mr. Daily want him to work for him until someone new took over the newspaper?

"To buy the paper and take over, of course."

Tom choked on the milk he'd just swallowed and slapped a napkin over his mouth as he coughed.

Ed thumped him on the back with enough force to loosen a few bones as he chuckled. "Took you by surprise, didn't I?"

Tom nodded. Another round of coughing ensued before he felt he could speak. "Sir, I'm honored by the offer, but I don't have that kind of money. Even if I did, I hadn't considered moving back to Hardman."

Mrs. Daily gave her husband an "I told you so" look before taking a bite of her roast.

Ed grinned and turned his attention back to Tom. "I know this is catching you unawares, Tom, but I want you to give it some thought. You'll be here a few more weeks before returning to Portland. Just let me know what you decide before you leave. If you are interested, we could work out the details. You wouldn't have to pay me a lump sum all at once. I'm not planning to retire until late spring or possibly summer, longer if I can't find a qualified buyer. At any rate, if you decide it's something you want to do, you could certainly come to work with me any time and I'll train you in all aspects of running the business.

You'll do fine writing articles and editing the work of reporters. I know you have the knowledge to run and maintain the equipment." Ed pointed to Tom's casted arm. "But there are other things you need to learn, like balancing the account books, creating advertisements, that sort of thing."

"Thank you, sir, for thinking of me and offering the opportunity. I really do need time to consider the possibilities." Tom looked at the man who had been a mentor of sorts to him. "I'll be entirely truthful with you. The kind of money required to purchase your business isn't something I have. I do well enough in my job, but not that well."

"I know that, Tom, but I'm also aware that you come from a good family, have strong morals, and work hard." Ed smiled and forked a bite of mashed potatoes. "If you decide you want to give it a go, we'll make it work."

Stunned by the offer, Tom could hardly swallow. He barely tasted the fine meal Mrs. Daily prepared and had no idea how he managed to carry on any sort of conversation as they ate.

After the meal, he lingered only a short while, answering Ed's many questions about the life of a reporter at a big newspaper before thanking Mrs. Daily for the meal and Ed for inviting him.

At the door, he shook hands with the man. "Thank you, again, Mr. Daily, for the opportunity. It certainly gives me a lot to think about."

"I hope your thoughts lean toward taking me up on the offer. Have a good evening, son, and we'll see you at the Christmas carnival."

"Good night, sir."

Tom strode out into the darkness, hunkering into his coat as snow swirled around him. On top of trying to decide what to do about his affections for Lila, he now had a whole lot more to consider.

If Ed had made the offer two months ago, Tom would have turned him down flat. However, after spending time back in town, after the news he'd finally have a sibling, after falling in love with Lila, life in the city didn't hold the same appeal it used to.

In truth, Tom missed the small town atmosphere, the friendly smiles, and the fresh air. He'd even missed snow, since Portland mostly received rain, rain, and more rain.

Weighed down by his thoughts, Tom returned to his house and huddled by the fire, contemplating his future.

Chapter Seventeen

Lila frowned at her reflection in the mirror, adjusting the bow tied at her neck and smoothing a hand down the expensive silk of her skirt.

Although the dress featured the latest style and was made specifically for her by a famous seamstress in London, she hated it.

Emerson had bestowed three gowns upon her after dinner the previous evening. It turned out he'd gone to Heppner to retrieve them because they hadn't arrived on the same train he'd traveled on a few days earlier.

Proudly carrying a trunk into the parlor as Lila sat with Luke and Filly, enjoying a cozy evening by the fire, Emerson beamed as he encouraged her to open it.

"Shouldn't I wait for Christmas?" Lila asked, unfastening the buckles and unhooking the latches.

"No. Consider this a gift to illustrate how much I missed you," he said, settling onto the settee next to her, closer than Lila liked. When she hesitated, he pushed open the lid, revealing three dresses packed among layers of tissue.

Exquisitely made, all three gowns featured expensive fabrics and beautiful trims. Any woman would be thrilled to receive them, and Lila tried to be. Nevertheless, she couldn't abide the color blue.

She didn't know why, but she'd never liked clothes in shades of blue. Even as a little girl, she adamantly refused to wear anything blue. She recalled telling her mother, "blue is for summer skies, jolly flowers, little birds, and deep lakes, but not for me to wear."

Emerson, on the other hand, favored blue. The three gowns in the trunk were the hue of pale blue he mistakenly deemed perfect for her. Lila thought it looked like someone had drained the color from the fabric and left behind a sad, faint reminder of what might have been. Had the gowns been crafted from cobalt or even navy-blue fabric, she wouldn't have minded. But the light blue shade made her fight to keep from wrinkling her nose in disgust.

Ashamed by her ungrateful feelings, she forced a bright smile and made over the gowns, showing them to Filly and discussing at length the famous dressmaker who created them.

"Wait until Abby sees them," Filly said, carefully fingering the skirt of one adorned with thick panels of lace. "She'll be beside herself."

"I somehow doubt poor Abby will muster that much enthusiasm over anything right now," Luke commented, glancing up from the newspaper in his hands.

Filly shot him a reproachful look then turned back to study the gowns. "I like this one best," she said, pointing to the dress without much adornment.

If Lila had to pick one to hate the least, it would have been her choice, too. An overskirt and a smart little jacket with oversized buttons topped a pleated dress with just a hint of rich lace at the hem and the throat. The style was one Lila greatly admired — if only it was in a different color.

"These are so lovely, Emerson. I can't thank you enough," Lila said, kissing his cheek and hoping he wouldn't notice her failure to wear the gowns. She planned to leave them in the trunk until she could find someone who'd enjoy them. Perhaps Ginny would like to have them for after the baby's arrival. Or maybe Junie Grove would appreciate them. The pale color would look wonderful on her.

Emerson kissed her cheek. "I'm so glad you like them. I look forward to seeing you wear one tomorrow."

Lila bit back a sigh and carried the gowns to her room, resolved to wearing one.

Now, as she stood gazing in the mirror, she wished she could toss it back in the trunk and never see it again. Emerson hadn't listened the first dozen times she told him she preferred any color other than blue. For reasons she couldn't fathom, he refused to accept the fact she didn't care for his favorite color.

Part of her wondered if he liked it so well because it accented his bright blue eyes and complimented his coloring. No matter how much she persuaded him otherwise, he was determined for her to wear blue. In the past, he'd given her an atrocious blue hat that Lila had eagerly given to Dora. The woman took it with great enthusiasm, wearing it with panache on top of her golden head.

Lila, on the other hand, looked like a washed out version of herself in the light hue. Her skin took on a sickly cast and her eyes lost their vibrant spark.

People would no doubt think she'd come down with some sort of ghastly illness once they saw her in the gown.

Determined to wear the blasted thing to make Emerson happy, she strode out of her room and hurried to the kitchen.

Filly offered her a concerned glance as she looked up from stirring a pan full of scrambled eggs. "Are you well, Lila?"

"I'm fine."

Filly gave her another long look. "But you don't look well. You appear rather pale."

Lila sighed and pulled on an apron. "It's this horrid dress."

At Filly's astonished expression, Lila offered her a wry smile. "I realize I'm probably the only girl on the planet who would hate such an expensive gift as the three gowns Emerson gave me last night, but I despise each and every one. As you can plainly see, I can't wear the color blue. It makes me look as though I'm about to perish from some incurable sickness."

Filly giggled and nodded in agreement. "They are lovely gowns, but I agree, they are not your best color. They would be better suited to Ginny or Dora's coloring. Does Emerson know you aren't fond of that shade of blue?"

Exasperated, Lila thumped plates down on the table. "In spite of me reminding him a dozen times I don't care for blue, he insists it is the perfect color for me." She glanced back at Filly with an irritated spark in her eye. "If he wasn't such a nice person, I would think he insists on this revolting shade because it complements *his* coloring."

Laughter rolled out of Filly. "That would be quite a vain thing for a man to do. I've never heard of a man purchasing gowns for his wife so they matched his complexion. Emerson doesn't strike me as the type to consciously do such a thing."

"I don't really think he would, either. It's just..." Lila glanced down at the gown. "I realize I sound like an ungrateful, spoiled wretch. He went to all the bother and expense of having Madame Beauchene make these beautiful gowns. If only they were any other color, I'd be so happy to wear them."

Luke strode into the room with Maura on his arm. "Good morning, Lila." He frowned at her and backed up a step. "Are you sick? You don't look well."

Lila huffed and threw her hands in the air while Filly laughed again.

He looked from his wife to his cousin. "What did I say? I realize that was rather blunt, but you are usually so full of life, it's quite a shock to see you appear rather subdued today, cousin."

Lila lifted a little apron from a hook and tied it around Maura so she wouldn't get her school dress dirty if she accidentally spilled something at breakfast. "I'm perfectly well, Luke, but thank you for your concern."

He gave her another look. "I probably shouldn't say it, but blue is most definitely not your color, Lila."

The icy glower she shot his way made him chuckle.

He rubbed a hand over his chin. "Ah, I see the problem now. That's one of the gowns Emerson insisted you wear. Is that it?"

Lila nodded, pouring a cup of milk for Maura and setting it at her place at the table. She tossed Luke a sassy grin. "And Chauncy said you aren't as smart as you look. You've just proven otherwise."

Filly swallowed her amusement, turning to scoop eggs out of the skillet into a serving bowl as Luke frowned.

Luke poured tea into three cups and set them on the table while Lila cut a piece of toast into four triangles for Maura. "Why don't you just tell Emerson you don't care for blue?"

"Apparently she has, multiple times," Filly said, placing the eggs and a platter of ham on the table. She sent Lila a sly glance. "She thinks he likes her to wear blue because it matches his eyes."

Luke snorted and set his cup of tea back on the saucer with a clatter. "What kind of man..." He caught the teasing grin on his wife's face. Slowly, he leaned back in his chair. "If you dislike the dresses that much, tell Emerson he can wear them."

Lila smirked. "Now that would be something to see."

After breakfast, Lila washed the dishes while Filly finished readying Maura for school. The little girl chattered about her teacher the entire time her mother styled her hair and washed her face.

"He's heaps of fun, Mama," Maura said, smiling at Filly. "He does good magics, too, like Aunt Alex."

Lila rather liked his "magics," too.

When she finished drying the dishes and putting them away, she went to her room to pin on a hat. She returned to the kitchen and slipped on her coat while Filly fastened the last button on Maura's.

With gloves in place and scarves wrapped around their necks, Maura kissed her mother's cheek then took Lila's hand.

"Have a good day, sweetheart," Filly said, waving to her daughter.

"I will, Mama. Bye!" Maura ran outside and hugged Bart as he sat on the back porch, then raced down the steps.

They'd just reached the boardwalk when Luke fell into step with them. "I can take her to school if you have other things you'd like to do this morning," he offered.

"I don't mind, Luke. I enjoy my strolls in the fresh air." Lila smiled at her cousin as he clasped his daughter's little hand in his and stopped so she could examine a white-frosted stick leaning against a fence.

"Are you sure you don't mind? I'd be happy to…"

"Good morning, Grangers!" Emerson called, striding toward them. He looked like one of the many dandies Lila had seen in New York with his narrow-legged trousers, blue brocade vest, dark blue frock coat, and a silver-tipped cane he carried in his gloved hands. With a grand sweep, he doffed his hat and tipped his head to Lila. "How does this day find you, lovely Lila?"

"Perfectly well, Emerson. Thank you."

"Excellent, my darling." He noticed the hint of blue peeping beneath the hem of her coat. "Oh, you wore one of your new gowns! You look magnificent, dear. Truly magnificent."

Lila didn't bother to inform him that if she looked anything beyond a specter of death it was because of the violet-hued scarf wrapped around her neck, not the dress she did her best to hide beneath a long coat.

"You always appear so beautiful, Lila, darling, but in that gown, you positively take my breath away."

Lila held several doubts about how much breath he'd lost since he continued to go on and on about the loathed gown.

Aware of her true feelings, Luke cleared his throat and looked at Emerson. "How would you like to spend the day with me at the bank, Emerson? Dad will be there today. We thought you might like to see how we conduct business."

With painstaking politeness, Emerson considered the offer then nodded his head. "That is a capital idea, Luke. I'd like that very much, as long as Lila won't mind my absence today."

She smiled. "Not at all, Emerson. Enjoy the bank with my blessing."

"Very well, darling. I shall endeavor to glean the most helpful facts of the bank business with this unique opportunity of an invitation of observance."

Lila wanted to roll her eyes at his formal manner of speech, but refrained. After the initial shock of seeing Emerson again passed, she found herself fighting constant annoyance with the man. It wasn't that he'd changed. He hadn't. Not at all. He was the same as he'd always been — polite, full of concerns about obeying every rule society imposed, and making his mark on the world.

She was the one who had changed. No longer a silly girl, the fact a handsome young man sought her hand failed to entrance her as it once had. She was a confident woman who'd survived devastating loss and finally arrived on the other side of it. The experience gentled her, added a deeper sense of gratitude and kindness, but also left her with a clearer vision of what mattered in life.

Love mattered greatly to Lila.

Truthfully, what started as an infatuation with Emerson no longer seemed an emotion strong enough on which to base a marriage.

In the few days Emerson had been in Hardman, he'd not once discussed their nuptials or setting a definite wedding date. He had mentioned that he wanted to return to New York right after the holidays, but didn't mind spending Christmas there with her family.

Much to her relief, Greg and Dora invited him to stay at their home. The fact they had meant Lila had a few waking hours without his hovering presence driving her daft.

Emerson was kind, attentive, and dedicated to her. He lavished her with compliments, and did his best to express his admiration of her.

Lila wondered why, then, she felt stifled by his presence. Her fiancé was everything a girl could hope for in a husband, but it suddenly didn't seem like enough. Or perhaps it wasn't a lack of anything specific about his personality. He just wasn't Tom Grove.

Startled by the thoughts popping up in her head, Lila sucked in a gulp of cold air and choked.

Both Luke and Emerson turned to look at her with concern. Luke tapped her back and offered her his handkerchief as she coughed.

Eyes watering, she dabbed at the moisture.

"Are you sure you aren't ill?" Luke asked, placing a hand on her shoulder.

"I'm fine, Luke, but thank you," she croaked, wishing she had something hot to drink to soothe her suddenly raw throat. "I'll be on my way and take Maura to school."

Luke shot her another observant glance, but he hunkered down and gave Maura a hug then kissed her rosy cheek. "Have fun at school today, honey, and be a good girl."

"I will, Daddy! Bye!" She glanced up at Emerson. "Bye, Mr. Lylan!"

"Enjoy your day, Maura." Emerson waved at her then smiled at Lila. "May your morning be filled with pleasantries, dear Lila."

"Thank you, Emerson." Lila offered a curt nod, then took Maura's hand in hers and guided the child down the boardwalk.

As they neared the church, Erin skipped outside and clasped Lila's other hand. "Guess what?" Erin said, looking up at Lila with excitement on her face.

"What?" Lila asked, working up a silly face that caused Erin to giggle.

"You're so funny, Lila," Erin said, then continued with her exciting news. "We have today and tomorrow at school, and then it's the Christmas carnival, and then church, and then the Christmas program, and then Saint Nicholas will come!"

"Is that so?" Lila asked, smiling at the little girl. "What do you hope Saint Nicholas will leave for you?"

"Oh, I want some chocolates, like the ones Aunt Filly likes, and a jump rope!" Erin jumped in the air three times before resuming her usual skipping gait.

Lila laughed. "Why do you want a jump rope? You can already jump high."

"I want to jump even better. That way I could practice!"

"Practice is important in reaching your goals," Lila said, as they neared the school. "You two go play while I take your things inside."

Lila took Erin's lunch pail and books, and Maura's little book bag, then walked up the steps to the school. Tom sat at the desk reading.

Quietly, she set down the girls' things. She would have left him undisturbed, but couldn't help studying him for a moment.

Intent on the book in front of him, dark lashes framed his eyes and fanned his cheeks as he turned the page. His hair was slightly tousled, as if his best efforts of subduing it weren't quite successful. The knot of his tie wasn't precise, but the somewhat disheveled way it rested beneath his chin only served to endear him to her.

Lila knew she needed to move past any thoughts or feelings she had about Tom, especially with Emerson in town, but she couldn't quite force herself to do it. Something about him, something gentle and kind and inordinately wonderful, continued to whisper to her heart in a way nothing about Emerson ever had.

So involved in studying him, she failed to notice when he lifted his gaze and observed her.

"Good morning, Miss Granger," he said, rising to his feet. His left hand went to his tie and he gave it a tug.

Lila grinned and moved down the aisle between the desks toward him. "I see you still haven't mastered the ability to execute a properly tied tie."

Tom chuckled. "I dare you to say that fast ten times in a row."

She gave him an exasperated look and retied his tie. He hadn't shaved that day and the scruffy stubble along his jaw brushed against her fingers. Thrilling little sensations zinged all the way to her head and down to her toes at the rough feel of it. Although she'd never admit it, she thought she preferred seeing Tom with a few days of unshaven growth on his face. It made him even more ruggedly appealing.

The outdoorsy scent of him filled her nose as she finished his tie and stepped back. "There," she said, resting her hand just above his heart. "Much better."

"Yes, I believe it is," Tom said, leaning toward her as yearning fired bright sparks in his eyes.

The thought of Tom kissing her again, of being back in his arms, nearly made her take a forward step that would remove every speck of space between them.

Instead, Lila stepped back, mindful of where they were and the fact Emerson should be the one filling her thoughts, not Tom. Desperate for a distraction, her gaze dropped to the book on his desk. "What are you reading?"

Tom slipped a scrap of paper between the pages to mark his place then handed her the book. She read the title and furrowed her brow. "A little light reading before class?" she asked with a hefty dose of sarcasm.

A derisive smirk met her teasing smile. "Something like that."

"I don't believe I've read much on the Boer War." Lila handed him back the heavy tome. "Do you like Arthur Conan Doyle's writings?"

"I do," Tom said, setting the book back on his desk. "This one came out just a few months ago. It gives a great deal of insight into the war, and the author injects quite a bit of commentary about the shortcomings of the forces since he was there for a few months."

"War seems like such a sad subject, especially this close to Christmas." Lila looked at the empty blackboard behind Tom. "Do you need help writing down the day's assignments?"

He smiled. "No. With just two days left before school releases for the holidays, I want to make them memorable for the students. This morning we'll have a spelling bee of sorts followed by a mock battle on the playground. After lunch, we'll engage in a few scientific experiments and then read several chapters in *The Wonderful Wizard of Oz*. I want to finish it before class releases tomorrow."

"I have a feeling the students will remain after class to hear the end if you don't finish reading it before release time." Lila smiled. "It sounds like you have wonderful plans for the students. If I was in your class, I'd be thrilled."

"You're welcome to stay," Tom invited, waving his hand to the chair she often occupied at the back of the room. His face lit up as he thought of an idea. "In fact, would you mind coming this afternoon? The students always enjoy it when you sing with them."

"I'd love to. And that gives me an excuse to linger and hear more of the story you're reading."

Lila tugged on her gloves and walked to the door with Tom right behind her. "Don't have too much fun this morning."

His deep chuckles warmed her from the inside out as she opened the door. "That would be impossible without you here, Lila Lilac."

Lila left with a spring in her step that had been absent since Emerson's arrival. After checking on Abby and running a few errands for her, Lila returned to Granger House and told Filly about Tom planning fun activities for the students.

"I think you should go back to the school and help him. The children have such a hard time paying attention this time of year and there are so many young ones in the class. Tom may need the assistance of another adult just to keep them all out of trouble today," Filly said. As she spoke, she packed a lunch for Lila and one for Maura into a basket she'd already filled with cookies. "If Maura wants to come home at lunch, you can always bring her, but I have a feeling she'll want to stay today."

"I think she will, too." Lila hurried back into her coat and tugged on her gloves then lifted the basket. "I'll see you later, Filly. Thank you for this." She motioned to the basket then hurried outside.

Bart started to follow her, so she stopped and scratched behind his ears and along his back. "Stay here with Filly, Bart. That's a good boy."

The dog woofed once then ambled around to the back door.

Lila hastened to the school and stopped in shocked surprise to see the children had constructed what appeared to be a fort made of packed snow on one side of the playground. Tom stood in front of it, wearing a hat fashioned from a sheet of folded newspaper.

"What do you think it would have been like to spend the winter at Valley Forge?" he asked.

Several students raised their hands. He pointed to Percy Bruner. "Go ahead, Percy."

"Cold," the boy said, drawing snickers from his classmates."

Tom hid a smile. "Yes, it was cold. What else would they have felt or experienced?"

Anna Jenkins raised her hand. Tom nodded at her. "Anna?"

"They were hungry, weren't they?" she asked in a quiet voice.

"They certainly were, Anna." Tom smiled at the girl. "What else?"

"Sick! Were they sick, Mr. Grove?" Erin Dodd asked, forgetting to wait until he called on her.

Tom grinned at her. "They were sick. Many had diseases, others suffered from battle wounds."

The children appeared to think on his words, growing more serious than Lila thought they should be.

"Don't forget about the unexpected fights," she said, setting the basket in her hands on the school steps then sauntering toward Tom and the children.

"Fights?" he asked, spinning around to look at her.

"Of the snowball variety." Lila scooped up a handful of snow, hastily packed it into a ball, and launched it at Tom, catching him on the chin.

He grabbed a glove full of snow and tossed it back at her, hitting her on the back.

Soon, all the students, from Maura Granger to the oldest in the class, engaged in a battle of snowballs.

Squeals of excitement and joyous laughter rang through the frosty morning air, making those close to the school smile in delight.

After Lila hit Tom in the face with a handful of soft snow, he grabbed her around the waist and threatened to stuff snow down the back of her dress.

In their playful mood, neither of them gave a thought to their behavior, acting like two children as they chased each other and joined in the battle.

Tom finally whistled loudly and all the students stopped. "Let's go inside and get warmed up. Your mothers will throttle me if you all take ill."

"Aw, don't worry about it, Tom..., er, Mr. Grove," Percy said, brushing clumps of snow from his mittens. "No one would gripe because we had such a fun time while learning our history lesson."

Tom directed the children to hurry inside the warmth of the school. Once they were all in their seats, he returned to his desk at the front of the room and motioned for Lila to join him.

He settled an extra chair close to his desk and held out his hand for her to take a seat. The warmth of his breath caressed her neck as he bent close to her. "Do you not feel well, Lila?"

"Never better," she said, exhilarated by frolicking in the snow with the children. "Why?"

"You just look rather pale, that's all."

Lila glanced down and swallowed her sigh. She'd forgotten all about wearing the hated dress. No wonder Tom thought she looked unwell. "I'm fit as a fiddle, Mr. Grove. Now, is there some reason you asked me to sit up here and face the students?" She cast him a wary glance. "I'm not in trouble, am I?"

"No. Not unless you want to be, in which case I'll have to keep you after class." The teasing wink he offered her did nothing to calm the nervous flutters in her midsection. Tom smiled as he looked around the room. "How many of you have heard of a telephone?"

Some of the students raised their hands but most stared at him with open curiosity. Tom pointed to one of the older girls. "Carol, would you please explain what a telephone is to the rest of the class?"

"Yes, Mr. Grove," the girl said, rising to her feet. "My Aunt Lucy has one at her house in Pendleton. It's the most fantastical thing. You hold the receiver to your ear, like this..." She held the fingers of one hand close to her ear. "Then you talk into the mouthpiece." Carol held her other hand in front of her mouth. "You can talk to people across town and even further away! I can't wait until we have telephones here in Hardman."

"Very good, Carol." Tom nodded to the girl then turned to Lila. "Do you have anything to add, Miss Granger, to Carol's description of how a telephone works?"

Lila smiled. "She covered the basics. A telephone is a handy thing to have, but it can also cause trouble. Some lines aren't private, so other people can listen to your conversations. Sometimes people misconstrue or misunderstand what is said."

Tom grinned. "And that's precisely the reason I'm glad we don't have them here in Hardman."

Percy Bruner raised his hand and waved it above his head.

"Yes, Percy?" Tom asked.

"Do you use telephones in Portland, Mr. Grove?"

"Yes, Percy, I do. We use them at the newspaper office every day."

"Wow! Do you talk to murderers and robbers and everything?" the boy asked.

Tom shook his head. "Not if I can help it." He glanced around the room again. "Can anyone tell me who invented the telephone?"

After they discussed Alexander Graham Bell and various types of telephones, Tom once again stood at the front of the class next to where Lila sat. "Let's play a game. I'm going to whisper something to Maura Granger. She'll whisper it to Sally, then Sally will whisper it to Maude, and so forth. When you reach the end of this row, Henry will whisper it to Vern across the aisle and up the second row. I want Billy to whisper it into Miss Granger's ear. We'll see if what I whispered is the same message Miss Granger receives. Are you ready?" Tom asked.

"Yes!" the children cheered, eager to play a new game.

Tom hunkered down next to Maura and whispered something in her ear. "Now whisper it to Sally, Maura."

"Okay," the child said in a subdued voice. She cupped her hands around Sally's ear and whispered the message.

Tom went to his desk and wrote something on a slip of paper. He folded it in half while the children took their whispering very seriously. Normally, whispering was frowned upon, so to be given permission to pass along a secret was something unique, indeed.

Finally, little Billy slid off his seat in the front row and scampered over to Lila's chair. She leaned over so he could whisper in her ear. When he did, her eyes widened and she stared at Tom.

"Thank you, Billy," Tom said, guiding the little boy back to his seat. "Miss Granger, will you tell the students what you heard from Billy?"

"I… I'm not so… I'd rather…" she stammered as pink filled her cheeks. Finally, she shook her head. "No, Mr. Grove. I won't."

Tom gave her a confused glance. "Why not?"

"Because it's not… that's to say, I don't believe…"

Tom's gaze swiveled from her to Billy. "Billy, what did you tell Miss Granger?"

The little boy shrugged. "Maybeth said 'Miss Granger is in love with you.' That's what I told Miss Granger."

Tom didn't blink for a full moment before he turned back to Lila. Her face flushed an even deeper shade of red. He snatched the piece of paper he'd written the original message on from his desk and handed it to her. "Please read that aloud, Miss Granger."

She took the paper from him and read, "Miss Granger is blue today." Lila looked at him then back at the paper in her hand. "Oh, that's what you originally said?"

Tom nodded then turned to the students. "Do you see how easily a simple statement can be completely misconstrued?"

The children nodded.

"What lesson did you learn from this experiment?"

Anna Jenkins raised her hand in the air.

"Go ahead, Anna," Tom said.

"Don't believe everything you hear?" the girl asked.

"Excellent, Anna!" Tom smiled at her then gave Lila a teasing glance. "Let's take a break for lunch and I'll find out if Miss Granger is really in love with me."

The children laughed and hurried to gather their lunch pails. Most went outside to eat while a few chose to stay inside close to the warmth of the stove.

Tom made room at his desk for Lila to set out her lunch. Maura climbed on her lap and chatted away as she ate the biscuit with jam, slices of cheese, and sliced apple her mother sent for lunch.

When she finished eating, Maura asked to be excused and hurried to get her coat to join the other children outside. Lila helped her fasten the buttons and wrapped a scarf around the child's neck and ears before sending her out into the sunny afternoon.

"I don't believe I liked your lesson about the telephone, Tom Grove." Lila scowled at him as she picked at a piece of cheese.

Tom leaned back in his chair with a cocky smile. "I rather liked the statement the students came up with." He waggled his eyebrows at her, making her laugh.

She sobered and gave him a reproachful look. "How did they take something simple, like I'm blue and twist it into being in love with you?"

"I have no idea, but perhaps they know more than we realize."

"What's that supposed to mean?" Lila asked as Tom snitched a piece of her cheese.

"It means, Lila Lilac, you like me more than you care to admit."

"Humph." Her spine went rigid and she looked away. "And I think you read far more into situations than you should."

Tom shrugged, pretending indifference. "Have it your way, but I do think you look rather blue today, and I don't just mean the color of that dress. Is it new?"

"Yes, it is." Her clipped tone didn't escape his scrutiny. She wanted to squirm as he studied her.

"Emerson gave it to you, is that it?" he asked, intuitively knowing she hated the dress. Oh, the style suited her well, but certainly not the color.

Lila nodded. "I'm not fond of blue."

"With good reason," Tom said, brushing the crumbs from his desk into his lunch pail. "As I said to the class, you look blue today. That color sucks all the life out of you. Surely Emerson noticed."

A sigh escaped her before she could hold it back. "No, he didn't notice. In fact, he thinks I look magnificent."

Tom couldn't help the snort of laughter that rolled out of him. "I didn't realize Emerson had problems with his vision. If he wants to see magnificent, you should wear that silvery dress you have with the lilacs on it. Now, that is a vision to behold, at least when you wear it."

Pleased, yet oddly unsettled by Tom's words, Lila rose to her feet and briskly marched toward the door. "I need a little fresh air before the children return for their afternoon lessons."

Lila snatched her coat and scurried outside, drawing in deep breaths. As she strode around the schoolyard, she wondered what was wrong with her. She cared for Emerson, a great deal. He'd make a devoted, loyal husband and do his best to give her a life of comfort and security. By marrying him she'd never want for anything.

Except passion and laughter.

Lila stopped, taken aback by her thoughts. Tom may never be wealthy or travel to exotic locales, he may not own fine suits or dine with royalty, but he made her laugh. Her heart felt lighter since she'd become his friend than it had for years.

Then there were Tom's kisses. Oh, there were his fervent, driven, demanding, deliriously marvelous kisses.

Lila's heart began to pound just thinking about them.

Was she in love with Tom? How could that be when she loved Emerson? She did love her fiancé. Didn't she?

Conflicted and confused, she shook her head to chase away her thoughts and went to push some of the girls on the swing.

The afternoon passed quickly. Lila led the students in singing a variety of songs, including a few Christmas carols.

Erin pleaded with her to sing a solo, so Lila stood at the front of the room and sang a hauntingly lovely version of *I Heard the Bells on Christmas Day.*

Stillness cloaked the room as the last note faded into the silence.

Tom gave her a look full of admiration and affection as he led the students in a rousing round of applause. "If you all settle down, I think Miss Granger has some treats to share while we read more in our book."

Lila passed out the cookies Filly had sent while Tom settled into his chair and turned to the page where they'd stopped reading the previous afternoon. Once the children contentedly munched on the cookies, Tom began reading the story. Quickly taking a seat at the back of the room, Lila was soon absorbed in the story every bit as much as the children.

Tom read for an hour, stopping only to get a drink of water to soothe his dry throat. He almost reached the end of the book, but a glance at the clock declared it time to release the class for the day. He placed a bookmark inside and closed the cover.

"Please keep reading, Mr. Grove. Please?" the students begged, but Tom shook his head.

"I promise we'll finish the story tomorrow, but I can't keep you any longer today. Have a good evening and I'll see you in the morning."

Although they groaned in protest, the students hurried to gather their things and be on their way. Lila helped

Maura and Erin with their coats and watched as the two girls raced outside to play for a few minutes.

She tugged on her coat before Tom could offer his assistance and yanked on her gloves. "I so enjoy listening to you read, Mr. Grove. You make the characters in the story come to life."

He smiled at her as he tidied the classroom. "I'm glad you think so. Will you come tomorrow?"

Lila grinned as she picked up the empty cookie basket. "I'll be here. I'm as eager as the children to know how the story ends."

Tom chuckled and pointed to the basket. "I don't suppose they left any crumbs, did they?"

She shook her head then took two cookies from her pocket, wrapped in a clean handkerchief. "You should know better than to even ask, but I saved these for you anyway."

"You are an angel, Lila Lilac. Don't ever let anyone tell you different."

A playful grin made her eyes dance with humor. Her heart did a flip every time he called her that name. "I've been told different more times than you could count. Have a pleasant evening, Tom."

"You as well."

She gave him a parting glance and hurried down the steps of the school.

As she walked Erin and Maura home, Lila's thoughts lingered on what Billy whispered in her ear. Was she in love with Tom? Or did her heart belong to Emerson?

Chapter Eighteen

"Hello?" Tom called, stamping his feet with unnecessary noise at the kitchen door of his parents' home as he pushed open the door. "Anyone home?"

His mother glanced up from where she stood in front of the stove and greeted him with a welcome smile. "What's all the noise about, honey? You know you can walk right in."

"The last time I walked right in didn't work out so well for any of us." Tom stepped inside the warm kitchen, redolent with the delicious aromas of baking bread and roasting meat.

Crimson colored Junie's cheeks as she turned away and fussed with stirring a pot on the stove. "Yes, well, um… what brought you out tonight, sweetheart? If we knew you wanted to come, your father would have gone into town to get you so you wouldn't have to walk in the cold."

"Oh, I didn't walk," Tom said, washing his hands at the sink and pouring himself a cup of coffee from the pot simmering on the back of the stove. "Fred Decker gave me a ride. He was making a delivery out this way and dropped me off."

"Fred's doing well, isn't he?" Junie asked, turning to glance at him.

Tom nodded. "Thankfully, he sure seems to be. He likes his job at the livery and he does other odd jobs around town. Tonight he needed to make a delivery for the lumberyard."

Without being asked, Tom set the table while his mother put the finishing touches on the meal. They discussed the students at school as they worked.

Tom looked over at her as he set silverware on the table. "Do you think Dad saw me come in?"

Junie shrugged as she buttered the tops of rolls, hot from the oven. "If he had, he probably would have come in already. He should be here any minute, though. That man has been working on something out in the barn and refuses to tell me what it is."

Tom had seen his father's secret project and knew his mother would be giddy with excitement to find the hand-carved cradle and matching high chair beneath the tree Christmas morning, but he certainly wouldn't spoil the surprise. "It's Christmas, Mama. You should know better than to ask questions or get nosy."

She grinned at him. "That's never stopped me before."

Tom chuckled. "Do you mind if I play a little joke on Dad?"

Junie propped one fist on her hip and studied her son. Despite the fact he was a grown man, she enjoyed it when the playful boy emerged. "Be my guest. What do you have in mind?"

Quickly, Tom shared his plan then snatched his things and hid in the pantry off the kitchen when they heard James' boots thud on the steps outside.

The door swung open, carrying in a draft of cold air. "June-bug, I'm so hungry I could even eat my own cooking."

Junie laughed and set the carved roast on the table. "Then you best wash up and sit down while the food's still hot."

"Yes, wife." James shrugged out of his chore coat and hung it with his hat and scarf by the door then washed his hands at the sink. He kissed Junie's cheek and let his hand trail from her waist over the curve of her hip. "I think you get prettier every time I walk in that door."

She lifted a bowl of green beans and set it on the table. "I'll make an appointment for you to see Doc next week," she said.

James gave her a baffled look. "What for?"

With a tender glance, she patted his cheek. "Because your eyesight is obviously failing, old man."

James grabbed her waist and attempted to tickle her, but she smacked at his hands and spun away from him. "What's gotten into you this evening, James Grove?"

"My beautiful wife, a warm home, a table full of good food, and a son who isn't quite as clever as he thinks." James winked at Junie and tipped his head toward the pantry. "You may as well come out here, Tom."

Tom opened the door and stepped out, giving his father a broad smile. "How'd you know I was here?"

"I heard the harness jingle on Fred's wagon and saw it out the window in the barn." James looked smug as he leaned back in his chair. "According to your mother, I'm practically blind, but at least I can still hear." He pointed to the table. "And even if I hadn't caught you climbing out of Fred's wagon, I noticed the extra plate on the table."

Tom laughed and took a seat. "I guess we aren't any good at pulling one over on Dad, Mama," he said, giving Junie a conspiratorial look.

"No, we certainly aren't." She set a cup of hot coffee in front of her husband then bowed her head as he offered thanks for their meal.

As his "amen" faded, Tom helped himself to a serving of meat and potatoes then added green beans to his plate. His father lifted the lid on the sugar bowl and stirred a heaping spoon of the white crystals into his coffee.

He leaned back and took a deep swallow. His eyes bugged and he choked, coughing and pounding his chest. Tom snickered while Junie tried to hold back her giggles.

"Told you he'd never suspect salt in the sugar bowl," Tom winked at his mother then reached out and slapped his father on the back. Junie handed James a glass of water, which he swigged down in a few gulps.

He glared at them. "Are you two trying to kill me?" The face he made caused both Tom and Junie to succumb to their mirth.

"I'm sorry, Dad," Tom said, attempting to curtail his laughter. "But you should have seen your face when you got a taste of the coffee. Boy, was it funny."

"I ought to toss you out on your ear, you ungrateful kid." James smiled at his son as his humor slowly returned. "It would serve you right for trying to bring about my premature demise."

"I'm fairly certain a little salt won't kill you, James." Junie grinned at her husband. "Maybe that will teach you not to use so much sugar in your coffee."

"Maybe I'll teach both of you something when you least expect it," he said, giving his wife a pointed glare.

"Most likely you'll try..." Junie looked to Tom, "but you'll have trouble keeping up with this one."

James shook his head. "I'm doomed if the new little one takes after her big brother."

Junie set a fresh cup of coffee in front of James then unconsciously rubbed a hand over her belly. "I sure hope it's a girl, although my only wish is to have a healthy baby."

"She'll be healthy and happy, Mama," Tom said. "When Jamie arrives, have you decided what her middle name will be?"

Junie shook her head. "No. We're still discussing options. I think we've narrowed it down to Jamie Meredith, Jamie Rose, and Jamie Viola."

James smiled at his wife. "And if it's a boy we like Jamie Robert, Jamie Harris, and Jamie Edward."

Tom nodded his head. "I vote for Jamie Rose. I'm not offering an opinion on a name for a boy because Mama is having a girl."

Junie laughed. "I hope you're right, sweetheart. From past experience, when you make up your mind about something, it's as good as done."

"That's right, so you might as well start crocheting pink booties."

James took a bite of his dinner then looked to Tom. "Other than to terrorize your dear old dad, what brought you out tonight? We didn't expect to see you until tomorrow evening."

"I know," Tom said, wiping his mouth on his napkin and looking at his parents. "Yesterday, Mr. Daily invited me for dinner and offered me quite an interesting opportunity."

"Oh, what's that?" Junie asked, setting down her fork.

"He's going to sell the paper and retire." Tom glanced at his father. "He wants me to buy it and take over."

"Well, I'll be," James said, broadly grinning at his son. "That's a fine idea."

"But, Dad, I don't have that kind of money. Mr. Daily said he'd work with me to figure out payments, but I'd hate to do that. I'm not entirely certain what I want to do. I enjoy my job in Portland, but it's been nice being back here in Hardman. If I stay here, would I toss away a great opportunity for my career to grow? If I go, would I lose my chance to own a newspaper?" Tom sighed and shrugged. "Even if I had the money, I'm not sure what to do. The fact I don't makes it seem like a far-fetched dream."

Junie reached out and squeezed Tom's hand. "If you decide you'd like to buy the paper and stay, you know we'll help you all we can."

A smile softened the worry lines on his face as he looked to his mother. "I know you would, Mama, but you've got a little one on the way to think about. I need to do this on my own, but I did want to let you know about the offer, to see what you both thought."

"I think," James said, studying his son, "that you'll figure out what's best for you and do it. As much as we'd love to have you stay here, Tom, we'll support whatever decision you make. Whether you return to Portland or start a new adventure here, we're so proud of you, son."

"Thanks, Dad." Tom offered his father a look full of respect and gratitude.

"What about Lila?" Junie asked, picking up her fork again.

Another frown settled on Tom's brow. "What about Lila?"

"Have you discussed this with her?"

Tom stared at his mother. "Why would I discuss it with her?"

Junie offered her husband a saucy look then smiled at her son. "She might like an opinion about where you'll live after the two of you wed."

"Wed? Are you delirious, Mama? She's going to marry Emerson Lylan, not me."

Junie shrugged. "If that girl was going to marry him, they'd be back in New York, getting ready for a wedding, not lingering here in Hardman. She can make all the excuses in the world, but I think she wants to stay. Just give her a good reason to, sweetheart."

Tom ate the rest of his meal in silence, contemplating his mother's words and the best way to make sure Lila remained in Hardman, with him. He was fast running out of time to win her hand.

Chapter Nineteen

"I want to thank you, class, for working so hard these last few weeks," Tom said, standing in front of his students as they neared the end of the school day. His final day of teaching.

Although the last thing he thought he'd find himself doing was teaching a variety of grades in a one-room school where he'd once been a student, Tom loved every moment of it. The students had worked hard, been respectful, and he'd miss them all when he returned to his life in Portland. Even if he stayed in Hardman and somehow figured out a way to take over the newspaper, he wouldn't see the students every day. Wouldn't listen to their excited chatter. Wouldn't see the wonder on their faces when they grasped a new idea. He'd even miss listening to Maura Granger's and Erin Dodd's silly little songs and hearing the lisping sweetness of those trying to talk around the inconvenience of missing front teeth.

"I know you are all excited to have Miss Alex return as your teacher in January, but it has been a pleasure to serve as your teacher this month."

Percy Bruner stood from his desk and gazed at Tom with a big grin. "You've been a good teacher, Mr. Grove. We've had fun with you and learned things, too." The boy looked around the room at his classmates. A sea of youthful heads bobbed up and down in agreement. "That's why we wanted to give you this." Percy nudged Anna and the girl hopped up from the desk, holding a small rectangular box in her hands.

Together, the two young people walked up to Tom and handed him the gift. The rest of the children rushed to the front of the room, crowding around him. "Open it, Mr. Grove," one of them encouraged.

Tom sat on one corner of the desk and untied the purple ribbon around the box. He dropped it on the desk then slowly lifted the lid to reveal a beautiful silver pen.

"Thank you, class," he said, smiling as he lifted it from the box and held it up for everyone to see.

Percy pointed to the side of it. "Fred engraved it for us."

Tom turned it until he could read, "To Mr. Grove, from your class."

"This is wonderful." Tom glanced around the faces of the students, warmly looking at each one while emotion clogged his throat. Lila stood at the back of the group, smiling in pleasure.

He had an idea she helped the students purchase the expensive pen because it was far more costly than most of them or their parents could afford. The purple ribbon around the box definitely made him think of her. He caught her gaze and held it. "I'll treasure this always, class. Thank you so much."

"You're welcome, Mr. Grove," the students said in unison.

Percy grinned and pointed to the book on top of Tom's desk. "Will you finish the story now?"

Tom chuckled. "Yes. If the gift was a bribe, I would have finished reading it to you all today, anyway."

Percy and a few of the older students laughed as the students returned to their seats.

"Since this is Mr. Grove's last day, I think we should make it seem more like a party," Lila said, carrying a box to the front of the room. Inside were enough shiny tin cups for each student to have one. Lila filled the cups with hot chocolate and passed out an assortment of cookies for the students to enjoy while Tom read the last few chapters of *The Wonderful Wizard of Oz*.

After Lila handed him a cup of chocolate and two cookies, he winked at her and settled at his desk to read.

The students quietly listened as Tom read about a girl named Dorothy and her friends. By the time he arrived at the part of the story where Dorothy and her comrades reached Glinda the Good Witch, the students hung on each word, eager to discover if Dorothy made it back to Kansas and her beloved Aunt Em.

Tom glanced around at the captivated faces and back at the book. "And she said, 'I'm so glad to be at home again!'"

With unhurried movements, he closed the book and stood. "Did you like the ending?"

"Oh, yes," several of the girls gushed. "Dorothy made it home."

"It's too bad there wasn't another mean ol' witch or a battle. Maybe Dorothy's friends could have gone at it again." Percy commented, forcing Tom to hide a grin behind a cough.

"Who can tell me one of the lessons you learned from the story?" Tom looked around the room and finally pointed to Anna Jenkins. "Did you find a lesson in the story, Anna?"

The girl nodded. "Yes, sir. I think the lesson at the end is that we have the power to do whatever we wish most, if we believe we can do it."

Surprised by her insight, Tom smiled. "That's absolutely right, Anna. You discovered one of the most important lessons in the story." He looked around again. "Does anyone else have ideas to share?"

"That it's important to have friends," Erin Dodd said, waving her hand in the air although she spoke without waiting for Tom to call on her.

"Very good, Erin."

"And to be in charge of the flying monkeys," Percy added with a cheeky grin.

"Indeed, Percy. On that note, I'll bid you all a fond farewell." Tom swept his hand around the room. "Thank you for being such a wonderful class to teach, and for my pen. Now, go enjoy the sunshine outside and have a very Merry Christmas!"

"Hooray!" the children cheered, rushing to pull on coats and hats and race out the door.

Chapter Twenty

"You did not, Tom Grove. That is so ornery," Lila said. She glanced back over her shoulder at Tom as he helped her with her coat after their final program practice at church. The children had all left and Luke had taken both Erin and Maura home, leaving Tom and Lila alone. "Did your father ban you from coming home again after you salted his coffee?"

"Actually, Dad took it well. He was even joking about it this morning as he gave me a ride into town." Tom's finger brushed against the soft skin of Lila's neck as he freed a wayward curl trapped beneath the collar of her coat.

The innocent touch made her catch her breath and work to hold back a shiver of delight. Determined to ignore the reaction the slightest touch or look from Tom stirred in her, she yanked on her gloves with more force than necessary. "You're lucky he didn't make you walk all the way into town this morning."

"He threatened, but after I talked Mama into making his favorite breakfast and helped with the chores, he was in a forgiving mood."

Lila laughed. "Nothing like buttering him up to get your way, is there?"

"Will a little buttering work on you to get my way?" he whispered, leaning close to her ear and enveloping her in his warmth.

Despite the teasing tone of his voice, Lila knew there was a world of emotion behind his words. Everything in her wanted to turn around and kiss him, but that would never do. Not at all.

Tamping down her yearning to be in Tom's arms, she wrapped a scarf around her neck and changed the subject. "What were you doing out at the farm last night? You usually stay in town until Friday."

"I had something I needed to discuss with my parents. Rather than walk back in the dark and cold, Mama talked me into spending the night there. It was nice. We played games and ate popcorn until we couldn't keep our eyes open."

Lila smiled, handing Tom the empty tin of candy he'd brought as a treat for the children. They'd eaten every last piece. "What did you play?"

"Dominoes, cards, and a rousing game of *Lost in the Woods*." Tom smirked and shrugged into his coat. "Mama likes to play the game, although it isn't my favorite."

"Oh, I love that game, with the colorful roads and the interesting places like the spring and the bridge. Who won?"

The light in his eyes as he smiled made Lila's knees feel weak. "Mama, of course. All three times we played it."

Lila giggled. "Did you boys let her win?"

"No, ma'am. We did not. She'd pitch a fit if she thought we let her win." Tom picked up his hat and leather satchel in his left hand then looked around to make sure the church had been set to rights after the children's practice.

"Good for her," Lila said, picking up a basket with her things and settling it over her arm. "You'll be at the Christmas carnival tomorrow, won't you?"

"I wouldn't miss it," Tom said. "Alex is still planning to do her magic show. I might be jealous she replaced me as her assistant if it was anyone other than Arlan."

"You were her assistant?" Lila asked, slowly moving toward the door. As soon as she stepped outside, she had to return to the reality where Emerson waited for her at Granger House.

"I was. She even let me wear her father's fancy suit and a top hat to perform. I outgrew them after the first two years I helped her, but it was fun while it lasted." Tom studied her as they lingered at the door. "How are you doing, Lila. You just don't seem quite like yourself the last week. Are you sure you're well?"

Tom's concern touched something deep inside her because she knew it was genuine. Oh, her family loved her, cared about, assured her safekeeping, but part of her felt as though Tom understood her in a way no one else could.

"I'm fine, Tom, but thank you for asking." Surprise shone from her eyes when he tugged off his glove and raised a hand to cup her cheek. For a moment, her lashes lowered as she allowed herself to indulge in the joy of his caress.

"I just want you to be happy, Lila Lilac. You still seem rather blue."

Blue.

Emerson had foisted more than three blue gowns upon her. Lila mused that his very presence had somehow stolen her inner sunshine and left her adrift in a turbulent sea of uncertainty. Perhaps when they returned to New York she'd feel differently. Ginny and Filly had both warned her that romance fairly danced in the air in

Hardman during the holiday season. That had to be the reason she felt so attracted to Tom.

However, if that notion held true, she reasoned her affections for Emerson should have multiplied instead of stretched to the very edge of their limits.

Emerson hadn't done a thing wrong, other than ignore her dislike of blue attire. In truth, he'd been wonderful, eager to please, and unfailingly kind. Yet, Lila found his presence more of an aggravation than a blessing.

Dismayed by her thoughts, she looked at Tom with a forced smile. "I'm well, Tom."

"I still don't believe you. However, the polite thing to do is to nod in agreement and pretend I don't know otherwise."

Lila giggled. "Tom Grove, the things you say! Why, your..."

The door opened and Emerson strode inside. "There you are, my darling. Luke arrived home with Maura, so I thought I'd escort you back to Granger House. Good afternoon, Mr. Grove." Emerson tipped his head to Tom.

Politely, Tom returned his greeting then gave Lila one last lingering look. "Have a wonderful evening, Miss Granger. I'll see you tomorrow."

Lila watched him leave, unaware of Emerson watching her. Finally pulling her thoughts back to her fiancé, she looped her arm around his. "Did you have a nice afternoon, Emerson?"

"I did, dearest. I availed myself of Luke's big desk in the library and wrote a number of letters, sent a wire to my parents, and offered my opinions on a batch of caramels Filly made."

"How were the caramels?" Lila asked, grinning at him, aware of how hard it was to resist Filly's confectionaries.

He tipped his hat to two women they passed on the boardwalk. "Delicious. She should sell them in one of those exclusive candy shops you like to frequent at home. Filly is a wonder in the kitchen."

"The wonder is how she gets anything done with three youngsters underfoot." Lila waved to Ginny Stratton as she stepped out of the newspaper office across the street.

"Three youngsters?" Emerson appeared puzzled. "Is there one I don't know about?"

Lila shot him a teasing look. "I included Luke. My cousin is hardly better than an overgrown child when it comes to sweets and staying out of Filly's way in the kitchen."

Emerson chuckled. "True, but it keeps things lively." The handsome man sobered and drew Lila to a stop outside the gate leading up the walk to Granger House. "I know you'll miss your family when we return to New York, Lila. I promise we'll visit them from time to time."

"Thank you, Emerson. I appreciate your understanding. They are such fun, I will greatly miss being around them. It's been good for me to be here the last few months."

He gave her a long, thoughtful look. "You seem more like yourself, like you've found your joy in life again. I'm so glad, Lila. I want whatever makes you happy, and if that means we make a trip to Hardman once or twice a year, then so be it."

A lump lodged in Lila's throat. How could she think anything ill of Emerson when he was such a good man? Convicted by her less than charitable thoughts toward him, she stood on tiptoe and kissed his cheek. "Thank you, Emerson. I'm sure at least Dora and Greg will come to New York to visit, too."

He grinned, eyes twinkling with mirth. "More than likely Dora will have to come to New York if she has any hope of purchasing new hats. I'm sure everyone around here has better sense than to make such monstrosities."

A giggle escaped her as she thought of Dora's odd collection of hats, none of them particularly appealing but all conversation-worthy. "I'll remind her of that if I get lonesome and want them to visit."

Although he wasn't one given to displays of affection where anyone might see, Emerson wrapped his arms around Lila and held her close. "Oh, Lila, my love, you'll make our home such a happy place to be. I think we should move the wedding date up from the spring and wed in February. Will that give you and Mother plenty of time for planning our wedding?"

"I suppose so," Lila muttered against the soft fabric of Emerson's coat. Her mind spun in a hundred directions, all of them refusing to settle on a wedding date. When she thought of standing at the front of a church and exchanging vows with the man she loved, she pictured herself in the church in Hardman with Chauncy officiating. Perhaps, she could talk Emerson into returning to Hardman for the wedding.

The folly of her thoughts caught up with her as she envisioned Emerson's parents and their friends traveling to the small town for a simple wedding. It would never happen, no matter how much she might like it to.

"Come on, darling, let's get you inside," Emerson said, releasing her, then cupping her elbow in his hand, guiding her toward the front door.

Throughout dinner, Lila remained subdued and distracted by her thoughts. Blake, Ginny, Dora and Greg were there, making for a lively atmosphere, but Lila didn't want to be part of the animated conversations.

Rather than join the family in the parlor after dinner, she used the excuse of having a headache and retiring to her room. In truth, her head did ache, mostly from her thoughts relentlessly traveling between Tom and Emerson, New York and Hardman.

She flopped down on her bed and curled up around one of the pillows, clutching it to her chest like a lifeline.

Before she could stop them, great sobs wracked through her. She buried her face in a pillow and let the tears she'd bottled up for so long fall. A dam of emotion burst free and she cried. She cried for the loss of her parents. She cried for the young innocent girl she used to be who had to suddenly grow up and deal with harsh reality. She cried for the ache in her heart caused by her inability to decide if she should allow herself to love Tom or remain loyal to Emerson. Torn by her affection for the two men, she wanted to make them both happy. No matter what or whom she chose, someone would end up with a broken heart.

A gentle hand on her back caused her to suck in a big gulp of air. She sat up and looked into the understanding face of Filly.

The woman held out a handkerchief and took a seat on the bed next to her. Lila mopped her face and drew in a shaky breath.

"What's wrong, Lila? And don't tell me you have a headache. I think the only one who believed that was Emerson." Filly rubbed a comforting circle on Lila's back as she spoke.

"I just needed some time alone," Lila said, wiping her eyes again. The tears she'd held back so long refused to cease trailing down her cheeks.

"We all need time alone. I'll go if you want me to," Filly said, studying Lila. "Sometimes, we just need a listening ear to share our problems."

Lila's lip quivered and she nodded her head as tears gushed from her eyes with renewed force. "Why is it so hard?" she asked between sobs.

Filly held her and let her cry, offering soothing words. When the storm subsided, Lila sat back and again mopped at her face.

"What's so hard, Lila? What made you so upset?" Filly continued to keep a hand on Lila's back, lending the girl strength.

"It's Emerson... and Tom... and leaving... and staying and... everything!"

Filly hid a smile as Lila continued dabbing at her cheeks with the soggy handkerchief. Filly opened the dresser drawer where she knew Lila kept her handkerchiefs and pulled out two, handing one to the distraught girl.

Once Lila wiped her face and blew her nose, Filly tried again. "What upset you, Lila? Did Tom or Emerson say or do something? And what's this about staying?"

Lila sniffled and knotted the handkerchief in her hand, twisting it into a tight little rope. "Tom and Emerson are both wonderful and neither of them has done anything but be kind and caring and..." Tears threatened to spill again, so Lila took a deep breath, then another. "They haven't done anything. It's just that I care for them both a great deal and I don't..."

"You don't know which direction to turn, is that it? The feelings you have for both of them has you torn between returning to New York with Emerson and staying here with Tom. Is that correct?" Filly asked with great insight into Lila's problems and the girl's heart.

Lila nodded and dabbed at her nose. "I just don't know what to do. Up until Tom arrived in town, I didn't give a single thought to remaining here or doing anything other than returning to New York to marry Emerson."

"But..." Filly coaxed, knowing there was much more to the story.

"But now, after spending time with Tom, after becoming his friend, I don't want to leave." Lila turned to Filly with a stricken look on her face. "How can I feel this way? It's not fair to Tom or Emerson to be so undecided about what to do or who to love."

Filly gave her a knowing look. "Oh, I think you know, deep in your heart, who you love. The question is, will you allow yourself to follow your heart. Only you can decide, Lila. You'll only ever know true happiness if you give your heart what it wants. Be certain, without a single speck of doubt about your decision, before you do anything rash. Listen to what your heart is telling you, Lila, not your head."

Lila looked at Filly with a watery smile. "So hiding out in my room until Emerson returns to New York and Tom goes back to Portland isn't the best decision?"

Filly laughed. "I should say not. You'll miss the Christmas carnival, the children's program, not to mention Christmas Eve services and Christmas Day. I happen to know you don't want to miss Christmas Day. Saint Nicholas might bring you something special."

"I don't think a ninny like me deserves anything special," Lila said, taking a cleansing breath.

"On the contrary, you deserve all the happy, wonderful things life sends your way, dear girl. Just be open to accepting the gifts with grace. You might be surprised by what you receive." Filly gave Lila a hug around her shoulders.

Lila squeezed Filly's hand and stood. "Are we still talking about Christmas presents or something else?"

"A little of both," Filly smiled and rose to her feet. "Just think about what I said, Lila. This is one time you should most definitely ignore reason and race in the direction your heart leads."

"If I didn't know better, I'd accuse you of reading those love stories Ginny enjoys so much."

Filly laughed as she walked to the door. "Maybe I have."

Lila watched her leave then took a seat in the plush chair across the room. She pulled her feet up beneath her skirt and hugged her knees, resting her cheek against them.

She had much to think about and wanted, more than anything, to decide what path her heart urged her to take.

Chapter Twenty-One

Tom smiled at his mother as they strode up the walk to Greg and Dora Granger's imposing home. Garlands draped the porch balustrades, accented with cheery red bows. Two big wreaths hung on the front doors and the sound of cheerful voices blended in an energetic harmony from inside the house.

Before James had an opportunity to knock on the door, it swung open and a butler greeted them with a formal bow.

"Christmas tidings to you all, Mr. and Mrs. Grove, and Tom," the man said with a friendly nod.

"Happy Christmas tidings to you, Mr. Callard," Junie said, smiling as they stepped inside the beautiful home.

"Allow me to take your coats. Guests are mingling in the parlor, the library, and upstairs in the ballroom. Mrs. Guthry will begin her magic show at precisely eleven. She wished to do it before we dine this year."

"She mentioned that the other day," Junie said, giving James a warm smile as he helped her remove her coat. "I'm always more than happy to watch her perform, regardless of the time."

Tom shrugged out of his and they handed their coats to the butler.

Mr. Callard smiled and bowed then handed their coats to one of the younger servants who hovered nearby. "Enjoy the Christmas carnival," the man said.

"Oh, we will, Mr. Callard," James said, placing a hand at the small of Junie's back and urging her toward the parlor. Tom spoke with a few friends and neighbors, glancing around for Lila. He saw Emerson deep in conversation with the owner of one of the outlying ranches, but she was nowhere in sight.

He made his way out of the room and down the hall toward the kitchen. Women laughed and talked as they bustled around the expansive room under Filly's capable direction. Although he hoped to find Lila there, she wasn't among those in the room. He peeked into the room being used as a nursery but she wasn't admiring the babies.

Highly doubting he'd find her in the library where many of the men preferred to gather before the festivities began, he made his way upstairs to the ballroom.

Arlan struggled to set up a heavy paneled prop on the stage where Alex would soon perform.

Tom rushed over to help him.

"Thanks, Tom. I wasn't certain if I was on the winning end of things for a moment." Arlan grinned at him. "How does this day find you?"

"Well, thank you. How are you and Alex?" Tom asked, setting the brace that would hold the prop upright.

"Alex is feeling well today. Late morning and early evening seem to be the times of day when she feels the best, so that's why we decided to move the time of her performance." Arlan opened a box that contained a number of props for Alex's magic tricks and removed a few, setting them on a nearby table.

Tom helped him, looking at him in concern. "Will Alex be able to return to teaching in January?"

"That is the hope, although I'm not certain how she'll manage. Most days, she requires an afternoon nap. Then there is the matter of her sickness. Sometimes it lasts all day, not just in the morning." Arlan noticed the worry creasing Tom's brow and thumped him on the back. "Don't worry about it, Tom. I'm sure everything will work out just fine."

"I hope so, sir." Tom helped Arlan set out the remainder of the props then glanced around the room. A few people lingered at the back, but Lila wasn't among them. He looked over at Arlan. "You haven't, by chance, seen Lila Granger, have you?"

Arlan grinned. "As a matter of fact, she's at our house helping my wife with her costume. Alex hasn't worn a costume for a while and had a slight problem getting one on in her... condition. Lila volunteered to help her since Abby has all she can handle right now."

"Yes, Mrs. Dodd seems to be quite..." Tom searched for an appropriate description. "Miserable."

Arlan nodded in agreement. "That she does." He leaned closer to Tom. "In fact, if that baby doesn't arrive before the new year, I'll eat my wife's top hat."

Tom grinned. "I'd bet on that if I didn't happen to agree."

A chuckle rolled out of Arlan. He placed a hand on Tom's shoulder and gave him a nudge toward the door. "Would you mind running over to our place and seeing if Alex is about ready? She wanted to sneak up the back stairs rather than do a grand entry through the front. Could you help make that happen, Tom?"

"I sure can, Arlan. Leave it to me." Tom hurried downstairs and didn't even bother with his coat. Rather, he jogged along the boardwalk, cut over two streets, crossed Main, and rounded a corner to arrive at the Guthry home.

A tap on the door was met with muffled voices then Lila swung it open.

Surprise registered on her face as she stared at him. "What are you doing here?"

Tom grinned. "Arlan sent me to fetch Alex the Amazing and escort her up the back stairs to the stage.

"Oh," Lila said, stepping aside so Tom could enter.

Alex appeared pale and wan as she desperately tugged on the buttons of an elaborately embroidered waistcoat, attempting to force it closed. "It's no use. I simply can't fasten them."

Tom bit back his amusement in the matter and studied Alex. "Do you have a long length of narrow ribbon, something that will match your costume?"

Alex gave him a puzzled glance, but nodded. "I think there's a piece of ribbon in my sewing basket, there by the rocker."

Lila hurried to upend the basket and retrieved a long piece of red ribbon.

Tom pointed to Alex's waistcoat. "Thread it back and forth through the button holes then around the buttons, like you would a…" He stopped himself. It wouldn't do at all to refer to a corset in front of either woman.

Alex and Lila both stared at him.

"Shoe lace."

Lila hurried to lace up the front of Alex's waistcoat then tied a bow at the top. She stepped back and critically eyed her work. "I think that will do quite nicely. Thank you, Tom, for that brilliant suggestion." She smiled at Alex. "What else do you need?"

"My cloak and hat. Arlan already took over the rest of my things."

Alex appeared woozy and grasped the back of a chair for support. Tom hurried to her side. "Are you sure you feel up to performing, Alex? You can cancel if you want to."

"No, I can do this," she said, taking a deep breath and reaching in her pocket for a peppermint. She popped it in her mouth and sucked on the candy.

"Does peppermint help?" Tom asked, taking Alex's cloak from Lila and draping it around the woman's shoulders.

"I'm not sure if it does or not, but I like to think it might." She settled her hat on her head at a jaunty angle and strode to the door. Tom held Lila's coat while she slipped it on and together, they flanked Alex as they walked to Greg and Dora's home.

Lila took them around to a back entrance and up the servant's stairs to the second floor. By sneaking down a hallway Tom didn't even know existed, they entered the ballroom from the back and Alex walked into Arlan's arms as he waited for her.

The volume of those waiting to watch Alex perform increased as more and more people filled the ballroom.

"Are you well, dear lady?" Arlan asked, leaning back to look into Alex's face.

"Well enough, Arlan. I'll have plenty of time to rest after the performance. You can coddle me all you like then."

Tom turned away to hide his amusement at Arlan's fussing over his wife. If he was this concerned now, he wondered what the man would be like when Alex reached the advanced stages of her pregnancy. As he considered the amusement Arlan's behavior would provide, Tom wondered if his father would act any differently when Junie reached her due date. He hoped he was around to see for himself, since Alex and his mother were due near the same time.

Alex moved away from Arlan and surveyed the props, set up just as she wanted them. "Shall we put on a magic show?"

"We shall." Arlan kissed her cheek then motioned to Tom and Lila. "Would you two mind announcing the show is about to begin?"

"Of course," Lila said, taking Tom's arm and stepping from behind the curtain out onto the stage. People filled the ballroom, excitement on their faces as they waited for Alex to perform.

Lila tried multiple times to get their attention, but the noise level was so high, no one heard her. Finally, Tom leaned down and told Lila to cover her ears. When she did, he emitted an ear-splitting whistle that immediately silenced everyone in the room.

"Go ahead, Lila," he said, giving her a nudge forward.

"Ladies and gentlemen, Alex the Amazing is ready to bring you phantasmagorical feats of spellbinding wonder and prestidigitation," Lila said, smiling at those gathered in the ballroom. "If you'll please be seated, the show is about to begin."

People poured into the ballroom, lining the edges of the room. Youngsters crowded around the stage, taking seats on the floor. Luke waved to Lila and she tugged Tom along with her, sitting down next to her cousin.

Tom took a seat next to her then reached forward and squeezed his father's shoulder. "I hoped you two had good seats."

James turned to his son and smiled. "We made sure to get seats early. I wouldn't want to miss one of Alex's shows."

"I'm excited to see this one," Tom said. He glanced over at Lila as anticipation added a happy glow to her face. Delighted to see she wore a silver-toned gown that matched her eyes, he found himself admiring the curve of her cheek, the determined set of her chin, the lush richness of her dark hair.

Lila Granger was a beautiful, intelligent, fun-loving woman. One he desperately wanted to claim as his own.

Thoughts of her fiancé made him glance around. Finally, he spied Emerson talking with the owner of the lumberyard near the door. Extremely pleased there wasn't room for Emerson to join them in their row of chairs, Tom draped his arm across the back of Lila's seat and leaned a little closer to her, inhaling her spring-like scent.

Lila laughed at Luke and smacked his arm. "You are hopeless, Luke Granger. The only reason you suggested Arlan ask me to introduce her was so you could beg me to use phantasmagorical and prestidigitation in the announcement."

"Guilty as charged," Luke said with a broad grin. "I can't help it if those are exceptionally fine words. Don't you agree, Tom?"

Tom nodded. "They are fun, Lila Lilac. Don't be so hard on Luke. It's not every day he can work those into more than once sentence."

Lila laughed and gave Luke an amused expression before turning to face the stage as the show began.

Alex, with Arlan's assistance, offered a show that left her audience awed. In fact, at one point in the performance, Tom was sure a pin could have bounced on the floor and everyone would have heard it.

Arlan and Alex came out on the stage to take a final bow. Alex cupped a hand around her ear and gave Arlan a questioning glance. "Do you hear that, Mr. Guthry?"

"What is it, Alex the Amazing?" Arlan asked, acting as though he strained to hear.

"I think it might be sleigh bells," Alex said, pointing toward the back of the room.

A large man dressed as Saint Nicholas entered the room, carrying a heavy pack over one shoulder and made his way up to the stage.

Children cheered and crowded around as he gave each one of them a small sack full of nuts and candy.

When he finished, Luke bounded up to the stage and invited everyone to return downstairs for lunch. Tom helped Luke close the curtains so Douglas from the livery could remove the Saint Nicholas costume. Alex plopped down in the chair Arlan slid beneath her a moment before her legs gave way beneath her.

"Alex, do you want me to take you home?" Arlan asked, concerned.

She shook her head. "No. Just give me a few moments to rest. I don't want to miss hearing you play in the band." Her gaze lifted to her husband's. "Aren't you supposed to be down there playing right now?"

"Yes, but I'm not leaving you until I'm certain you're well."

Alex smiled and sat up. "Go on, Arlan. I'm fine and even if I wasn't, Doc is here, so there is nothing for you to worry about. Go play that trumpet. I'll be there in a moment to listen."

Arlan kissed her cheek then raced out of the room.

Lila hurried over and fanned Alex's top hat in front of the woman's pale face. "Are you sure you don't want us to take you home, Alex?"

"No. I really do want to hear Arlan play. If I can make it to the parlor, I'll be fine."

Tom gave Alex a hand and she stood. Lila preceded her down the stairs, hiding the fact that Alex was unsteady on her feet as Tom and Luke flanked the magician, helping her down the stairs and into the parlor. Ginny motioned for Alex to sit next to her on a comfortable sofa. Filly appeared and gave Alex a cup of tea, patted her on the shoulder, then disappeared back down the hall to the kitchen.

Chauncy's booming voice carried throughout the house as he asked a blessing on the meal then people began filing through the line in the dining room to fill their plates at the massive table loaded with food everyone contributed for the community lunch.

In the milling crowd, Tom quickly lost track of Lila. Ducking into the dining room, he found his parents filling plates and visiting with friends. Hungry, he decided to find Lila after lunch because he had something important to say to her.

Determined to follow his mother's advice, he wanted Lila's opinion on the possibility of him purchasing the newspaper from Ed Daily. Tom spent several hours devising a plan to pay Ed half the money up front and make payments on the rest. If he lived frugally, Tom could make it work. Nevertheless, the idea would hold much greater appeal if Lila would agree to stay in Hardman with him.

Before the day was over, he planned to propose to her.

Tom caught a glimpse of Emerson speaking to Aleta and George Bruner. His competition for Lila's hand was a fine man, one Tom might even consider a friend under other circumstances.

As it was, he couldn't help but see Emerson as a rival. One he wanted to best, not for the sake of winning but because he loved Lila with his whole heart.

Tom couldn't imagine how dismal and horrible life would be if Lila did return to New York with Emerson. The thought brought such an onslaught of pain to his chest, Tom had to draw in several breaths to chase it away.

Wandering into the parlor, he saw Lila sitting on the floor next to Ginny. Carefully making his way through the crowd, he took a seat beside her.

"Did you already eat?" he asked, pointing to his plate.

Lila shook her head. "No. I snitched a few bites in the kitchen."

Tom tried to hand his plate to her, but she refused. "Go on and take it, Lila. I can fill another."

"No, Tom, you eat. I'll get something later," she said, bumping his shoulder with hers. "A growing boy like you needs his strength, right?"

The teasing smile she shot his way zipped straight to his heart and exploded with a shower of warmth.

He forked a bite and held it out to her. She took it and licked her upper lip. Tom's gaze fused to her mouth as he recalled how delicious her kisses had tasted. How he wanted to taste them again, to savor the sweet ripeness that was solely Lila Granger.

But the middle of her family's home during the town's annual Christmas carnival wasn't the time or place to do such a thing.

As he shared his food with her, his mind spun, plotting a way to get her alone to declare his intentions and confess his love.

Once most everyone had eaten, Luke and Blake began the annual charity auction. Each year, the children made items to donate to the auction and the funds went to help those in need in town.

Tom had participated in the auction as a student. Now, as the teacher who oversaw many of the projects, he took pride in the clever abilities of his students. Everything from a wooden nativity set to a lacy apron sat on a table, waiting to be auctioned.

Lila rose up on her knees, anxious to see all the children's creations.

"Oh, look at that," she said, placing her hand on Tom's arm when Luke held up a roughly carved shepherd boy with a lamb.

Tom enjoyed watching the emotions flit across Lila's face as much as he did the students as people bid on their items. Tom knew he couldn't bid on anything because it wouldn't seem fair, but he'd coached his parents on a particular item that had caught his interest. A shawl, made by one of the older girls, in a lovely shade of lavender, reminded him of Lila and he'd decided she needed to have it.

Fortunately, the bidding stayed within his budget and his father claimed the item, giving Tom a pointed look, although everyone assumed the man bought it for Junie.

Tom watched as his father turned right around and bid on a yellow scarf that would match Junie's fair complexion. He cheered loudly when his father won that bid as well.

"Give the rest of us a chance, James," one of their neighbors good-naturedly teased.

"Dig a little deeper in your pockets, Peters," James said with a cocky smile.

Lila almost sat on her hands to keep from bidding when a picture Maura Granger drew went up for bid. Of course, the little girl's doting grandfather claimed he had to have it and paid an unheard of amount for it, but everyone clapped and cheered as Maura hugged Greg Granger.

The auction was just winding down when Horace Greenblum from the telegraph office raced in as fast as is bandy legs could carry him. Instead of quietly finding the intended recipient of the telegram, he climbed on a chair and shouted "message for Emerson Lylan. It's urgent!"

Emerson rose from where he sat by Douglas McIntosh and hurried over to retrieve it. Quickly scanning the message, he frantically looked around the room, as though he suddenly recalled Lila's presence. She was already on her feet, making her way to him along with the rest of the Granger family and Tom.

"What is it, Emerson? What's happened?" Lila placed a hand on his arm, staring at him with compassionate concern.

"It's my father. He slipped on the ice. It says he broke his leg and suffered a head injury. Mother wants us to journey home right away." Emerson glanced from Lila to Luke. "If we hurry, can we make the evening train in Heppner?"

"Just barely. I'll hitch the team to the sleigh while you pack," Luke said, racing outside with Blake accompanying him.

Emerson took Lila's elbow in his hand, propelling her out of the room toward the front entry. "Will you be ready to leave in fifteen minutes?" he asked, glancing down at Lila. "Please, Lila? I need you to go with me."

"Of course, Emerson. I'll gather a few essentials and be ready to leave. Filly and Luke will ship the rest of my things later."

"I'll be at Granger House as quickly as I pack. It will only take a few minutes." He kissed her cheek then charged up the grand staircase, taking them two at a time to the guestroom where he'd stayed since arriving in Hardman.

Mr. Callard appeared with Lila's coat, holding it while she slipped it on.

As she tugged on her gloves, she looked over the faces around her. "Thank you all for your hospitality, making me feel like a true member of the community here in Hardman. It was a pleasure to meet each one of you. May the joys of the holiday season rest tenderly in your hearts throughout the coming year." Lila spun around and sailed out the door.

Rooted to the floor, Tom watched her go while his dreams for a happy future crashed around him. She was really going to leave. With Emerson.

A nudge to his back made Tom turn around and look at his mother. "Don't stand there like an idiot, Tom, go after her. If you want that girl, you need to fight for her." Junie pointed her finger in the direction of the door.

The butler tossed Tom his coat as he raced to the entry and down the front porch steps. He shoved his arms in the sleeves as he ran to Granger House.

Desperate to talk to Lila, he hurried around to the back door and knocked loudly. When no one answered, he opened it and stepped inside. "Lila? Lila! It's Tom!"

Drawers slammed with enough force the noise carried down the hall. Tom followed the sound through the kitchen and along the back hallway. "Lila?" he called again.

Her face appeared around the edge of a doorway at the end of the hall. "Tom? What are you doing here?"

"I couldn't let you leave without saying goodbye."

She waggled her hand at him, motioning for him to come into the room. He realized it was highly improper for him to be in her bedroom, but considering the fact she frantically packed a bag to leave and he may never see her again, he didn't give it more than a passing thought.

Hastily, she stuffed a few articles of clothing into an expensive leather bag. "I'm so glad you came, Tom. Emerson's request I go with him caught me unawares and I realized after I left I didn't even take time to speak to you." She snapped the lid closed on her bag and picked up a dark coat and hat.

Tom lifted the bag and followed her to the front entry. After he set it by the door, he took the coat and hat from her hands, setting them aside before grasping her arms, forcing her to stand still for a moment. "Lila."

She lifted her silvery eyes to his. Tears brimmed beneath her dark lashes and her lip quivered, making pain throb in his heart.

He pulled her to his chest and buried his face in her fragrant hair. "Please don't go, Lila. I want you to stay. Mr. Daily offered to sell me the newspaper. If you stay, I'll figure out a way to buy it and move back to town. We can build a good life here, in Hardman."

Lila pulled back and stared at him. "What are you saying, Tom Grove?"

A smile started at his mouth and worked its way up to his eyes. "I'm saying I love you, Lila Angelique Granger and want to marry you. Don't leave. Stay here, Lila Lilac. Stay with me and be my wife. I may not have a fancy education or a lot of money, but I love you with all my heart and then some. I'd give you a happy life."

"Oh, Tom, I…" The lump in Lila's throat kept her from speaking what was on her heart, so she rose up on her toes and kissed Tom with all the love she'd harbored for him the past several weeks.

The stamping of boots outside the door forced them apart. Before Tom quite knew what happened, Luke and Emerson stormed inside. Emerson draped Lila's coat around her and grabbed her hat while Luke took her bag. They herded her outside to the waiting sleigh.

Lila glanced back at him, so Tom raced down the steps, intent on stopping them.

Emerson settled Lila in the sleigh and climbed in beside her. He held out a hand to Tom. "Thank you for your friendship, Mr. Grove. We both wish you well in all your future endeavors."

Woodenly, Tom shook Emerson's outstretched hand and gave the man a stiff nod of acknowledgement. Shocked speechless by the fact Lila really was leaving, he started to take a step back.

Lila grasped Tom's hand in hers, squeezing it so tightly he thought his fingers might break. "Be happy, Tom," she whispered.

"That's not possible without you," he replied and took an envelope from his coat pocket, shoving it into her hands as Luke snapped the reins and the sleigh lurched forward.

Lila turned in the seat and gave him one long, last, remorse-filled look before Luke guided the horse around a corner and she disappeared from sight.

Tom stood as still as stone for so long, his fingers and toes felt numb. Finally, Bart bumped against his leg, bringing him back to the present.

He brushed a hand over the dog's head and released a weary sigh.

"It looks like the battle is over, Bart, and I did not win."

Dejected, angry, and hurt, Tom walked off into the chilly afternoon air.

Chapter Twenty-Two

"Tom, you need to eat something," Junie said, placing a hand on her son's arm and offering a sympathetic squeeze. "I know you don't feel like it, but you have to keep your strength up."

He picked up his fork and shoved the food around on his plate. Since Lila left with Emerson the previous afternoon, Tom had fallen into a state of such despair, he couldn't see anything but a long, bleak future awaiting him.

Numb from the inside out, food tasted like sawdust, everything smelled unpleasant, and he couldn't even remember if he'd brushed his teeth or combed his hair before his parents insisted he go to church with them that morning.

Before anyone could offer sympathetic glances or words about Lila's abrupt departure, Junie and James hurried him back out to their wagon and returned home.

Tom spent the afternoon moping in the barn, only coming in for the evening because his father insisted he would freeze to death if he spent more time outside.

The nearly frostbitten state of his toes and fingers failed to register as he washed for supper and sullenly slid into his chair.

Tom replayed every moment from the point where he confessed his love to Lila to her staring at him as Luke's sleigh carried her away.

Her eyes said she loved him even if she failed to speak the words. Would she really marry Emerson because she'd already promised him they'd wed? Was she that concerned about her social status that she'd forsake love for a life of wealth and luxury? Tom didn't think that was something that would even cross Lila's mind. Unaffected by the things most people of her class would find important, Lila appeared to be a genuine, sweet, caring person.

Perhaps her caring heart drove her to go through with plans to wed Emerson. He'd certainly appeared thoroughly enamored with Lila, and Tom couldn't blame him. Not when he felt the same way.

Attempts to understand how she'd kissed him so feverishly, so passionately, when he confessed his love, and then turned around and left with another man, made his head throb. Each time he mulled over the possibilities, he grew angrier and more despondent.

He should never have come home for the holidays. Most certainly, he should not have allowed himself to fall in love with Lila Granger. His head told him it was pure folly from the start. He should have listened to it instead of allowing his heart to lead him on a merry chase that ended so painfully.

He'd been so sure, so absolutely convinced of Lila's affections for him, he never thought she'd actually leave.

But she had.

She'd left him standing in the snow with his heart bleeding in a ruptured, broken mess that might never heal.

"Please, Tom, just eat a few bites of something," Junie encouraged, casting James a worried glance. He shrugged then shook his head.

Tom took a bite of the chicken and dumplings just to make his mother happy.

After dinner, he sat in the parlor with his parents, largely ignoring their discussion about Christmas Eve the following day. With all that had happened over the last few days, they still needed to cut down a Christmas tree and decorate it.

Desperately, Tom wished he could fall asleep and wake up in his apartment in Portland with the past month nothing more than a horrible dream.

Only every moment of the last several weeks was real, including his stupidity of falling in love with another man's intended bride.

What was he thinking?

Clearly, he hadn't been.

Agitated, he paced around the room, fingering keepsakes, but not really seeing anything.

"Thomas James Grove, sit down before you wear a hole in my carpet," Junie demanded.

"Sorry, Mama," Tom said, returning to his seat by the fire.

James leaned forward from his spot next to Junie and thumped Tom on the leg. "Look, son, I can't pretend to know what you're going through. I don't. And I'm so sorry about what happened with Lila. We encouraged you to pursue her, so we feel partially at fault. But for the sake of the children who are so excited about Christmas and the program tomorrow night, a program you are now solely in charge of, you have to pull yourself together."

Tom sighed and ran a hand through his short hair. "I know, Dad. It's just hard. I was so sure she'd stay when I asked her to marry me."

"You proposed to her and she still left?" The knitting needles in Junie's hands stilled. "What did she say?"

Another sigh rolled out of Tom and he stared into the flames of the fire. "I asked her to stay, to stay and marry

245

me. She kissed me, then the next thing I knew, Emerson herded her outside to the sleigh and she was gone."

"She kissed you?" James said, glancing at Junie.

"Yes, but she didn't say anything. Not a word."

"I see," Junie said, a faint smile lingering around her mouth as she returned to knitting a soft pink blanket.

Tom glared at her. "What do you see, Mama? Because all I see is that she didn't care enough about me to even dignify my proposal with a reply."

"Maybe she was too overcome to answer and before she could, Emerson whisked her away."

A derisive snort escaped Tom. "Have you both met Lila Granger? If she didn't want to go somewhere, there isn't a force on this earth that could make her. Emerson didn't drag her out to the sleigh like a cavedweller. She went willingly, of her own accord."

James patted Tom's leg then leaned back. "I know it hurts, Tom, more than anything you've ever experienced, but time really does heal all wounds and things will look better soon. I'm sure of it."

Tired of listening to his parents' encouragement, Tom went to his room and crawled into bed, spending restless hours wondering where Lila was and praying she'd at least be happy.

The following morning, James insisted Tom go with him to cut down a Christmas tree.

As they walked into the woods at the far end of their property, James kept up the bulk of the conversation. He talked about the crops he planned to plant in the spring, the things he wanted to update on the house before the baby's arrival, and asked Tom if he thought it would be possible to add a bathroom at the back of the house.

Tom stared at his father. "You're really thinking about adding indoor plumbing. With a bathtub and everything?"

"Everything," James said with a grin. "I don't want your mother to have to go through all the work of hauling water for a bath or traipsing out to the privy when the baby is close to due. She practically lived in the outhouse the last month before you were born and I don't want her to go through that again." James looked at Tom. "Do you think you might like to help me do the work?"

"If you let me know when you're planning to do it, I could probably arrange to take a few days away from work." Tom pointed to a grove filled with perfect-sized Christmas trees.

James gave him a long look. "Are you sure you don't want to take Ed Daily up on his offer? Your mother and I have some money set aside. We'd be happy to help you purchase the paper."

"I appreciate the offer, Dad, but all things considered, I think it best I go back to Portland. At least for now," Tom said, setting down the pack he'd carried on his back.

He removed a flask his mother filled with hot chocolate and handed it to his father. James took a swig then handed it back to him.

Tom took a drink before returning it the pack he'd carried. "Despite everything that happened, this trip home has reminded me how much I like being here and what a good community we have."

"Well, I'm glad to hear you got something good out of the last several weeks. I think the students at the school will be sad to see you leave, even though they love Alex. I wonder what will happen after she and Arlan become parents. I doubt she'll return to teaching." James took out an axe and motioned to a bushy tree. "Will this one do?"

Tom walked around the tree and shook his head. "Mama won't like bare branches on this side." He studied three other trees before choosing one. "This is the one."

"Stand back and let me at it," James said, wielding the axe and striking near the base of the tree.

Tom would have liked to get in a few chops just to work out some of his aggression, but it would most likely do damage to his healing arm.

After James felled the tree, they finished drinking the hot chocolate and ate a few cookies Junie sent along for their enjoyment. Tom tied a rope around the trunk of the tree and dragged it toward home while his father carried the axe.

They hadn't even made it up the porch steps before Junie opened the front door and excitedly rushed outside.

"Oh, it's beautiful! You two outdid yourselves this year." Junie kissed James' cold cheek as he settled a hand around her waist.

"You say that every year, June-bug," he said, stamping snow from his boots so they could carry the tree inside.

"I mean it every year," she said, giving him a hug. "It really is a marvelous tree."

"You'd say that if we brought home a stick that only had bare branches," Tom teased, bouncing the tree on the walk to shake the snow off the limbs.

Junie crossed her arms over her chest and glared at him. "I would not and you know it, smarty."

Tom grinned and hefted the trunk while his father lifted the tip of the tree, carrying it inside the house. Junie had a bucket of sand ready in a corner of the parlor to hold the tree.

When it stood straight, she added a few rocks to help keep it upright then poured water into the sand to keep the tree from drying out too quickly.

She took a deep breath and brushed her hands as she surveyed the tree. "It smells so good."

"That it does," James agreed, shrugging out of his coat.

An hour later, even Tom laughed as they decorated the tree. The ornaments they owned were not expensive or fancy, but they all held great sentimental value.

Tom fingered a little stuffed bear ornament his mother had made for him when he was about six. It wore an embroidered smile of red thread and a bright red bow around its neck.

"I see you found Bobo." Junie pointed to the bear.

"I did, Mama. It wouldn't be Christmas if he wasn't on the tree." Tom hung the ornament on a branch then reached for another. He lifted a heart-shaped ornament his father made by cutting a series of sticks in graduated lengths then gluing them together.

"Oh, my heart," Junie said, taking the ornament from Tom and placing it on a branch with loving care. "We've had that one since our very first Christmas together."

"Well, we couldn't afford much more than sticks and glue that first year," James said, wrapping his arms around Junie's waist and kissing her neck. "Things have changed a lot, haven't they, June-bug?"

"They have, Jimmy, so much, but I wouldn't trade anything for the experiences that brought us to where we are today." She turned and smiled at her husband, giving him a light kiss.

Tom rolled his eyes and feigned disgust although it pleased him to see his parents so much in love.

He'd planned to spend his life loving Lila and envisioned being just as enthralled with her twenty years down the road as he was now.

Only, that was not meant to be.

Aware of the maudlin mood about to settle over him, he forced away thoughts of the beguiling girl and instead asked his mother to tell him about some of the ornaments on the tree. He knew the story behind each one, but Junie loved reminiscing and Tom gratefully embraced the distraction her stories provided.

If he hoped to make it through the holidays with his sanity intact, he'd have to seek out every distraction he could find.

Chapter Twenty-Three

"Mr. Grove?" Maura Granger tugged on the hem of Tom's suit coat, gazing up at him with pale green eyes.

"What is it, Maura?" he asked, hunkering down and smiling at the adorable little imp.

"Is it time?" she asked, referring to the children's program. To keep the children from restless anticipation of their performance, Chauncy agreed to schedule the program before the Christmas Eve service started. Without the addition of live animals, it simplified things immensely. Although, the rascal wearing the donkey costume was determined to wear holes in the knees of it before the program ever started by crawling around the floor and kicking out his hind legs with a sound that vaguely resembled a donkey's bray.

Tom had given up trying to get the boy to sit still and moved him to the end of the stage where he wouldn't cause damage to the props or fellow actors in the performance.

"It's almost time, Maura," Tom pretended to tug on her nose, making the child grin.

She leaned against him and sighed. "I miss Lila," she said. Her lip puckered into a pout.

"Me, too, but she'd want us to have fun tonight, don't you think?" Tom hugged the little girl.

Maura nodded and pointed to where one of the shepherds got into a shoving match with the sheep.

"Stay here, Maura," Tom said, rushing over to break up the two boys and restore order. Blake and Arlan stepped behind the curtain and helped get the children into their proper places. Dora volunteered to oversee the music and Ginny, from years of helping with the program, offered to fill in for Lila.

Percy Bruner and Anna Jenkins did their best to keep the younger children occupied.

When Tom gave the signal they were ready, Filly Granger hurried behind the curtain and handed Anna her sleeping son. "Just don't set Cullen in the manger or drop him," she cautioned the girl.

Anna nodded, taking the safekeeping of the baby seriously. She held the infant close to her chest with Percy huddling beside her.

As Luke and Blake pulled back the curtain, the program began.

Erin Dodd stole the show when, in her role as an angel, she smacked one of the misbehaving wise men on the head with a pasteboard star she held in her hand.

Snickers and subdued chuckles echoed throughout the church. Tom had to work to keep a straight face as he and Ginny led the children through the remainder of the program.

Fred Decker, who won the camera the Bruner's gave away at the store, did his best to take a few photographs of the children in their costumes.

Cullen stretched and awakened just as Anna finished her last line. Unaccustomed to seeing her face, the baby let out a wail and fussed, effectively ending the program when Anna gave Filly a panicked look.

Filly took the baby and the audience joined in a hearty round of applause.

Tom waited until the children joined their parents in the audience before he took a seat next to Junie and James.

Chauncy moved behind his pulpit, one Blake had generously carved as a Christmas gift a few years prior, and ran his hand across the smooth wood before he cleared his throat and smiled at the congregation.

He delivered a heart-felt message of hope and love that left many dabbing moisture from their eyes.

"Will you all rise and join me in singing '*Hark the Herald Angels Sing*?'" Chauncy asked.

As the congregation blended their voices in the familiar carol, Tom was sure he picked out Lila's sweet, clear soprano, but that was impossible. She was probably halfway to New York by now.

They neared the end of the last verse when Percy Bruner stepped beside Chauncy and whispered something in his ear. The pastor grinned and nodded.

"Please be seated," Chauncy said, motioning the congregation to return to their seats. He led them in a brief, emotional prayer, then raised his gaze and grinned. "We have a unique request. Someone would like to sing a special song before we all leave this evening."

Chauncy took a seat next to Abby and lifted Erin on his lap as a beautiful voice sang from behind the curtain where the children had performed their program.

The love song, pouring out a promise of devotion to last a lifetime, wasn't what anyone expected, but the voice singing it was so beautiful, no one thought to dispute the appropriateness of it.

Afraid to dream, but filled with hope, Tom stood when Lila Granger moved from behind the curtain and continued singing. Her silvery gaze locked with his and he stepped into the aisle, rushing to her.

The last note of the song lingered in the air as he wrapped her in his arms and rained kisses on her face. Her hair hung down her back in a disheveled mess and her hands felt like ice, but she was there. She was really there, proclaiming her love in a way that left everyone in the church aware of her feelings for him.

"You came back," he said, lifting her up and whispering in her ear. "How did you get here? When did you get here?"

Lila laughed and leaned back, still held in his arms. "I woke up yesterday morning and realized what a mistake I'd made, especially after I read your poem, Tom." She held out a piece of parchment in her hand. "I should never have left. I'm sorry. Emerson agreed I needed to return to Hardman. I got off the train at the next stop and bought a return ticket. I missed the stage in Heppner, so I rented a horse at the livery and rode all the way here as fast as I could."

He breathed in her fragrance, soaked up her essence. "I'm so glad you came home, Lila Lilac."

Her heart was in her eyes when she bracketed his face with her hands. "I love you, Tom Grove, with all my heart, and if you haven't withdrawn your proposal, nothing would make me happier than being your wife."

"Oh, Lila," he groaned, kissing her in a way that made Chauncy clear his throat and many members of the congregation whistle and cheer in a boisterous manner.

Lila's face glowed as red as the holly berries decorating the front of the church when she pulled back, but she kept an arm wrapped around Tom when he finally set her on her feet.

He smiled at the congregation, his family, and friends. "In case you didn't figure it out yet, Miss Granger has agreed to be my bride."

More cheers and clapping filled the church. People surged forward to extend their well wishes.

Junie rushed up to them and engulfed them both in a hug. She pulled back and smiled at Lila. "What made you come back?"

"This," Lila said, handing Junie the sheet of paper.

Junie's hand went to her throat and she blinked back tears as she read the words her son had written to his sweetheart.

Beneath the frosty branches
Buried deep in winter's snow,
There lived an empty man
In a place no life could grow.

He wandered in the darkness,
A vessel dimmed by night,
Until the day he met
A sweet fairy made of light.

Her smile held summer sunshine,
Her lips a hint of dew,
Springtime lilted in her voice
And the lonely man then knew

One glimpse of silvery heaven,
One taste of succulent bliss,
Snow melted in the lilacs
Hope blossomed in her kiss

The fairy full of laughter
Would forever change his life,
If she returned his love
And vowed to be his wife.

"Oh, son," Junie gave Tom a watery smile. "No wonder Lila rode through the cold and snow to reach you."

"And I'd do it again in a heartbeat," Lila said, leaning against Tom. "I'm sorry I left, Tom. I should never have gone."

"I know," he said, kissing her chilled nose. "But the important thing is that you're here now, on one of the most blessed nights of the year."

The festive atmosphere carried through the next hour as they shared mulled cider, punch, cake and cookies in the church's basement.

Most everyone had left, anxious to return to their homes for Christmas Eve dinners, when Erin screamed. "Mama sprung a leak!" she yelled, pointing to a puddle at Abby's feet. "Mama's leaking!"

Chauncy clamored over chairs, knocking aside tables to reach his wife. "Is it time, Abby?" he asked, taking in her ashen skin and beads of perspiration dotting her upper lip.

"Yes," she panted, bracing both hands beneath her extended belly.

"Why didn't you say something earlier?" he demanded, wrapping his arm around her to offer support.

"Because you were in the midst of delivering a beautiful Christmas Eve service, that's why. We've got plenty of time before this little one will appear, but I'm ready to go home, Chauncy."

Luke ran for the doctor while Filly rushed next door to the parsonage to ready Abby's bed.

Lila found herself holding Cullen while Blake and Ginny herded Erin and Maura upstairs to put on their coats and take them to Granger House.

Tom glanced over at his parents and they nodded, understanding he wanted to stay with the Grangers.

"Please, Tom, ask your folks to come with us," Lila said, smiling at Junie and James as they approached.

"Mama, Dad, we're going to help keep an eye on the children. Would you like to join us at Luke and Filly's place?"

"We'd love to, son," James said.

Alex and Arlan stayed behind to set the church to rights so Chauncy wouldn't need to worry about coming back later.

Together, the Grove and Granger families prepared to leave. Junie held Cullen while Tom helped Lila slip on her coat, then they all strode down the boardwalk to Granger House. Tom ended up carrying Maura while Blake held a sobbing Erin.

"My mama's leaking to death," the child cried. "Why's she leaking?"

"She'll be fine, sweetheart. No need to carry on so," Blake said, rubbing the child's back. "Your mama is in good hands with Uncle Luke and Aunt Filly and Doc. They'll take good care of her. I promise."

Her sobs lessened to sniffles.

Blake kissed her cheek. "Do you remember watching my horse have a baby back in the spring?"

Erin nodded and scrubbed a hand across her eyes.

"The horse leaked, didn't she?"

Another nod.

"And both she and the baby were fine. So don't worry, Erin. Your Mama will be fine and you'll soon have that baby you've been eager to meet."

"I will?" Erin asked, leaning back to look at Blake.

By the time they reached Granger House, Erin had calmed considerably.

After divesting the two little girls of their coats, Ginny took them into the parlor to admire the towering fir tree.

Lila once again gave Cullen into Junie's keeping while she shrugged out of her coat. Tom caught her hand, concerned by how cold it felt.

"Before you do anything else, Lila, I think you best change your damp clothes," Tom said, giving her a nudge toward the hall. He kissed her cheek and offered her a warm smile. "I can't have my bride-to-be taking sick."

She returned his smile. "I thoroughly like the sound of being your bride, Tom. I'll be right back."

While she changed, Tom held the baby. Blake and Junie made hot tea and poured cups of milk for Erin and Maura.

Blake set everything on a big tray and carried it to the parlor. With slow, steady steps, Tom followed his parents down the hall as he held Cullen. He rather liked the feel of the little one in his arms and envisioned holding his own son someday, one with gleaming dark hair like Lila's and her silvery eyes.

Cullen remained asleep, much to everyone's relief. Once they settled in the parlor, Junie took the baby, rocking him as she sat by the fire.

"Well, we've had many interesting Christmas Eve experiences in the last several years," Blake commented, wrapping an arm around Ginny's shoulders and pulling her against his side.

"That's right. You two wed on Christmas Eve," Junie said, dragging her gaze away from the baby long enough to smile at them. "Happy anniversary."

"Thank you, Junie," Ginny said, grinning at her husband. "We all thought Arlan and Alex would wed on Christmas Eve, too, but they waited to see if Adam could make it. Then there was the Christmas Eve Toby's grandfather kidnapped him. Now, Miss Lila has ridden back into town and Tom's heart while Abby and Chauncy will welcome a new baby. What a wonderful way to welcome Christmas!"

"It is indeed wonderful," James said, smiling at his wife and the baby in her arms.

Tom saw the looks of love the two of them exchanged. By summer, they'd have their own baby to cuddle and hold. He looked forward to being there to spoil his baby sister, or brother.

Lila breezed into the room in a dark purple wool dress. Much to his dismay, she'd pinned all that lovely, shiny hair back up on her head instead of leaving it loose to tempt him.

She sat next to Tom, near the crackling fire. He took her hands in his and brought them to his lips, blowing warm air on them. "We need to get you warmed up, Lila Lilac, before you turn into an icicle."

Blake smirked. "I'm sure if we left you two alone in here for five minutes, you'd figure something out."

Lila blushed while Tom gave Blake a disparaging look. Just because thoughts of kissing Lila until they both reached a feverish level filled his mind, he didn't appreciate any comments along those lines.

James waggled his eyebrow at his son, making them all laugh.

Maura and Erin wandered over from where they'd been looking at the decorations on the Christmas tree and sank down on the floor by the table where Blake had placed the refreshments. The girls each took a cup of milk and a cookie, quietly eating their snack. When they finished, Ginny cupped Maura's chin in her hand.

"I think it's time to put you two to bed, or Saint Nicholas won't visit."

"I's not tired yet, Aunt Ginny," Maura said, battling to keep her eyes open.

"Of course you aren't," Ginny agreed, winking at Lila. "But it's time for bed just the same."

Weary, Erin rose and looked around. "May I go home to my mama and daddy?"

Lila pulled the little girl onto her lap and kissed her cheek. "You get to stay here tonight. Won't that be fun? You and Maura can share her bed and when you wake up, it will be Christmas!"

"But what if Saint Nicholas doesn't know where to find me?" Erin's lower lip rolled out in a pout. "What if my mama needs me?"

"Oh, your mama has all the help she needs right now," Lila said, hugging Erin close and kissing the top of her head. "As for Saint Nicholas, he always knows how to find good little boys and girls, no matter where they might be."

"Okay," Erin said. The child spoke without a speck of enthusiasm as her shoulders sagged.

Maura yawned and slumped against Ginny's side while Erin leaned into Lila.

Blake stood and lifted Erin in his arms while Lila picked up Maura. He held out a hand to help Ginny to her feet. "Let's get these girls ready for sleep so they can dream of sweet surprises."

While the three of them left to tuck the girls into bed, Tom smiled at his parents. "Just think, by this time next year, little Jamie will be here, all decked out in pink."

James shook his head. "I don't think my boy will be wearing pink."

"Our Jamie will be because Mama's having a girl," Tom said, winking at his mother. "You want a girl, too, and you can't deny it."

James laughed. "Girl or boy, makes no difference to me. We'll love the baby no matter what." He kissed the top of Junie's head. "You look mighty pretty sitting there in the firelight rocking that baby, June-bug. Makes me think of old times when Tom was that small."

"Are you sure I was ever that little?" Tom asked, kneeling next to the rocker and studying Cullen's tiny features.

"You sure were, Tom, and you had the longest eyelashes that fluttered on your cheeks like butterfly wings," Junie said, giving her son an adoring look. "I used to sit and hold you for hours, so in awe of the beautiful, precious gift God gave us in you."

"Aw, Mama, there you go getting all sentimental on me," Tom said, kissing her cheek.

"If you can talk Lila into marrying you soon, you could be well on your way to having your own baby to hold, Tom," James teased.

Tom grinned at him. "I don't know, Dad. Are you sure you can handle having a newborn and a grandchild close together. They won't know what to call you. Maybe we should start practicing by calling you gramps right now."

Junie laughed. "The boy does have a point, James. We could very well have a daughter and a grandson less than a year apart."

"I wouldn't mind. Since Tom has decided to stay in Hardman, those two kids could grow up like siblings." James thumped Tom on the back. "We're mighty happy Lila will be joining the family, and that you'll both stay in Hardman."

"Will you have to go back to Portland for a while, son?" Junie asked, shifting Cullen as the baby began to fuss.

"I figured I'd wire my boss after Christmas and let him know I don't plan to come back to work there. I will need to go to Portland to clear out my apartment, but I thought perhaps Lila would like to go with me and we could make it a honeymoon trip."

"That's a fabulous idea," Junie said, rising to her feet and rocking the baby in her arms, trying to get him to quiet down. "I think this one is hungry. Should we take him back to Filly?"

Lila hurried into the room. "I thought I heard him fussing. Filly has a few bottles prepared for emergencies. I'll warm one for him."

She returned a short while later with a bottle and flannel cloth that Junie draped over her shoulder. She fed the baby then lifted him to her shoulder, gently patting him on the back. His loud burp drew smiles from the adults.

"I guess that means he enjoyed his meal," Tom said, draping his arm around Lila's shoulders as she rested against his side. He pulled a throw off the end of the sofa and tucked it around her. With a devilish grin, he leaned down until his breath caressed her ear. "I can think of any number of ways to warm you, but until Chauncy pronounces us man and wife, I suppose a blanket and the fire will have to do."

Heat seared her cheeks and she narrowed her gaze with mock offense as she looked at him. Her feigned affront gave way to a flirtatious wink. "I hope Chauncy will be up to the task very soon."

Thrilled that she wanted to wed immediately, Tom banked his yearning for her and enjoyed the light conversation as Blake and Ginny returned to the room. Junie finally settled Cullen in his cradle then she and Lila washed the dishes.

When they returned to the parlor, Blake and Tom played with a zoetrope Luke had purchased for Maura. By changing the slides that fit inside it, they watched a horse gallop, a couple dance, and a monkey swing from tree to tree.

"This is quite a toy," Tom said, grinning as he turned the handle and made the horse run faster. "Maura will love it."

"If she ever gets it away from her uncles. Arlan and Blake have nearly worn it out playing with it," Ginny said, giving her husband a pointed look.

"Then perhaps Saint Nicholas should deliver one to our house," Blake said, tossing Ginny a cheeky grin.

She tipped her head back against the cushions of her chair and watched them set Maura's gifts beneath the tree.

"Should we fetch Erin's gifts from her house? I'd hate for her to awaken and not have anything from Saint Nicholas," she said, stifling a yawn. The clock in the hall struck eleven.

"Let's wait a while longer, love. If necessary, I can run fetch a few things before we go home." Blake kissed Ginny's temple.

It was almost midnight when Luke and Filly arrived, both bearing looks of excitement on their faces from having witnessed the miracle of birth.

Everyone looked to them, eager to hear how Abby and the baby were doing.

"How's Abby?" Junie asked, as Filly and Luke walked into the room.

"She's doing very well, and pleased at the arrival of their son."

"Oh, it's a boy." Ginny clasped her hands beneath her chin. "I bet Chauncy is about to bust his buttons."

"Indeed, he is."

"What did they name the baby?" Lila asked. She knew from time spent with Abby that she and Chauncy hadn't settled on any names for the baby.

"Owen," Filly said, beaming with joy. "Owen Andrew Dodd. And he has dark hair like Erin."

"I bet he's adorable," Ginny said, leaning against Blake.

"He is," Filly said, walking over to check on Cullen. Satisfied he was well, she turned back to the group. "Is Erin asleep?"

"Yes, but we were debating what to do about her gifts from Saint Nicholas," Blake said, glancing at Luke.

He nodded. "Chauncy had us fill her stocking and place presents beneath the tree before we left. I'll carry her home. She'll want to wake up Christmas morning in her own house," Luke said.

"If we wrap her in a blanket, we can tuck her straight into bed," Filly said, starting for the stairs with Luke right behind her.

While they bundled up Erin, Blake and James went outside to harness their teams. Ginny asked Junie if she'd noticed the arrangement Filly made for the dining room, purposely leaving Lila and Tom alone in the parlor.

"I thought they'd never all leave," Lila whispered, wrapping her arms around Tom's waist and leaning against his chest.

His hands rubbed tantalizing circles across her back. "I'm so glad you came home, Lila. You broke my heart when you left without saying a word." He tipped her chin up so he could look into her face.

Tears glistened in her eyes. "I know, Tom, and I'm so sorry. I wanted to tell you then how much I love you, but I felt obligated to go with Emerson. I'm sorry I hurt you."

A rakish grin made her knees weaken. "You can make it up to me by marrying me tomorrow afternoon. Until someone tells me otherwise, I've still got the teacher's house all to myself and I need to make a trip to Portland to clean out my apartment there. Do you think you'd like to take a little honeymoon trip between now and New Year's Day?"

"Oh, I'd love that," Lila smiled at him. "I would be honored to marry you tomorrow. Do you think Chauncy will leave Abby's side long enough to perform the ceremony?"

"I bet we can talk him into giving us a few minutes of his time." Tom lowered his head to hers. His sweet, gentle kiss, held a heart full of promises. Before it could turn into anything deeper, his father and Blake stomped snow off their boots at the front door, and Luke and Filly returned with Erin.

"I guess this is goodnight, Lila Lilac. Merry Christmas to you."

She kissed his cheek and smiled. "And to you, Tom. May tomorrow be the beginning of many, many happy Christmases we'll share."

Chapter Twenty-Four

The steely strength of Greg's arm helped Lila remain upright after she stepped into the back of the church and caught sight of Tom standing at the front with his father and Pastor Dodd.

Incredibly handsome in his suit, he wore a festive green tie and a smile just for her. She couldn't believe how much her life had changed in a few short days. When she boarded the train heading to New York, her heart had remained in Hardman, with Tom.

Even though she hadn't been able to tell him the truth, it didn't change how she felt inside, how much she loved him.

Now, she walked down the aisle of the church, eager to become his bride.

She had no idea what their future together would hold, but she knew they'd spend it holding each other, supporting each other, loving one another.

And that was more than enough for her.

Tom's heart threatened to burst with joy as he watched Lila walk down the aisle of the church on Greg Granger's arm.

She wore his favorite gown, the one with lilacs embellishing the front. Although it was not a particularly festive selection for a Christmas wedding, it perfectly suited his bride.

He meant the heartfelt words he'd written in the poem to his soon-to-be bride. Lila was springtime, bringing sunshine, fresh air, and new life to his heart. A heart he hadn't even realized had turned so frosty and barren as he wrote about the calamities and horrors that took place in Portland on a daily basis.

Thanks to the beautiful, effervescent woman, he was ready to return to Hardman and build a good life there with her.

Despite their plans to have a small wedding with only close family and friends, it seemed as though half the town had shown up at the church that afternoon.

Fred Decker took photographs with his new camera, as did Percy Bruner. The boy's wishes came true when his parents gifted him a camera that morning.

James nudged Tom with his elbow as he stood beside him in the role of best man. When his father waggled his eyebrows as Lila neared them, Tom grinned.

Lila took the arm he held out to her and smiled, eyes brimming with love. She nodded to Filly who served as her matron of honor then moved forward to stand beside Tom.

Throughout the brief ceremony, Tom battled to keep his focus on Chauncy's words. His attention drifted to Lila's tantalizing fragrance and her beautiful appearance. He couldn't wait to get her alone and show her exactly how alluring he found her.

Mindful of his wayward thoughts, he pulled them back to the moment when Chauncy asked if he had a ring. His father placed a wide gold band set with a single diamond on his palm, a ring that had belonged to Tom's grandmother. He slipped it on Lila's finger, pleased it was a perfect fit.

Surprised by the simplistic charm of the ring, Lila admired it a moment before repeating her vows.

"I proudly present to you Mr. and Mrs. Tom Grove," Chauncy boomed, smiling at them both. "You may now kiss your bride."

Tom wasted no time in pressing his lips to Lila's, kissing her just long enough and with enough emotion to cause everyone to clap and cheer.

Filly glanced at Luke who nodded and stood. "Please join us all at Granger House for refreshments."

Tom glanced at Lila and she shrugged.

As guests filed out of the church and either returned home or ventured to Luke and Filly's home, Tom and Lila turned to Chauncy.

"Thank you so much for performing the wedding for us, Chauncy."

The pastor smiled. "You are most welcome. Congratulations to you both." He thumped Tom on the back and grinned at Lila. "Now, if you'll excuse me, I'm going home to my wife and children. Merry Christmas!"

"Merry Christmas!" Lila echoed. She took Tom's hand in hers and together they walked to the door. "This has been the most wonderful Christmas, Tommy."

He pulled her against him and dropped his head to nuzzle her ear. "I have a feeling it will get even better before the day ends, especially if you keep calling me Tommy."

Pink suffused her cheeks from embarrassment, but she didn't pull away from him. Instead, she leaned into him and wrapped her arms around the back of his neck. "I'm looking forward to having you show me around Portland."

"I'm excited to share my favorite places with you," he said, trailing kisses along her neck. "I hope you don't mind staying in my apartment."

"Actually, I thought we could get a room at a hotel. Luke recommended one where he and Filly stay." Unconsciously, Lila tipped her head to the side to give Tom better access to her neck as he made his way to her ear again.

He raised his head and frowned. "I want to give you the best of everything, Lila, but I won't be able to afford that. All of my money will go to Ed Daily for the newspaper."

"About that..." Lila grinned. "The newspaper is no longer for sale."

Tom's amorous mood evaporated as he straightened and stared at her. "What do you mean? He said he'd wait until after Christmas for my decision."

"Well, that was before he received an offer he couldn't resist." Lila handed Tom her coat. He held it while she slipped it on.

"Who made him an offer? How do you know about it?" Tom tugged on his coat and lifted his hat in one hand, taking Lila's small hand in his other.

"I know, because he told me this morning when I went to see him." Lila hid her smile as Tom closed the church door and offered her a puzzled look.

After opening gifts with his parents, he'd gone to Granger House to see Lila. Ginny and Filly refused to allow him to see the bride before the wedding, so he'd returned home and waited with his parents until it was time to head to the church. He wondered when, in all the busyness the day had brought, Lila had time to visit the owner of the newspaper.

"Why would you go see Mr. Daily?" he asked, clearly perplexed and slightly perturbed.

"So I could tell him we wanted to buy the paper and agree to meet him at the bank tomorrow to make payment for it. Luke said he'd have his attorney meet us there to draw up a simple agreement."

"But, Lila, I can't afford to buy the paper outright. I was hoping Mr. Daily would be open to accepting payments." Distraught, Tom ran a hand through his hair.

Lila's laughter rang like a bell in the crisp wintery air. "Perhaps you can't afford to purchase the paper, but *we* can."

"You aren't making sense. What do you mean we can?"

She looped her arm around his and sauntered down the church steps. "My parents left me a wealthy woman, Tom. I can afford to buy a hundred newspaper businesses and still have money left over. And what is mine is now yours."

He gaped at her. The fact the Granger family had money was common knowledge, although exactly how much remained a mystery.

In truth, Tom hadn't given a thought to Lila having her own funds. She'd never, not once, put on airs or flaunted her fortune, so he'd conveniently forgotten she came from wealth and affluence.

Uncertain what to think of the idea of being married to a wealthy woman, Tom let the notion sink in a few moments. Pride demanded he refuse to accept a penny of her money, but common sense prevailed.

"Thank you, Lila. For making all my dreams come true." He shot her a rakish look as the hand he settled on her waist dropped lower, caressing the curve of her hip. "Well, almost all my dreams. Anticipation of how well you'll fulfill the rest of them before the day is over makes me want to carry you back to the my house right now."

Playfully, she swatted at his arm. "Tom Grove, you best behave yourself, at least until this impromptu reception is over."

He smiled and draped his arm around her shoulder. "I hope you know how much I love you, Lila. I may not bring much money to this marriage or anything of great material value, but the one thing I can give you is an abundance of unconditional love."

Lila pulled his head down and kissed him with unbridled emotion. "I love you so much, Tommy. More than you can imagine. We're going to have a wonderful life together."

"Yes, ma'am, we are," Tom said, grinning at his bride. He shook his head in disbelief. "I can't believe you bought me a newspaper for Christmas."

Mischief sparkled in her eyes. "Just wait until you see what I have planned for New Year's Eve."

Cinnamon Rolls

These cinnamon rolls are so delicious, they freeze well, and they make wonderful holiday gifts (if you can keep your family from eating them all before you can give some away!)

Dough
2 cups milk
½ cup vegetable oil
½ cup sugar
1 package active dry yeast
4 ½ cups flour
½ tsp. baking powder
½ tsp. baking soda
½ tbsp. salt

Filling
1 cup melted butter
¼ cup cinnamon
1 cup sugar

Icing
4 cups powdered sugar
¼ cup milk
3 tbsp. softened butter
8 ounces cream cheese, softened
1 tsp. vanilla extract

Scald the milk, oil, and sugar in a medium saucepan over medium heat (bring milk to nearly a boil, but don't let it boil!). Set aside and cool to lukewarm (temperature of milk in a baby's bottle).

Sprinkle yeast on top of milk and let rest for one minute.

Add four cups of the flour and stir until just combined. It is going to be sticky. Cover with a tea towel and set in a warm place for an hour.

Remove the towel and add baking powder, baking soda, salt, and final ½ cup of flour. Stir to combine.

On a floured surface, roll the dough into a large rectangle, somewhere in the proximity of 10 inches by 30 inches.

Pour melted butter over dough. Use your fingers or a knife to spread evenly. Sprinkle on cinnamon and sugar. You can also mix cinnamon and sugar into the butter before pouring over dough. Either way works fine.

Beginning at the long end farthest from you, roll the rectangle tightly toward you. Use both hands and work slowly, keeping the roll nice and tight. Some filling may ooze out and that is okay. It gives you something to snitch later.

When you have the roll finished, pinch the outside edge of the roll to create a seam. You should now have a long log. Transfer to a cutting board and cut into 1 1/2 inch slices. You should get about 25 rolls.

Spray a pan with non-stick cooking spray and place rolls in the pan. I like to use smaller pans and freeze them. If you want to give cinnamon rolls as a holiday gift, put them in disposable aluminum pans, then they are ready for gift giving!

Preheat the oven to 375 degrees. Cover the pans with a tea towel and set aside for about 20 minutes.

Remove towel and bake for about 15 minutes or until rolls are golden brown. Do not overcook! While the rolls are baking, whip up the icing.

Mix the powdered sugar, butter, cream cheese, milk and vanilla in a bowl. Icing should be thick but pourable.

When the rolls come out of the oven, pour on the icing. Make sure you cover every bit of roll. This step is vitally important for the overall happiness of your taste buds.

Author's Note

It's such fun for me to return to Hardman for another holiday season with the fun-loving families who reside in this fictional world.

When I first introduced Tom Grove in *The Christmas Calamity*, I knew he eventually would have his own story.

The thought of a girl for Tom made me ponder who would be just right for him. She needed to have spunk and charm. She had to be fun and sweet. I think Lila fit the bill quite well. And I don't know why, but the name Lila always makes me think of lilacs and springtime, so that's why Tom calls her Lila Lilac.

I try to include some historical facts in my works of fiction, and this story is no exception.

The first United States automobile show really was held in November of 1900 at Madison Square Garden. Varieties of autos were on display with any number of fascinating demonstrations. From the articles I read, many thought the gasoline engine would never be more than a passing fad. I wonder what they'd say now.

The World's Fair did take place in Paris that year. I found an article in the Heppner newspaper that talked about one of the local farmers attending with his sheep for a display. The man reported the "Turkish dancers" as one of his favorite exhibits. The first Olympic games outside Greece were held there.

I also found in the Heppner newspaper archives about the painting of Abraham Lincoln falling off the wall. It's amusing to see the types of news that used to make headlines!

If you are wondering why I was reading the Heppner newspaper instead of old issues of the Hardman paper, I have been unable to find any archives from Hardman.

Recently, I came across a book of Victorian morals and manners. Among the many "dos and don'ts" was a list for teachers, which inspired the list of rules Tom reads through.

Oh, and the whole thing about a gypsy came from a fun photo I found on Pinterest. A gypsy woman claimed to have hexed a bunch of police officers for arresting her son.

My dad had an old stereoscope that was always fun to look through. That's where I got the idea to include it in the story. I think Luke will like those slides Ginny purchased him for Christmas. Don't you?

If you've never seen a zoetrope, peek at them online. Some of them look like elaborate works of art.

As always, thank you for reading my books. If you have ideas for future Hardman stories, please let me know!

Hardman Holidays Series

Heartwarming holiday stories set in the 1890s in Hardman, Oregon.

The Christmas Bargain *(Hardman Holidays, Book 1)* — As owner and manager of the Hardman bank, Luke Granger is a man of responsibility and integrity in the small 1890s Eastern Oregon town. When he calls in a long overdue loan, Luke finds himself reluctantly accepting a bargain in lieu of payment from the shiftless farmer who barters his daughter to settle his debt.

The Christmas Token *(Hardman Holidays, Book 2)* — Determined to escape an unwelcome suitor, Ginny Granger flees to her brother's home in Eastern Oregon for the holiday season. Returning to the community where she spent her childhood years, she plans to relax and enjoy a peaceful visit. Not expecting to encounter the boy she once loved, her exile proves to be anything but restful.

The Christmas Calamity (Hardman Holidays, Book 3) — Arlan Guthry's uncluttered world tilts off kilter when the beautiful and enigmatic prestidigitator Alexandra Janowski arrives in town, spinning magic and trouble in her wake as the holiday season approaches.

The Christmas Vow (Hardman Holidays, Book 4) — Sailor Adam Guthry returns home to bury his best friend and his past, only to fall once more for the girl who broke his heart.

The Christmas Quandary (Hardman Holidays, Book 5) — Tom Grove just needs to survive a month at home while he recovers from a work injury. He arrives to discover his middle-aged parents acting like newlyweds, the school in need of a teacher, and the girl of his dreams already engaged.

Baker City Brides Series

Determined women, strong men and a town known as the Denver of the Blue Mountains during its days of gold in the 1890s.

Crumpets and Cowpies (Baker City Brides, Book 1) — Rancher Thane Jordan reluctantly travels to England to settle his brother's estate only to find he's inherited much more than he could possibly have imagined.

Thimbles and Thistles (Baker City Brides, Book 2) — Maggie Dalton doesn't need a man, especially not one as handsome as charming as Ian MacGregor.

Corsets and Cuffs (Baker City Brides, Book 3) — Sheriff Tully Barrett meets his match when a pampered woman comes to town, catching his eye and capturing his heart.

***Bobbins and Boots** (Baker City Brides, Book 4)* — *Coming in 2017!*

ABOUT THE AUTHOR

SHANNA HATFIELD spent ten years as a newspaper journalist before moving into the field of marketing and public relations. Self-publishing the romantic stories she dreams up in her head is a perfect outlet for her lifelong love of writing, reading, and creativity. She and her husband, lovingly referred to as Captain Cavedweller, reside in the Pacific Northwest.

Shanna loves to hear from readers.
Connect with her online:
Blog: shannahatfield.com
Facebook: Shanna Hatfield's Page
Pinterest: Shanna Hatfield
Email: shanna@shannahatfield.com

If you'd like to know more about the characters in any of her books, visit the Book Characters page on her website or check out her **Book Boards** on Pinterest.

CPSIA information can be obtained
at www.ICGtesting.com
Printed in the USA
FSOW03n0618221216
28769FS

9 781539 860242